I0607650

THESE SMALL HOURS

GLORIA HERRMANN

These Small Hours
ISBN # 978-1-83943-729-8
©Copyright Gloria Herrmann 2021
Cover Art by Erin Dameron-Hill ©Copyright July 2021
Interior text design by Claire Siemaszkiewicz
Totally Bound Publishing

THESE SMALL HOURS

Dedication

To my wonderful readers, 2020 was a rough year for all of us. However, one good thing came out of it for me—this book. With the encouragement of my amazing readers and author buddies, I found my way back to writing during this bleak time. Simply put, writing makes me happy and so do all of you. Thank you for the laughs and tremendous amount of support when I needed it the most.

Sarah Flanagan, I'm not sure I would have been able to finish this book without you. Your kind words, enthusiasm and positivity were greatly appreciated during all those moments when I doubted myself. You made me remember why I write, and thank you is not enough.

Chapter One

"You can't possibly be serious?"

"I am, and it will be good for you. I promise. You need to trust me on this."

Charley — also known as Charlene Vanderberg, a bestselling author — was currently experiencing writer's block for the first time. The words were there, locked somewhere in her mind and refusing to come out when she sat down every night to free them. *Nothing.* Just a blank page staring back at her, taunting Charley with the blinking cursor of where words should form. It had been months since Charley had written anything that hadn't ended up on the wrong side of the delete button. At this rate, she feared there might never be words again.

"It's the perfect solution," Pamela beseeched.

Her agent was a force of nature and had the manipulative power of getting her way. That's why Charley had agreed to sign on with Pamela Mansfield once her second manuscript had been complete. Charley had needed someone fierce to land her a book deal and steer her career in the right direction. Rejection letters didn't help her fragile writer's ego, and it was challenging enough to be recognized by any publisher without an agent. That's why she needed one like Pamela. That woman knew her way around the publishing world and had seen something in Charley.

Her advice and encouragement had pushed Charley and ultimately launched her into the success she was now enjoying. Over the years, they had become good friends, almost like family. Charley had learned a great deal from this tiny woman who was set on building a brand and empire with the clients she represented. Pamela only worked with the best, most talented people in the industry, and Charley still couldn't believe she was among them. She didn't want to disappoint Pamela and worried that if those words didn't start making an appearance soon, there would be some ugly consequences. They both had reputations to uphold.

Charley eyed Pamela curiously from across the table, half-hoping to break her agent's resolve. It wasn't going to happen, and they both knew that. The unwavering but tender stare as Pamela held her ground on what a great idea this was showed Charley that it truly was in her best interest.

"So, you honestly think by shipping me off to some lake resort in the middle of nowhere, I'll really get this book done? That magically all of my creative juices will start to flow again because you've got me locked up in some hillbilly cabin?" Charley scoffed. "Sounds like all the makings of a Stephen King novel, and we both know how those go," Charley teased as she poked her straw at a bobbing ice cube in her sweaty glass of water.

"Not just any cabin, Charley. My nephew owns the cutest little resort in Crescent Lake. The best part is that it's only a few hours from here. Just imagine, all these quaint cabins around that gorgeous lake. Besides, you know very well that you give Stephen King a run for his money." Pamela winked and turned her attention to the plate in front of her. "I thought nature was sort of your *thing*? Aren't you some kind of country girl?" Pamela countered playfully as she stabbed her colorful salad of varied bright leaves and vegetables.

"It was. I mean, I like it well enough, but I'm hardly a country girl," she answered with a touch of sophisticated sass.

"That's right. You're a famous writer now and living in your fabulous apartment with a perfect view of the Seattle skyline." Pamela smirked with her fork to her lips. "Too good for the great outdoors?"

"What I meant was that I haven't done anything remotely *outdoorsy* for years."

"Then you're long overdue."

"I just don't see how it will help." Charley shook her head and looked away. The restaurant with its elegant lighting and décor was filled with patrons all sipping wine and dining on extravagant dishes. Her writing had afforded her this lifestyle. *Maybe I'm a little out of touch.* The years of success and landing movie deals had pampered her with opportunities she'd never dreamed possible, especially for a girl who'd grown up on a rural farm town in the middle of Washington. She gazed back and saw a peculiar flicker in Pamela's hazel eyes.

"What?"

Pamela squirmed ever so slightly in her seat and bit her mauve-painted bottom lip. All the playfulness abandoned her face and was quickly replaced with something else. Charley studied her and tried to figure out exactly what it was. She could sense her agent's nervous energy.

"They want that book before fall," Pamela stated bluntly as she gently placed her fork down.

"And if they don't get it by then?" Charley asked. Her belly began to do anxiety-induced flip-flops. So many *what ifs* ran through her mind that her sense of reason started to trip over them.

She clasped her hands together in prayer form. Pamela exhaled but kept her eyes locked on Charley. Through a forced smile, she calmly replied, "Let's just focus on getting this book done."

"Nothing like a little pressure to add to my already-growing problem." Charley nibbled on a dry piece of skin on her bottom lip.

"You need a change of scenery and a little quiet inspiration then that ridiculous writer's block will be gone. Every author goes through this at some point," Pamela reassured Charley but nervously twirled a strand of her chestnut hair between her fingers. "I've had clients who've been down this road before."

"I haven't ever had this problem," Charley confessed in a near whisper. "I've never had an issue with writing—like...ever, Pamela." Charley's heart beat a little faster with a sudden pang of anxiety. "The stories always kept coming, the characters made their demands well known and now poof, they're gone. Writing is what I do—what I did." As the words left her mouth, Charley realized the severity of her problem. If she didn't pull it together and find a way to get her writing mojo back, Charley didn't know what would become of her career. By the look on her agent's face, it definitely wasn't good. "Fine... I'll go to your nephew's little resort." Charley defiantly speared the lemon wedge that rested on her perfectly cooked salmon. She no longer had an appetite as her brain developed images of her impending failure. She could lose it all—

her swanky apartment, ridiculously expensive SUV and her famous name. It could all be gone.

Pamela smiled. "Don't worry. We'll get this book done and you'll be back on top again. Everyone wins."

Charley hoped Pamela was right.

* * * *

Charley had been sitting in front of her laptop for hours. The remnants of cold coffee in her favorite mug sat forgotten next to her. Her butt had gone numb and she'd lost track of time as she stared at the stark white screen with no words. Her fingers rested on the plastic keys, waiting and ready to pounce at the first hint of an idea. Charley was beyond frustrated. She moved her neck in slow, gentle circles, hoping to release the tension that seemed to have stuck around long after her lunch date with Pamela. Charley felt even more stress than before, which definitely wasn't helping the words come any faster. *How will a trip to some lake town really solve this?* Charley had her doubts about being holed up in a cabin all alone. She'd seen movies like *The Shining* and *Misery*, and she knew how those tales went. *No thanks. Why can't these words just find their way back to me?* Charley rubbed her temples and begged her brain to come up with something. *Anything.*

"It's useless. I'm screwed," she muttered in defeat in the silent space. The room was mostly dark, except for the dim light of an old lamp near a large bookcase. She glanced over at the cherry-stained bookcase containing all her books, words that had all magically turned into bestselling thrillers. *My* words. Deliciously wicked stories that had somehow sprouted from the dark crevices of her mind. Tales that no one could believe had come from a perky and happy-go-lucky girl like her.

She'd had a nice childhood, better than normal by anyone's definition. Her parents still lived in the charming farmhouse she'd grown up in with her older brother and sister. So, where had all these twisted and demented stories of abduction, murder and crimes so gruesome stem from? Maybe she had been a serial killer in a past life. The notion caused her to giggle loudly.

Charley knew exactly where all the vivid images and horrific ideas had come from...real life. Charley had taken a job as a reporter for a fairly large newspaper in the Seattle area. For her, it had been a ticket out of the sprawling hay fields and sleepy town she'd become tired of. That opportunity had offered her a chance to do something exciting with her life and to see how different the rest of the world was. Little had she known how in just the few short years she'd spend covering the homicide beat, it would implant story ideas into her brain, shifting her world completely.

Being a journalist wasn't exactly what Charley had planned on becoming. Her love of books as a child and having spent all those nights reading until the words had become blurry had been just the start of what had become a secret passion. She had then begun writing short stories and poems. Charley had always wanted to capture and create that same magic her favorite authors had done for her. They all had put her under a spell spun from their words, charming her to believe they'd taken her to faraway places and introduced her to so many incredible people.

Those short stories and poems Charley had written soon found their way into the hands of overly impressed teachers. With a little prodding from them,

Charley had agreed to write for her high school newspaper. The creative outlet had only spurred her passion as she had become an even better writer, honing her craft and, unbeknownst to her, shaping her future. The only drawback had been having to cover stories ranging from the awful cafeteria food to Friday night football games.

Charley had discovered that she was actually quite good at reporting—and so had the local newspaper. They'd offered her a job right out of high school and it was there that she had begun her life as a small-town reporter. She had gone from covering football games to town hall meetings. Nothing too scandalous had ever happened in their farming community, other than maybe a few cows wandering out of their field. Charley had grown bored with just reporting the facts of this simple life. The itch to write bigger and better things had always been there but it had intensified as the years had gone by.

She'd tinkered with the notion of writing a novel and had even begun to work on a few rough drafts of a silly romance story. Then an opportunity from out of nowhere had knocked on her door. She'd just about reached her breaking point in her mundane career and jumped at this once-in-a-lifetime chance with gusto— only it hadn't quite turned out to be what she'd hoped. It had ultimately been the start of her fabulous new life, but the nightmares that haunted her had clung onto Charley. The stories she'd covered—the awful news of kidnappings, murders and a slew of violent crimes she'd reported—had shaped her into the writer she'd become. She'd turned into a successful one who'd grown into an overnight sensation by retelling all those awful events with her own personal twist.

Her books were now found on nearly every bookstore shelf around the globe. She'd risen to fame quickly with her descriptive encounters of sinister minds and plots so demented that it had been no wonder Charley found herself being offered movie deals and opportunities to write for television. Part of that success was due to Pamela being the pit bull that she was, but those ideas had all come from Charley — or rather the criminals of the Pacific Northwest.

So, where were those ideas now? Was Charley drained of all her inspiration because she was no longer a reporter and a witness to the cruel and evil nature of humans? Something had definitely changed, and it couldn't have come at a worse time. The last book her publisher released had flopped, big time. It hadn't even hit any of the bestseller lists. She'd wanted a break from the gore and had tried her hand at a sweet romance. Her fans had been blown away by her new release — and not in a good way.

It was no wonder her publisher was after her to write something more like her previous work. Her fans craved storylines with not-so-happy endings and lots of blood. Charley had tried to revisit those ghosts and had hoped a new bestseller would magically appear. She'd never seen this struggle happening in her career. She knew other authors had gone through it, just not her.

Charley banged her head lightly on her desk. "Why, God?"

Being an author wasn't only about the actual writing. There was a whole other animal involved — marketing and sales, keeping relevant and engaging with fans. It was never just about the books. Charley had learned that rather quickly and found herself immersed in the social media frenzy that was now part of her everyday life. Whether Charley was posting pictures of her morning coffee or sharing videos of her typing away on her trusty keyboard, she had to let readers know what she was up to.

Tweets and posts were only a small portion of it, though. Charley had to go on book-signing tours and radio shows to promote herself. She also had taken it upon herself to personally answer emails, messages and letters from fans and readers. It was important to Charley to stay grounded and not forget those who had given her this lifestyle. *Charlene Vanderberg* wouldn't be where she was today if it weren't for all those readers. But those readers had been so quick to turn on her when she'd tried to venture outside her norm. The only way to gain their love again was to go back to telling those horrific stories. Charley felt like a misbehaving child who was suffering some kind of deserved cosmic punishment.

Charley yawned and reached for her phone to check the time. It was late, the time when she'd normally be so utterly consumed with words dripping from her fingertips. Those small hours during the night before the sun robbed the moon of its glory was that magical time when the world sleeps and creative souls work best. In those quiet moments of darkness was when artists painted masterpieces, writers and poets found the light of their words to illuminate the world around them and the hours when the soul was most honest. It was the time when imaginary monsters were safely keeping watch under beds and hiding in closets while the innocent dreamed. Those precious late hours were when the real monsters were lurking in the shadows, strangling life or causing it to bleed away. Only now, for Charley, those monsters were tucked away somewhere, keeping themselves hidden, not letting their heinous deeds be seen for her to tell those hungry readers. She gently closed her laptop. Another night with no words.

* * * *

Charley spit the minty toothpaste out into the sink and swished cold tap water around in her mouth. The splattered semi-runny mixture wasn't pretty against the expensive glass-bowl sink and she quickly washed it away with more water. She peered at the mirror and examined the dark mask around her sapphire eyes. Charley poked at the puffy skin and released a heavy sigh. The stress was beginning to take its toll.

There was one person who Charley knew that she could turn to, the person who Charley always ran to when she needed the best advice. After splashing more cool water on her face in hopes to revive her sleep-deprived soul, she pulled her hair into a semi-decent ponytail. Charley was on a mission. She walked barefoot on the porcelain-tiled floor, a rich mahogany color with artificial wood grain that was throughout her home. The dark tones of the large apartment didn't seem to fit the normally sunny disposition of Charley's personality, but as of late, they were a perfect match.

The furniture was sleek, modern and an expensive reminder of how well Charley had done for herself. Plenty of warm, muted light filtered in through the large living room windows to restore the contrasting balance.

After becoming a working author, Charley had turned into a nocturnal creature who survived off caffeine, take-out and sleeping in until well past noon. Her apartment was practically untouched and could easily grace the cover of an interior design magazine.

The only space she cared about anyway was her office — which she affectionately referred to as her 'writing cave'. It was located in the corner of the apartment and had incredible built-in bookcases that Charley had fallen instantly in love with. The room was so unlike the rest of the sterile apartment. There were beats of color, splashes of her personality reflected by the art on the walls and knick-knacks that sat on the many shelves. It was *her* room and not a place she often shared with others. It was small and perfect for trapping those brilliant plots in her mind. It had been a haven for several years but now had become a self-imposed prison of sorts. It had been her pilot's seat on the many journeys her characters had kidnapped her away to, a place where ghosts spoke to her and recounted the ways they'd met their demise.

Against one wall was her helm, a desk she'd been using ever since her first completed manuscript. It was a beat-up old piece of furniture Charley had rescued from a second-hand store, one that Pamela had insisted she should dispose of and replace with a proper workspace. It didn't matter how many dollars were in her bank account. She'd never part with that desk. It held a special place in her heart and contained a magic that only a writer understood. Charley smiled at the thought of it as she strolled past her office then quickly frowned. It had also recently become a torture device — a spot where she sat and stared at a blank screen for hours, pleading for the magic to return. All the conjuring and banging her head against the shabby solid wood wasn't cutting it.

Charley entered the tiny kitchen of her apartment. Everything was shiny and looked professionally staged. She couldn't even recall when the last time was that she'd cooked any kind of real food in that space. It didn't even appear that Charley actually lived there. It was nothing more than a cold shell and fancy representation that she'd made it, something Charley could show off to friends on the rare occasion she wanted to entertain. All those hours of working on new books had left little time for friendships.

Charley rambled in the apartment all alone. Glass and bright metal were the cold contemporary and very industrial theme in this building. It was nothing at all like the charming kitchen back home, the fond place where Charley had written short stories at the dining table while her mother had made chocolate-chip pancakes on Saturday mornings. She could almost taste them now. Nostalgia was funny like that. It just hit out of nowhere and could make one begin to miss the little and simpler things — those things Charley maybe had taken for granted.

"Hi, Mom," Charley spoke softly into her phone as she prepared her first pot of coffee of the day. She caught sight of the time on the small digital display on her oven. It was a little after four in the afternoon. She was still in her pajamas but had brushed her teeth. *That has to count for something, right?*

"Hello, my precious girl," her mother answered sweetly, which stirred an instant longing in Charley's heart that she hadn't felt in a long time. She wasn't one for getting homesick, but the sound of her mother's voice toyed with her vulnerability. "Daddy says hi."

Charley bit down hard on her quivering lip and attempted to steel her emotions before the waterworks came. "So, what have you guys been up to?" She stared at the dark amber liquid as it dripped silently into the glass pot.

"Nothing much. Daddy just got done cutting the field. It's been terribly warm here." Her mother rattled on about the usual boring details of their life back home. Charley answered with the appropriate sounds and found her mind wandering. "Honey, what's on your mind? You seem distracted."

"Oh, Mom, I'm really struggling with this book. My publisher wants it before fall and that's barely three months away. They're already preparing some huge launch for something I haven't even written yet," Charley blurted out in one rambling breath. All the stress that had been festering had come to the surface. She wiped away hot tears that traveled down her cheeks like a flash flood. "What am I going to do?"

"Baby girl, I have complete faith you will not only come up with a fantastic book but that it will be your best one yet," she replied with confidence that only a mother could deliver.

"My last book tanked. I think I'm done, Mom." Charley felt the defeat course through her. Her chest felt heavy as she sobbed into the phone.

"Now quit that nonsense. You're a gifted writer and this is just an awful case of writer's block."

"That's what Pamela said," Charley sniffled.

"And she's right. That agent of yours is a smart woman. You really should listen to her."

Charley allowed a laugh to escape. "I'll be sure to tell her you said that."

"Well, since she's so smart, has she got any ideas on how to help you through this little crisis?" her mother asked with a touch of sharpness in her voice.

"Actually, she came with this grand plan for me to hide out at some cabin. Her nephew owns a small resort on Crescent Lake."

"Well, that sounds lovely and a pretty darn good idea."

"It sounds like it's in the middle of nowhere and a last-ditch effort before she lets me go," Charley whined.

"Oh, you stop. Pamela adores you."

"Yeah, but if I don't come up with another bestseller..." Charley started and was quickly interrupted by her mother.

"You've made that woman a lot of money," she pointed out. "Getting rid of you would be like throwing out her golden goose."

Charley reached for a paper towel and blew her nose. She tried to inhale deeply and calm herself. Her mother was right. She'd been Pamela's golden goose for a number of years now and that had to have earned her some credit — or at the very least bought her some time.

"But it's more than that, honey. Pamela knows you're talented, and she's been there with you this whole time. She must sense this is what you need to get back on track."

"What if I just came home instead?" Charley asked, hoping her mother would suggest home as a refuge and better alternative.

"I wouldn't mind you popping over for a visit, but this lake idea sounds quite nice — and exactly what you need," Charley's mother replied. "You could always swing by here on your way to Crescent Lake. I know Daddy would love to see his little girl." Charley could hear her father in the background and imagined him giving her a hug.

"You really think I should go? Will it even help?" Doubt and excuses tried to root themselves deep in her mind.

"It certainly couldn't hurt any."

Charley considered the idea silently as her mother continued to add reassurance, gently stroking her brittle writer's ego. After being fed to contentment, she said, "Thanks, Mom."

"What for, dear?" The sugary laugh from her mother caused Charley to smile.

"For everything. You always know exactly what to say."

"And here I thought you were the one who had the way with words."

* * * *

Charley yawned and rubbed her achy eyes. The light from her laptop illuminated the small room in a dull whitish hue. No words were reflected back to her. It was another night where she sat and waited for something to crawl out from her mind.

"This is seriously getting old," she groused aloud in a breathy huff. Charley stretched her arms into the air and wiggled her fingers. She exhaled and defiantly crossed her arms. *How much longer can I carry on like this?* She hadn't strayed from her strict routine. Here she sat every night until well after dawn, just waiting and praying the words would find her.

Tomorrow everything would change—and hopefully for the better. Charley would be leaving to go to that damn lake cabin. First, she would pay her parents a long overdue visit. Charley secretly hoped that somehow being back home might magically restore her literary powers. If not, then on to the cabin. Pamela had called earlier in the day to check on her progress. There had been none, and Pamela had insisted more firmly that this trip to the lake was exactly what Charley needed. Pamela called back a few hours later, letting Charley know that all the arrangements had been handled. There was no turning back now.

Charley had spent the remainder of the day reluctantly packing for her trip. Long after the sun had set and the vibrant city of Seattle had come alive, she'd set about her nightly routine, planting herself in front of her laptop with an assortment of sugary snacks and a steaming mug of gourmet coffee. She was eager to work. This definitely wasn't a case of laziness. She had never considered writing a chore, a job or any kind of torture…until now. Hours crept by. It was as though she were waiting for a lover to pay her a secret midnight visit — anxiously anticipating their arrival, her nerves tight with want and desire for this special rendezvous.

At first, Charley distracted herself by checking emails and scrolling through the seemingly endless posts on social media. Her theory was if she could just numb her brain long enough from all the worry, maybe it would open up and give her what she needed. As Charley waited with no sign of her inspiration, she decided it was best to step away from her laptop. After a few stretches and punching at the air, she wandered over to her bookcase. She grazed the paperback spines lined up like perfect soldiers, all with titles so cryptic and intriguing that it still amazed her that they had come from her. Her name stood out in a bold elegant font. *Charlene Vanderberg. How did this happen to me? How is it possible for my words to fall victim and become kidnapped? What ransom do I have to pay for them to be returned?*

She went back to nibbling on her snacks and cracking her knuckles to interrupt the silence that was driving her crazy. The screen from her laptop was bright as she summoned any inspiration, attempting to pry it from her mind. Despite the hummingbird sensation inside her, the hunger for those words to write, Charley had never felt more alone or abandoned.

Her lover never showed up. She feared they may never again.

* * * *

Her phone buzzed somewhere near her head as Charley slapped at it to make the annoying sound cease. Groggy and irritated, Charley saw on the ultra-bright screen it was her best friend and personal assistant Victoria calling her.

"Hello," her voice croaked.

"Rise and shine, cupcake," Victoria ordered sweetly. Charley groaned, her brain fuzzy and exhausted. "So, any luck last night?"

"No," Charley answered slowly, her throat dry and thick with sleep. She rolled over in her plush bed and wanted to bury herself in the heavy comforter.

"Well, that's okay. I'm on my way up and figured I'd see you off before you left for your big adventure."

"Please tell me what I want to hear," Charley begged.

"That I brought coffee? Of course. And I even snagged a few of your favorite cinnamon rolls. You're welcome. Now get your lazy ass up and let me in."

Victoria was way too perky. Granted, it was past ten o'clock and any normal person would already be awake and have already begun their day by now. She covered her face with one of her fluffy pillows. *Maybe I should just suffocate myself, then I'd be rid of all my problems.* The sound of her doorbell interrupted her plans of suicide. Charley sluggishly removed herself from the comfort of her bed and made her way to the front door.

"You look like hell," Victoria said with a tight smile as Charley let her in.

"You might want to work on your wake-up call." Charley led them to her small dining area where she snatched one of the coffees from Victoria. Raising the heavy paper cup, she chortled. "This is the only reason I keep you around."

"And these," Victoria replied as she shook a small white paper sack. Victoria went to one of the glass cabinets and fetched two plates. Victoria joined Charley at the round table and stared at her with concern. "You really look like crap, doll."

Charley rolled her eyes and sighed. "What do you expect?"

"That if you're not getting any writing done, then at least get some damn sleep."

Charley let out a laugh. "I can't. I need to be writing and the lack of it isn't helping my sleep either."

"Maybe you need a break, like a real one, and some time to recharge your batteries — maybe an opportunity to wear something other than those awful pajamas." Victoria motioned to Charley's flamingo-covered nightgown.

She suddenly felt self-conscious and tried to ignore the judgmental scowl on Victoria's face. Her friend was right. Charley lived in her pajamas most of the time. She probably owned more flannel bottoms and comfortable cotton shirts than any real adult attire. She hardly left her apartment these days and didn't see the sense in being in anything that wasn't comfy.

"This trip is just the thing you need."

Charley fiddled with her cell phone, only half listening to Victoria. "Except I have a deadline and like a million other things I need to be doing." Charley maneuvered her coffee cup into position and aimed her cell phone at it.

"And what exactly is it that you're doing right now?" Victoria asked sassily, with a slightly annoyed look on her pretty face.

"Posting a shot of this delicious coffee," Charley exulted as she cropped the image on her phone.

"I think it's so ridiculous that you do that. I don't get it." Victoria tucked a stray strand of her black bob behind her ear, revealing long gold earrings that had been a gift from Charley the previous Christmas.

"Because my readers love it and it's all about keeping them happy," she answered as she returned her attention to the coffee. She could sense Victoria's irritation. Charley snapped another perfect image of her cinnamon roll and set to work on creating clever hashtags she knew would soon get hundreds of 'likes' from her fans.

Victoria snatched the phone from her hand. "Just drink the damn coffee."

"As my assistant, you should know how very important this is," Charley argued as she tried to retrieve her phone. Victoria kept it out of her grasp.

"As your best friend, I also see how utterly stupid it is. You're overextending yourself. Isn't that enough?"

"What is?"

"All the books you've given these fans. Why do they need to know what flavor your coffee is? How much more of *Charlene Vanderberg* do they need to have?" The genuine concern in Victoria's smoky gray eyes hit Charley hard.

"I guess I'm so used to doing it," she admitted as she took a sip of her coffee. "I don't want to disappoint anyone." Charley shrugged as she avoided Victoria's eyes.

"Girl, they will survive not seeing a post of what you're eating or drinking. You've attracted enough creeps. Trust me." Victoria darted her gaze away as she reached for her cup. "Heck, just last night we received a message on our website from a total weirdo."

"Really?" Her body tingled with intrigue as she swallowed her coffee, enjoying the surge of warmth as it traveled down her throat. Sure, she had some weirdos who would write some pretty strange messages or make odd comments. That was the nature of the beast and not all that surprising, considering the genre she wrote. "Go on." Charley was curious about this latest one.

"Honestly, some of the emails and online messages we've been getting lately are a little concerning. You've got more than a few angry fans, honey." Victoria's shiny hair shook as she spoke. She moved her slender fingers silently across the screen of Charley's phone as she searched for the message. "Well, he was a big time creepazoid and pretty pissed about your last release."

"Who isn't? Evidently, everyone hates that book. I mean, I liked it. That was why I wrote it." Charley took another swallow of her coffee. It didn't taste as delicious as it had a moment ago.

Victoria rolled her eyes and shoved the phone back into the pocket of her black jeans. "It's great that you wanted to try something different. You should be allowed to. You're the author, after all," Victoria agreed as she sipped on her coffee.

"Thanks. That's what I'm saying. Like, leave some room for a little creativity and quit pigeonholing me."

"But, you gotta admit that you've pretty much only written crime thrillers since the start of your career.

Your fans weren't exactly expecting a sweet, contemporary romance," Victoria pointed out.

"True." Charley nodded as she considered Victoria's words.

"I'm just saying maybe you should keep some of your life private. Like, maybe don't tell anyone where you're headed this weekend," she suggested softly.

"So, no posts of the lake and stuff like that?" Charley rolled her eyes. "Gosh, is it really that bad?"

Victoria frowned slightly. "It's not super bad, but there are definitely some people out there who aren't loving you and your work right now."

"That's exactly why this new book has to be friggin' spectacular, Vic. It's also why Pamela is forcing me to go to this stupid lake town. Everything is riding on this book." Charley felt herself grow angry. "It's all about making other people happy—the fans, the publisher, my agent. What about *me*?" Charley asked, her nerves tight and angry.

"That's why you need to take this time to really find yourself and get back to what you're amazing at. Don't share this moment with everyone, except for maybe me. I'm totally dying to see this place." Victoria grinned excitedly.

Charley pinched off a piece of the sticky cinnamon roll. "I don't know if I'll ever be able to write again. I've never dealt with anything like this before."

"It's a little strange, I'll admit," Victoria concurred as she popped a piece of the pastry into her mouth.

"A little? I've been writing for years and not once during all that time have I never been unable to come up with something. It's like it's gone."

Victoria shook her head. "Nope, I don't entirely agree. I just think you've spent so much time constantly working that this is just your brain's way of saying you need a vacation. A real one."

"Trust me. This isn't a real one. Pamela says they need this book by fall. This is a working vacation," Charley said, hearing the disappointment in her own voice. "They've already started to come up with a launch for something that's not even written yet." Charley released a hearty groan.

Victoria matched Charley's groan with an even louder sigh. "Yeah, I see how you feel pressured. Obviously, that's not going to help matters. If anyone can do it, though, it's you. You've written amazing books in just a few weeks. Remember, *In the Dark of Night*?"

Charley smiled at the memory. It was during the early years of her career, and she'd been given a ridiculous deadline. She'd not only killed that deadline, but that book had ended up being one of her first to be offered a movie deal. It had changed her life as an author and thrust her into success she hadn't known was possible. The drive and confidence it had instilled in Charley to create more books were powerful.

She'd quickly penned nearly twenty more books since then. All of them had topped every bestseller list, except for one—her last release. Charley's attempt of trying something a tad different had completely failed. It had tanked so bad that Charley feared this could very well be the end of her career. Numbers didn't lie, and now everyone was waiting for this comeback book, especially her publisher. She found herself frowning again and Victoria reached for her hand from across the table.

"You've got this, girl."

Do I? It certainly doesn't feel like it.

"You all packed?" Victoria asked as she shifted the heavy conversation in a lighter direction.

Charley nodded. "Yeah, I figure I'll spend a day or two at my mom and dad's place."

"That's nice. I bet they miss you. Gosh, when's the last time you were home?" Victoria asked with one of her perfect eyebrows arched.

"I know. There's no excuse. They only live a few hours away and I should visit more often." Charley couldn't even come up with a valid reason for not having visited them for months, though she couldn't help but recognize that it had been shortly after her last trip back home when this whole writer's-block nonsense had started.

Perhaps deep in her subconscious Charley somehow associated the last visit home with when the words had suddenly gone missing. Was it the Hallmark movie feel of being home with her parents and older siblings? Those home-cooked Sunday dinners, seeing her siblings' children play and being swarmed by feelings of domestic inadequacy?

Charley's parents were beyond proud of her accomplishments, but it was difficult to ignore the normal questions they'd asked about her personal life. Her sister had asked innocently enough if she'd been seeing anyone or what her thoughts were on marriage and children. Charley had been so focused on writing and creating her little empire in the fiction world that it honestly gave her little time to socialize, let alone date anyone. She wasn't opposed to the notion of romance — white picket fences and mini versions of her and her dream husband running underfoot.

Charley was too busy living among ghosts to think that far ahead into a rosier shade of happiness. It was in the darkness where she found herself most happy.

That spectacular time before dawn when she traveled through the veil of her deviated thoughts and words that led her on a journey into the world where people felt safer reading or watching on a big screen.

But that world was very much real and had become such an important part of who she was. Now it was during those midnight hours when Charley just sat. She felt lost and absent from the person she thought she was.

"You okay?" Victoria's broke into her mind, scattering her thoughts like loose pages plucked from an ancient book.

"To be perfectly honest, I don't really know," she admitted as she held her cup to her lips.

* * * *

With the radio blaring and the highway stretched out in front of her, Charley's mood had lifted considerably. She tapped her fingers on the steering wheel of her over-priced SUV along with the beat of the song and belted out lyrics she'd probably sung incorrectly dozens of times. She didn't care if she knew the words of the song or not. She felt free and was having a blast. It bordered on that feeling of being tipsy, that fun kind of intoxication where all the problems in the world have temporarily floated away. She savored the joy that coursed through her and danced in her seat after she turned the radio up a tad louder. Her visit with Victoria had given her a bit of peace. Maybe when this whole book nonsense was behind them, they could take a much-needed girls' trip somewhere.

Charley peered through the windshield to see feathery white clouds across the sky like strewn pieces of cotton. The sky had become an even brighter shade of blue as she'd driven farther from the city and entered the expansive fields and rugged terrain of central Washington. With summer approaching, the fields were fading from their springtime bright green to a more muted shade. It wouldn't be long before the summer heat scorched them and everything would be in varied tones of dry brown. Charley had been on the road for a little over an hour and the afternoon sun was high in the sky, delivering its warm rays through her sunroof. She'd just gotten off the phone with her mother, promising to arrive at the house no later than dinnertime. Charley smiled at the thought of how excited her mother had sounded and found herself driving a little faster now.

Being alone with her thoughts was nothing new to Charley, and today hadn't been any different. After she and Victoria had packed her car with all her essentials and a few dozen things she probably didn't need, Charley had set off on this very reluctant trip. She kept hearing the theme song to *Gilligan's Island* play in her mind as she navigated through the busy traffic of Seattle. *Sit right back and you'll hear a tale. A tale of a fateful trip… A three-hour tour*. The silly song kept her mind occupied until she found herself on the nearly vacant highway. It was then that she confronted her brain. She demanded to know why it was sheltering all her ideas and holding them for ransom. Charley bribed it with delicious carbohydrates and caffeine. She even made false promises of self-care, all in exchange for what she and her publisher desired.

"Come on and just gimme the book," she pleaded. She was met with silence and no response.

Charley decided there was no point in trying to coax a deal out of her brain. What did she actually expect? Instant answers? That somehow by being away from her beloved writing cave everything would suddenly rush back to her? Her brain wasn't going to surrender that easily. Might as well look at this like Victoria had suggested — a long overdue vacation. She cranked up the stereo again and let her SUV fill with funky music. Soon Charley wasn't even thinking about a completed book due in less than three months — or really much of anything else other than seeing her family. She had missed them and realized that there was no way her last visit had anything to do with this absence of words.

After another two hours on the road, Charley saw the exit that would lead her along a small main street lined with trees and hanging baskets overflowing with purple-and-white flowers. A surge of happy excitement flooded her entire body as she steered the SUV toward the single traffic light. Everything seemed untouched, whereas back in Seattle, perpetual change was constant with the endless construction and new growth in the city. Cranes and heavy equipment were now a part of the Seattle skyline. This place had remained the same since she had been born and when she'd left. There was a strange comfort in that.

Lost in thought and driving the few turns on autopilot, Charley arrived at her childhood home. Her tires crunched over the white rock-coated driveway. Charley couldn't stop grinning as she parked her SUV and hopped out. Her mother was sitting on the porch of the sunny-yellow painted house with its stark white trim and matching shutters. Three children bounded excitedly off the steps of the porch and with huge smiles raced toward her.

"Auntie Charley," they all squealed in enthusiastic unison. They almost knocked Charley over as they encircled their arms around her waist.

"Hey, kiddos," Charley replied happily as she attempted to hold steady and keep her balance.

With the small children clinging to her legs and arms, Charley slowly made her way up the porch. Her mother shooed them away and quickly wrapped her arms around Charley in a tight embrace. "Oh, how we've missed you, sweetheart."

"I know... I'm the worst daughter ever," Charley babbled as she inhaled her mother's perfume. The light floral scent was the same one her mother had worn for as long as she could remember.

"Nonsense. You're a busy one, that's for sure." Her mother patted and released her. "You hungry? How was the drive?" Questions seem to pour from her as she opened the old screen door that creaked loudly. "Your sister is inside with the baby, and your brother is out in the barn with Daddy."

Charley entered the house as the children ran back outside to play. She breathed in this moment with her entire being, taking in all the scents and sounds of this very special place. It wasn't as though she'd been gone for years, but in so many ways it almost felt like it.

"Hey, there's that famous kid sister of mine." Charley looked toward the sound of her sister's voice. She was seated on the couch, nursing her baby. "Come sit."

"Look at how much he's grown," Charley exclaimed in a hushed wonder as she reached out to stroke the tiny bare foot.

"He's almost five months old." Pride washed over her sister's face.

"The girls are taller than heck too," she added, not taking her eyes off her baby nephew. "What are you feeding them? Miracle-Gro?"

Her sister laughed. "They've been so excited to see you. It's all they've talked about since they woke up this morning."

"That's so sweet." Charley couldn't stop smiling.

"So, Mom says you're just staying a day or two then you're off to Crescent Lake." She turned the milk-drunk baby and lifted him gingerly to her shoulder to burp him.

Charley shrugged. "That's the plan."

"Just curious why you're headed out that way?" her sister frowned slightly. "You could always just come home and write, you know?"

Charley smiled tightly and nodded. She could, but would she actually accomplish anything? "My agent arranged it under the advisement of our publisher," she partially lied.

"Mom says you're really struggling with this book. That's not like you. What's up?" Her sister patted the baby's back in a steady rhythm. Charley tried to summon an excellent excuse when the baby suddenly released a loud burp. "That's Mommy's good boy," she cooed sweetly as she kissed the baby's head.

Charley turned to the sound of loud voices heading in their direction and rose off the couch quickly. "Daddy," she squealed like a happy child as she ran to the giant of a man who had open arms.

"Baby girl," he replied in his gruff voice and swung her around, causing her feet to lift from the floor. "It's been way too long."

As he reluctantly released her, he smiled at Charley, his caramel-colored eyes twinkling. Instantly guilt flooded her. She could see that since their last visit he wore more wrinkles on his happy face and had much more silver in his hair.

"I know," she replied softly.

"Well, you're here now, and from the wonderful smells, I'm thinking your mama has dinner just about ready." His jovial face was full of light and love. He extended his hand to lead her to the dining room.

They say parents weren't supposed to have favorites, that they were to love all their children equally, but there was no doubt she was his favorite and always had been.

They were all seated around the long table. Charley traced the embroidery on the tablecloth, knowing it hid the marred surface of the table beneath the beautiful linen. They'd spent so many holidays and special moments here at this very table. She remembered sitting there and telling her parents when she was leaving for Seattle. Charley could still recall both of her mother and father having damp eyes. Even she'd shed tears and asked if she was making the right decision. They supported and encouraged her to chase her dreams. Charley remembered sitting in the very same seat when they had celebrated the very first time her book had hit the bestsellers list. Her dreams had come true.

Charley stared down at the plate in front of her, now filled with golden and perfectly fried chicken with a mountain of fluffy mashed potatoes. She spotted her mother's famous biscuits only a few inches away. As she spooned a mouthful of the delicious potatoes and relished the creamy texture and buttery taste, Charley knew one thing for sure about coming home. *Nothing beats a home-cooked dinner.*

* * * *

The house was quiet except for the constant ticking of her grandmother's ancient cuckoo clock in the living room. The strange clock had always bugged her, and tonight was no different. If anything, she was more keenly aware of its rather annoying sound. Charley blinked hard at the laptop that was situated on her lap as she sat on the couch. Her pajama-clad legs were tucked under her as morning approached. She'd hoped the words would find her after the nostalgic dinner and wonderful evening she'd spent visiting with her family. There were none. Maybe they weren't going to come back, and Charley just needed to face the facts and accept it. She doubted her publisher would be okay with that.

A yawn escaped her, and Charley realized how truly exhausted she was. The drive from Seattle and not sleeping well over the last few months had taken its toll. Maybe the clean air of the country was working its magical sleep-inducing powers on her. She closed her laptop as the cuckoo clocked chirped loudly. The urge to rip the clock from the wall consumed her. The accumulation of frustration, lack of sleep and stress were creating a rage-filled monster. Charley stomped off to bed with every intention of hiding her head under the pillow. She hated that cuckoo clock more than ever now, and for a split second, a sliver of inspiration twinkled in her brain but quickly ducked out of sight. *Damn, almost.*

Charley forgot just how early the house came alive in the mornings as she squeezed her pillow over her ears. The scents of bacon frying along with freshly brewing coffee danced together in perfect harmony. It tempted Charley to leave the bed she'd only climbed into a few hours earlier. *Is there any hope of falling back to sleep? Not in this house.*

There was a gentle tap on her door as it slowly moved open. Her mother peeked from behind it. She wore a lilac-colored apron and her strawberry-blonde hair was pinned neatly behind her ears.

"Good morning, sweetheart. Breakfast is ready." Her voice was soft as she smiled at Charley with love. It was the same look that had greeted her so many mornings as Charley had grown up.

"Thanks, Mom." Charley stretched and sat upright in the bed.

"How late were you up last night?" Her mother entered Charley's childhood bedroom that had since been converted to a sewing room. Only a few reminders of her childhood remained — trophies and ribbons from her days in school. Then there were the scrapbooks that were proudly filled with articles Charley had written. Her mother had collected every single one and treasured her daughter's printed words.

As her mother sat down on the corner of the full-size bed, Charley felt another yawn coming and covered her mouth. "Just normal business hours."

"And were those hours productive?" She shook her head and her mother patted Charley's blanket-covered leg. "It'll come. Just be patient, dear."

"It's kind of hard when you have a deadline breathing down your neck," Charley answered.

"That may be true, but right now you're here, and I intended to feed you. You've lost too much weight. You're all skin and bones now."

"Stress will do that to a person," Charley quipped.

Her mother tossed her knowing look. "Come… Let's feed you, and maybe after you're properly nourished, you'll feel inspired."

"And if I'm not?" Charley asked as she got out of the bed.

"Then you can help your daddy out in the barn. Maybe some good old-fashioned farm work will get those juices movin'," she teased as she wiggled up from the bed.

"At this point, I'm willing to try anything." Charley let out a hearty laugh and followed her mother out of the room.

The moment Charley entered the dining room she spied a stack of her mother's famous chocolate-chip pancakes. Had she known those were waiting for her, she might've hurried to breakfast a little quicker.

After one of the best meals she'd eaten in a very long time, Charley threw on some jeans and a comfortable hoodie. She braided her long, strawberry-blonde hair and made her way outside in search of her father.

The late-morning air held only a hint of a chill, a simple reminder that summer hadn't quite arrived yet. Birds chirped, waking the world up with their happy song. Charley couldn't help but smile as she became bathed in a sense of peace. She wondered how it was that she'd ever grown to hate this place. This very simple place seemed like heaven. It was staged beautifully with everything wholesome and homegrown. Charley couldn't resist snapping pictures with her cell phone of the glorious morning sun, drenched fields and the weathered barn that stood proudly. She had just posted the pictures online to a few of her favorite social media platforms when her phone rang.

"Hello," she answered, knowing full well the reason behind the call.

"Seriously? Did we not discuss you posting stuff?" Victoria's voice wasn't exactly perky this morning as she scolded Charley. "You've been gone less than twenty-four hours."

"I couldn't help it. Do you see how pretty it is here?" Her eyes feasted on the spread of land as she tromped down a gravel path to the barn.

"We discussed this. No posting on social media. You need to focus on the task at hand. Do I need to contact Pamela?" Victoria threatened playfully.

"Okay, I'll try to be better. At least I didn't post any pics of my coffee or the amazing pancakes I just ate," she offered sweetly.

"I'm actually shocked you didn't. You need to inhale that fresh air then get some words down, girl."

"Jeesh, someone's a little bossy this morning."

Victoria exhaled loudly. "Let's call it job security."

"For who? You?"

"Both of us. Now, go enjoy the day with your family without posting pics. Remember… You're headed to Crescent Lake tomorrow and need to be ready to work. I'll try to sneak over and check up on you," Victoria offered.

"That'd be cool. You're right, Vic. I need to stay off social media."

"That's why you hired me. I'll keep your fans plenty fed with some book giveaways or something while you're away. Don't worry…just write."

"I love you, you know," Charley said sweetly as she arrived at the side door of the barn.

"Love you too. Call me tomorrow." Victoria disconnected their call and Charley shoved her phone in the back jean pocket.

"Dad?" Charley called out as she entered the barn. The musty scent of hay and aging wood filled her nose.

"Come to work with your old man?" He was wiping his hands on a shop rag and his overalls were dusty and with a few streaks of grease. "I was just fixing the tractor." He motioned toward the bright red machine with its enormous tires. "Hop on, kiddo."

Charley hadn't sat in the tractor seat in years. She'd spent most of her childhood on one, sitting on her father's lap as they made laps around their fields. They didn't talk much when they were busy working, but she'd never felt more connected than when they'd been together on a tractor. Charley hoisted herself up and nearly lost her balance.

"It's been some time since you've been on a tractor." Her father stood there proudly with a giant smile on his face, like all was right in his world in that very moment.

A brief sensation of a fear swept through her, along with the temptation to snap a picture and post to her fans that she was still a true farm girl. She fought the urge as her butt found the seat and she held on tightly to the steering wheel. A flood of happy memories came to her as she closed her eyes. She could almost feel the vibration of the powerful motor or the slow movement of the giant wheels. Charley imagined disappearing in a field they'd worked in so many times, and she envisioned the uniform lines as they passed each row.

"You miss it, don't you?"

Charley opened her eyes and looked down at her smiling father. "Gosh, I really do. I think those are my happiest memories."

"They are some of mine too."

Charley looked ahead, the imaginary field was gone, only wooden slats with various tools hung on it stood in front of her. A pinch of sadness hit her as the nostalgia wore off.

"Need some help down?" Her father offered a now partially clean hand.

"Thanks," Charley replied as she accepted his help and eased herself off the machine.

"So, what's all this nonsense about you having trouble writing?" he asked as he closed the hood to the engine. The shop rag dangled from his back pocket as walked to the other side of the tractor.

Charley's anxiety returned. "I can't really explain it, Dad. Writer's block, I suppose."

"You're just overthinking it, sweetheart."

"I don't think it's that simple, Dad." Charley leaned against the tractor and tucked her cold hands in the butt pocket of her jeans.

He stared at her and asked, "Why can't it be?"

She fought to come up with a good rebuttal. *Maybe he's right.* Charley didn't want to admit that it could be something as simple as that holding her back, that it could be her own fault. It was a heck of a lot easier to find something or anyone else to blame.

"I think this trip is going to do you some good." He wandered across the barn and returned with something that instantly brought a smile to her lips. "Here. This will help while you're at Crescent Lake."

Charley curled her fingers around the old fishing pole, one she used anytime they'd went fishing. "I can't believe you still have this," she said in awe.

"It's your pole. I wasn't about to get rid of it. I knew it would come in handy one of these days. Don't overthink things when you go to that lake tomorrow. Take some time to see if the fish are biting." He winked at her and squeezed her shoulder softly. Charley almost teared up as she gripped her pole with one hand and carried it with her as they exited the barn arm in arm.

This man always had a way of always knowing exactly the right thing to say in every situation.

Maybe he should write my book.

Chapter Two

"You can't be serious."

"I am, and quit making such a big deal out of it."

Nick Capra rubbed his jaw and sharp stubble met his palm. The morning had started off pretty shitty, but then again, most did for him nowadays. He had no idea how he had just landed the position of babysitter, but he was less than thrilled. Nick was an uncover agent, a 'had been' being more like it. He'd fled Portland after his entire world had imploded only a few short months before. His cover had been blown in a major sting operation, his partner of the last ten years killed in cold blood, and guilt had been eating him alive ever since. Nick had requested a transfer, anywhere to get his head right. Little did he know he'd be sent to the sleepy community of Crescent Lake.

He hadn't known towns this small even existed anymore. It was in the middle of nowhere, surrounded by towering pine trees and featured a decent-sized lake. There was a diner where he'd eaten most of his meals for the last three months, a few small shops mostly for the tourists during the summer months, a single gas station and a well-equipped grocery store. Everything else was over thirty-plus miles away in either direction. This wasn't exactly the place where he had pictured himself starting over. But nonetheless, there he was, living in a crappy little cabin on the lake, twiddling his thumbs because nothing ever happened in Crescent Lake. Nick should be grateful this assignment had been tossed into his lap, but he was bored.

"You want me to basically babysit this so-called celebrity?" Nick asked gruffly.

"You ever watch that movie *In the Dark of Night*?" asked the sheriff and Nick's commanding officer for the last several months.

Nick shrugged. "Hell, I don't know. I don't really spend a lot of times at the movies. Why?"

The sheriff, who was in his mid-sixties, laughed aloud and the sound irritated Nick that much more. "Well, son, if you had, you'd know this so-called famous celebrity is the author who wrote the book to that particular movie. It was a damn good one too. A lot of her books have been made into movies."

"Okay, I get it. She's a *big* deal. Why do I have to keep an eye on her?" Nick leaned back in his seat across from the sheriff and crossed his jean-clad leg.

"For starters, her agent has personally requested we provide some kind of security to her client. Apparently, there's been some backlash from her last book," he explained carefully.

"So, she's got a few upset fans? What? Are they actually after her? Is an angry mob of box-wine-drinking housewives going to storm the town with pitchforks and torches?"

"Not necessarily. But Pamela Mansfield is definitely a big deal in these parts, son. Hell, in the entire county. Her nephew owns the cabin you're renting."

"Tucker? That's her nephew?" Nick gibed.

"Yep. They're old money, the Mansfields."

Nick grew even more agitated and wasn't the least surprised to learn this new bit of information about Tucker. It all made sense now, especially with the snotty way Tucker carried himself.

The sheriff leaned forward and stared at Nick intensely. "Listen, Capra. We like things quiet here. Having a celebrity around is going to cause some kind of stir, there's no denying that. But just imagine if things did get out of hand with an angry fan. That could mess things up here real good. You don't exactly have a lot going on here." The sheriff paused and took hold of his coffee mug. "Let me remind you that you were the one who requested a transfer and weren't by any means forced to come to Crescent Lake."

"I know, sir," Nick lamented. He didn't need to be reminded. He lived with those reasons and ghosts every day.

"Ms. Charlene Vanderberg will be arriving sometime tomorrow. Make her feel welcome, but more importantly, protected. Keep an eye on things."

"Does anything even happen here?" Nick joked.

The sheriff shrugged his broad shoulders. "Not really, but we'd like to keep it that way."

After grabbing two burgers from the diner to take back to his cabin, Nick purchased a six-pack of his favorite beer, Olympia, and planned to forget about this whole bodyguard bullshit he'd been signed up for. As he arrived at his tiny cabin on the lake, the sun was casting a tangerine and soft golden light on the dark, shimmering surface. Nick had to admit it wasn't exactly the worst view in the world. Maybe he'd eat his solitary meal outside and watch the sun get swallowed by the moon-shaped lake.

Nick let himself in and was instantly greeted with a bark. "You're such a good guard dog, aren't ya?" Nick looked toward his feet and smiled down at the little dog pawing at him. Ruger, a black-colored pug and gag gift from his partner and all the guys at his old station back in Portland, was now his only friend. They'd been through a lot together and as hard as Nick's exterior may seem, he was an absolute softie when it came to this little guy.

Feeling lazy, Nick decided against making the effort to eat outside and instead plopped himself onto the worn plaid couch that had seen better days, probably back in the 70s. He popped open a can of Olympia beer, the metal sound echoing in the small space. The moment the cold, bitter taste hit his tongue, Nick closed his eyes, pushed himself deeper into the couch and put his feet up on the rustic coffee table. He quickly finished his beer and cracked the tab open on another before he set to work on his now-cold burger. He contemplated not even eating the pathetic-looking patty cradled on limp lettuce on a cheap bun. Nick removed the meat and offered it to Ruger, who gobbled it up quickly. Nick guzzled more beer and waited for the feeling of a buzz to numb his brain. It seemed a lot harder these days and took more alcohol to forget everything he'd been through. Nick knew he'd eventually have to deal with all the issues instead of drowning them. But for now, the Oly was working its magic.

* * * *

45

"I promise to call after I get there," Charley called out as she waved goodbye to her parents.

Her mother had packed her enough food to host a small banquet and hugged her at least a million times. It was bittersweet leaving them. The last two days had been lovely, but she was growing anxious. A few ideas had popped into her head for this highly anticipated book. This whole break from Seattle might actually be starting to work. Charley could almost feel that familiar itch to type again and was eager to follow this urge down whatever rabbit hole it would drag her. Maybe the words were finally coming back.

As she carefully backed her SUV out of the driveway and waved once more, Charley couldn't help but feel as though she were leaving a small piece of herself behind. Soon her parents disappeared from her sight. Charley blinked away tears and tried to fix her now-blurred vision. She concentrated on getting to the highway and making sure she was on the right one. This part of Washington could be a little tricky if one missed their exit, something she had done plenty of times. It wasn't long before she found herself on the major highway with the early afternoon sun spilling its golden light in front of her. It was time to focus on the real task at hand. She pressed her foot down on the gas pedal and smiled as the engine purred a little louder.

The scenery began to change, the endless fields of agriculture morphing into sharp mountains and thick woods. The sun barely broke through the canopy of trees as Charley traveled down a single-lane road that would lead her to Crescent Lake. Green metal signs indicated it wasn't much farther to the lake resort.

Up ahead she barely spotted a deer dart across the road. She'd been distracted for only a moment as she adjusted the stereo. Charley was grateful she and the deer hadn't gotten up close and personal.

"I think it's safe to say I'm definitely not in Seattle anymore," Charley nervously commented as she slowed down and paid closer attention to the road. Her heart was beating a little quicker and she felt a tad on edge.

Relief consumed her as a wooden welcome sign to the town of Crescent Lake came into view. This place was definitely small, only a few shops lined a pleasant-looking main street. A decent-sized grocery store was to one side and a gas station across from that. As she ventured farther down the main street, in the distance Charley could see a twinkling glow that was moving. The lake. It was quite beautiful and larger than she had expected. Charley approached the resort slowly — the speed limit signs were practically a crawl — but this allowed her to take in the sights, even though there weren't many.

She finally came to the lake, which was at the end of the town. The pavement had turned into a narrow dirt road. Charley followed the trail to a large building near the shore and parked her SUV. It was the lodge where Pamela had told her to check in. The A-framed windows were massive and faced the best possible view of the water. The sweet scent of pine tickled her nose as Charley inhaled deeply before setting foot inside. She could hear lake birds making their calls and insects singing their own distinct song. Pamela had been right. This place was gorgeous. Charley stood in front of an intricately carved wooden door. A skilled artist had created a scene that captured a buck standing majestically behind a doe not much different than the one that had darted across the road earlier. Charley reached out to touch the wood when the door suddenly moved open. A handsome man stood in front of her. His movie-star good looks greeted her and caused her to stumble in place.

"You must be Charlene," he greeted kindly and motioned for her to enter.

She nodded but found her feet frozen on the welcome mat. Charley 's body grew warm, her hands clammy as she stared him. He was more than just good looking. There was something about the way he'd said her name. His voice was silky and there was careless sexiness about him. Pamela should've warned her just how attractive her nephew was. At least she could've been a little more prepared, worn something a tad cuter than her current road-trip outfit—a faded Seattle Mariners baseball tee and jean capris. A sharp prick brought her back to reality and she rubbed her arm.

"The mosquitos start coming out around this time. Come on in before they eat you alive."

Charley followed him in and her eyes were immediately drawn to taxidermies that were displayed throughout. Large game such as elk, a moose and a few bucks stared down at her with their glossy eyes and their plastic mouths open in panic. She grew nauseated at the sportsman décor.

"Don't worry. Those guys don't bite," he teased as he led the way past a large leather couch and river-rock fireplace. They arrived at a counter where Pamela's nephew began to type on a small laptop.

"This is really some place you've got here," Charley politely commented in hopes of breaking the ice. The lodge was incredible with its rustic charm. It smelled of spicy cinnamon and something else she couldn't quite decipher.

"Thank you." His nearly crystal-clear blue eyes appeared to twinkle. "I'm Tucker, by the way." He extended his hand and she quickly wiped her sweaty palm on the back of her capris before shaking his.

"Charley," she replied nervously.

"I know." Tucker winked and Charley's knees grew soft.

What is my problem? Am I that starved for some male attention? Pull it together, woman.

Tucker turned around and retrieved a key from a series of small hooks mounted on the wall. "Well, Charley, I'll walk you over to where you'll be staying."

"Great," Charley managed and followed him again.

It had grown darker since she'd arrived and it frightened her a little, oddly enough. Maybe it was just being in an unfamiliar place — or the fact that Bigfoot could very well be lurking out in the woods that sheltered the cabins. Charley kept close to Tucker, nearly at his heels as they walked past several identical cabins. Each one was near the shore and had a fantastic view of the massive lake that almost appeared to be the shape of a crescent moon. Charley almost opened her mouth to comment if that was the reason behind the town's name and thought better of it, realizing her brief moment of stupidity.

"Here we are," Tucker announced as he stopped in front of a cabin made of cedar or redwood — Charley wasn't sure which — but there was an obvious red hue that even stuck out in the dusky night.

"Wonderful," Charley said but then remembered she hadn't grabbed anything from her SUV. "What about my car?"

"You can park next to your cabin over there," Tucker answered and pointed to a vacant spot.

"Do you mind walking me back to get it?" Charley asked as a chilly shiver coursed through her.

"Of course, I'd be happy to." Tucker guided her back to the SUV, and as soon as she was safely inside, said goodnight.

Charley started up her SUV and crept slowly to her cabin. She didn't want to disturb any of the other guests. The resort seemed mostly unoccupied, but Charley figured that once summer officially hit—which would be soon—the place would probably be swarmed with lake-goers. She'd better enjoy the peace and quiet while it lasted. After she parked the SUV, Charley gathered her first load of bags to bring in. With her hands full, she was grateful that Tucker had left the door unlocked.

"I could kill you, Pamela," she growled loudly once inside. She took in the shabby furniture and sparse cabin. "Cute, my ass." This place wasn't exactly a dump, but it was definitely not what she'd expected, especially after having seen the stunning lodge. This was not one of those fancy glamping types of cabins, but it could be a whole worse.

Charley dropped her bags onto an old couch that had seen better days and prayed there weren't any bugs camping out in the furniture. She gathered the rest of her belongings and set the alarm on her SUV. She winced at how loudly it beeped, but old habits died hard. She lived in Seattle and it didn't matter how great the neighborhood. It was smart to always lock and set an alarm. Maybe out here it wasn't necessary.

As Charley started to put things away, she noticed small curtains framed the windows, giving away a complete view inside. She could've sworn she felt someone watching her.

"You're being paranoid," Charley told herself as she set up shop. There was a small dining table that would have to do as a makeshift desk.

This paranoia she felt was in a weird way a good sign. All those tingly feelings and creepy sensations were the things she'd written about. The hairs on the back of her neck rose in attention as her body became keenly aware. Her skin was instantly cold, and another shiver moved down her spine, despite the humid and muggy warmth inside the cabin. Her back was to a window, and as tempted as Charley was to turn around, she didn't. A prickle of fear had a hold of her and her instincts warned her to not move.

"If I'm going to be here a while, I think I'm going to see if I can buy curtains or something," she said to the empty room. "Get a grip and focus. We've got work to do." Feeling truly inspired for the first time in months, Charley sat down carefully on an ancient-looking chair she'd moved in front of her makeshift desk. She opened the laptop slowly and half expected the Boogey Man to jump out at her. *Yeah, this place might actually do the trick.*

So, that's her. Nick removed his eyes from the binoculars and went back to the couch. He had to admit that even though he completely loathed the very notion of babysitting this little author diva, she was sort of pretty. More than just pretty... Her hair was an odd shade, almost pink, but not quite red, at least from what he could make out in the dim light. He'd watched her as she moved around her small cabin like a skittish bird, fluttering around, which made it difficult to follow her. *Surveillance, a little recon, not being a creep.* Nick wanted to get to know his subject before she had a chance to know him, not that she'd ever fully get to know him. No one would ever have that opportunity again, not if he could help it.

Nick tried to focus on the author lady when his pant leg was tugged. "Ruger, do you mind? I'm trying to concentrate here, buddy." Ruger whined and Nick gave up on trying to keep the binoculars steady on his subject. "Some partner you are. See if I ever take you on a stakeout." Ruger cocked his head to the side and wagged his curled tail. Nick smiled down at Ruger. "Okay, let's go outside."

Ruger's business completed and once they were back inside, Nick drained another beer and his eyes grew heavy as he stroked the soft, round head of his pug. Nick often fought the urge to sleep because that's when the nightmares came, forcing him to relieve one of the worst days of his existence—one he'd never forget. He shifted on the couch and melted into the tough fabric. The warmth of his dog next to him caused him to become far too comfortable and almost too paralyzed to move. *Stay awake.* Nick soon succumbed to relentless exhaustion and the dreams began to play behind his closed lids. He would spend the rest of the night trying right the wrongs and stop senseless deaths—a torture he endured every single night.

Chapter Three

I watch as she exits her car and casually scans her surroundings. She hasn't the slightest clue I'm here, hidden in the shadows and waiting patiently. She gingerly slides the credit card in and tucks it back into the front pocket of her white shorts. Her legs are a shade of almost-harvested wheat against the brightness of the material. Slender fingers with nails painted a coral pink press the plastic PIN pad. I close my eyes for a brief moment and can almost feel her touch. It's almost too much to bear but I must. I inhale deeply from my station and take in the sounds that surround us both.

She lifts the heavy gas pump handle from its cradle and gives her small car the nourishment it needs. She locks the pump into place and leans against her car. Her arms are too thin. They are crossed at her chest that is much too big for her frame. She has no idea what is coming. The slight breeze gently moves her dark hair. I desperately want to feel the tendrils at her nape. My fingers itch to touch her, but there will be time for that.

I begin to move from my place, walking ever so quietly. The moment has to be perfect. I must be precise. She has no clue I'm near. I catch a whiff of her cheap perfume and fight the urge to gag. She twists her body back to her car, her back now staring at me. In one swift movement, I cover her mouth. I feel her scream into my hand as I drag her away from the bright fluorescent lights where the night bugs gather to feast. They are drawn to the light, as she soon will be.

She kicks at the ground, chipping the asphalt and causing pieces of the black rock to fling up into the air. She's a fighter. She knows what's next. We both do. I've read it. This is how it must happen. I'm doing this for her — not for this woman struggling in my arms but for someone who needs me to do this. It's all for her.

I can feel her tire as we enter the wooded area not too far from where her car will be discovered when the sun is up. I throw her to the ground and her will to survive is not nearly as strong as it should be now. She stays there, looking up at me with fear in her eyes. Her mascara is running down her cheeks. She is bartering inside her mind. I can almost feel the gears turning in her brain as she attempts to figure out a plan of escape. I kneel down next to her and am half-tempted to assure her that this won't hurt. But I don't want to lie to her. What if I'm wrong? This is my first time.

She remains frozen stiff and pleads for me to let her go.

"I can't do that," I answer calmly.

I reach out and a zing of electricity courses through my veins and into my fingertips as I touch her skin. It's warm and velvety soft. I press gently at first then circle my palms around her neck. The tips of my fingers meet at her nape. I desperately want to touch her hair. There will be time for that. I place my thumbs firmly on the front of her throat. I swear I can feel her blood rushing under them. Her pulse is fast, and I can feel her heart beating hard inside her chest. My own heartbeat matches her rhythm.

She begins to claw at me, but I manage to keep my arms rigid and my face away from those sharp coral-painted fingernails. I squeeze. She moves frantically under me as I bear down. The strength in my hands is no match for her as I squeeze even harder. I peer down at her eyes. They are wide and beginning to bulge from their sockets. This only encourages me. I'm almost there. We both know it.

She squirms, resisting me with every last drop of her will to survive until it finally leaves her in one last flail. I feel something snap underneath my thumbs. A loud pop. I curl my fingers around the silky strands I wanted to play with so badly. I toy with their softness but feel nothing. I stare at her. Her eyes are open and looking off into a distance. Heaven maybe?

My body isn't sure why it feels an odd sense of pleasure mixed with a sick adrenaline-fueled rush as I walk away. I leave the woman there on the cold earth, her bed for these small hours until they find her.

I did this for her, not the corpse. She'll soon see this is what she needed, someone who was willing to help her, to save her from herself. I've taken on that role — of being her savior and giving her this sacrifice.

Chapter Four

Light pierced through Charley's eyelids no matter how hard she tried to squeeze them shut. Curtains were the priority of the day. She stretched, decided there was no use in trying to battle the brilliant rays and crawled out of the surprisingly comfortable bed. Last night, Charley had managed to write. *Well, a little anyway.* Granted, those words had been deleted and retyped more than a dozen times until she'd finally surrendered. Despite waving the white flag, the good news was there had been words. The bad news was that they weren't the right ones. As she'd studied them until almost dawn, Charley had found that they didn't even begin to convey what she needed them to. But she wasn't going to wallow in this. Charley was celebrating that she was finally somewhat back on track. She'd happily accept that as a win.

She lied. Curtains weren't a priority this morning. Coffee was. Charley looked at the small single-serving coffee pot on the ugly Formica counter. *That's not going to cut it.* She remembered seeing a restaurant as she'd driven along the main street. Charley could definitely eat, as her stomach loudly reminded her that she'd only snacked on a few chips the night before. Leftover fried chicken and the other assortment of food from her mother wasn't exactly calling her name. However, the idea of an omelet or even a cheeseburger sounded really great right about now. Charley dressed quickly in jean shorts and a pale-pink tank top. She slipped her arms through a warm flannel, relishing the feel of the soft fabric against her skin. She ran her fingers through her slightly tangled hair and decided to leave it down. She was a woman on a mission and didn't care how she looked. Right now, coffee was of great importance then finding something to cover the windows of the cabin. Charley planned on squaring off with her laptop and forcing herself to write at least one Chapter today. If she could at least knock out a decent word count, something to build up her confidence, Charley knew she'd be well on her way to actually writing the novel.

She grabbed her purse and exited the cabin, making sure to lock the door behind her. Charley was greeted again with the sweet scent of pine and brisk morning air. She paused to take in the view and told herself she needed to make sure to enjoy this place. The dark blue water rippled and slapped against an inviting sandy shore that she hadn't really noticed the evening before. She spied a dock between her cabin and the neighboring one. Her dad's words echoed in her mind and reminded her to add bait to her list. A little retail therapy would do her some good. She actually looked forward to tackling the day, and it wasn't even ten o'clock yet. *Maybe getting up early isn't all that bad. Gosh, who am I?* Charley giggled as she headed into the main part of town.

Where is she off to this early? Nick peered through his cabin window as Miss Fancy Pants got into her expensive SUV and left the resort. She had only taken her purse with her. Nick knew she wasn't leaving for good. *Too bad.* He drank the bitter black coffee in his mug and kept his gaze trained on the cloud of dust left behind from her SUV.

He was beyond exhausted. Nick felt it deep in his bones and in his soul. He'd been plagued by nightmares and had woken up stiff and achy on that shitty old couch. He'd never made it to his bed, not that the lumpy mattress that was too short for his tall frame was any better. Nick peeked over and saw Ruger snoozing loudly with his head elevated on the arm of the couch. Nick decided to move his coffee, his third cup of the morning, outside. His pug wasn't about to let him go out alone, woke and quickly hopped from the couch. He let out a heavy sigh as he took a seat on the camp chair on the porch of his cabin. Ruger found his place on Nick's lap and resumed his morning nap.

Nick should tail the woman and find out where she was going. But where could she really go? The town wasn't all that big, and he wasn't in the mood to chase her. He doubted she'd get into any real trouble.

The lake was empty of any boats, and the breeze brushed against the surface, causing tiny waves to crash on the shore only a few yards away. Nick relished quiet moments such as these when peace had a sneaky way of finding him. Birds chirped as the slight wind whistled through the trees. Nick looked up at the towering pines with their bristly branches of sharp green needles. Discarded dead needles littered the dirt paths beyond the lake. Nick took in the scenery and slipped into a state of complete relaxation. His cell phone chimed loudly and ruined the moment.

"Capra," he answered gruffly. Ruger's bulging eyes glared up at him. The scowl on his small black face didn't hide his annoyance.

"We need you down at the Fill n' Go," the sheriff ordered sternly.

"What's up?" Nick asked casually as he took a long and leisurely sip of his coffee.

"We've got a body."

Nick coughed and coffee sputtered from his lips. He'd not expected those words to come from the sheriff. "I'll be right there."

A body? I thought nothing ever happened in Crescent Lake.

* * * *

Charley soon discovered that Crescent Lake was even smaller than she'd originally thought. The quaint restaurant was literally one of the only places to eat. It was like a throwback from the 1960s with its ugly brown vinyl booths and wrap-around counter. She inhaled the greasy scent of nostalgia that hung in the air. Charley felt eyes on her as she located a spot by the window. *Maybe they aren't exactly fond of newcomers.* Charley slipped into one of the few unoccupied booths, and the worn material squeaked as she made herself more comfortable. She was quickly served coffee and given a laminated menu that had seen better days. The young waitress didn't announce any specials as she smacked her gum and trotted away. Charley perused the menu. She was debating whether to go with biscuits and gravy or a patty melt when a shadow covered it.

"Hey, sweetie," a slender waitress said as she paused at Charley's booth. She held a pot of the blackest coffee Charley had ever laid eyes on. "You're that writer lady, aren't ya?"

Charley smiled and reluctantly nodded. "Which one might that be?" she teased.

The waitress quickly sat across from her. In a hushed voice, she whispered, "I thought so. Charlene Vanderberg, right?"

"In the flesh," Charley smirked as she held a beige speckled mug to her lips.

"I knew it. We'd heard a rumor you were going to be here. Something about writing a new book."

"Word travels fast." Charley laughed.

"Have you seen the size of Crescent Lake, honey?"

"You've got a point there." Charley offered her hand politely. "I'm Charley. Nice to meet you?"

The waitress gripped her hand firmly. Her brightly painted lips turned upward into a broad smile. "Molly."

"So, have you read any of my books?" Charley asked. That was always the hard part. Most of the people she met these days were obsessed with her books or the movies. It was just easier to ask if they had read or seen her work and get it out of the way.

"Truthfully, I'm not much of a reader." Molly blushed with embarrassment and Charley smiled with relief. "I did watch one or two of the movies they made out of them, though."

She couldn't explain why but Charley felt instantly comfortable with Molly. Maybe it had to do with the bright fuchsia lipstick on her crooked front teeth, the cheap box-dye of blonde her hair was colored or the honesty that shone in her ordinary-looking hazel eyes.

She exuded a genuine realness about her, something Charley missed. "I kind of like the fact you haven't read my books."

"You're not offended?"

"Gosh, no," Charley reassured her.

"Wow, Charley, I gotta be honest. I think we all were worried you were going to be some snotty Hollywood type."

Charley laughed a little too loudly at the accusation. "I actually grew up on a farm just a few hours from here."

Molly slapped the table softly. "Get out. Well, that explains it. You're a country girl."

"I think my agent may disagree. Seems I've been in Seattle a little too long and have forgotten my roots."

"Don't you worry. You seem sweet as apple pie to me." Molly winked. "If you need anything, you just holler," she said as she scooted out from the booth.

"Actually, yes. Do you know where I could maybe find some curtains and few things for the cabin I'm staying at?"

"The closest fabric store is almost fifty miles away. If I were you, I'd see if the grocery store has any dish towels. That would probably be your best bet," Molly suggested as she shrugged her shoulders.

Charley watched her hurry to the counter and refill the coffee mug of a grumpy looking older gentleman. The waitress had to be in her fifties, was in decent shape overall but with plump hips and didn't seem to be a stranger to hard work. The old guy was hunched over his plate, but Charley could make out his craggily face lined with deep wrinkles and the permanent frown that was attached to it. Charley constantly assessed people, building a catalog of would-be characters. She took in all the physical features and personality traits and mentally stored them for later use. Charley had always found people fascinating. They came in so many varieties, no two the same. Even with identical twins, there was always something to help one tell the difference, but a person just had to look for it and be observant.

The young girl reappeared to take her order of biscuits and gravy and sprinted back to the kitchen. Charley scrolled through her phone as she waited. Fellow colleagues in the industry were releasing more books than she could count, and all the glossy-looking covers caused an anxious pit to form in her stomach, not that Charley was envious that these authors were putting their books out there. That was the name of the game. She usually championed new releases and supported her writer pals. That was just another reminder that Charley should be doing the same thing right now — releasing a brand spankin' new book for readers to gorge on. Maybe if she were completely honest with herself, she was a tad jealous. She was relieved when an oval plate loaded with food was placed in front of her.

Charley enjoyed her strong but doctored-up coffee — her mug never seemed to go empty — and focused on the delicious meal. The gravy was salty and creamy and seasoned with large bits of sausage. The biscuits weren't as good as her mother's but were pretty darn close. She surveyed the diner as she feasted. Everyone was engrossed in their meals. She could hear the whispers of conversations in neighboring booths and forks scraping against plates as folks finished their breakfast. She almost felt inspired as she absorbed all the sounds around her.

Charley turned her attention back to the plate of scrambled eggs and charred bits of bacon in front of her. She was beyond full, not used to consuming this much food in one sitting. Charley pushed the plate away and stared out of the dirty window. A police cruiser raced by, its lights swirling in a blur. Charley didn't hear any sirens. She wasn't the only one who noticed. Every patron in the diner had shifted in their seats and gazed out of the large windows to get a better view. Charley heard whispers as to what that had been about. She was certain that whatever was happening would soon be known.

Charley couldn't deny the sense of curiosity that invaded her. That was the reporter in her who still wanted all the details. Maybe a terrible accident had happened on the highway. The cruiser was definitely in a hurry to wherever it was headed, but the silence of the sirens created goosebumps on the skin of her arms. The absence of sound was meant to not cause notice, which was never a good thing. The sight of them should be enough for drivers to pull over and out of the way. Charley fought the urge to follow the cruiser and do a little of her own investigating. She looked back at her plate, but her eyes weren't taking in the leftover breakfast. She saw blurry words in her mind in black typewriter font. She smiled. Her words were coming back.

* * * *

By the time Nick arrived at the scene, several police cruisers were already there. Their red-and-blue lights shone brightly against the mid-morning sun. He had the familiar sensation of nervous adrenaline making his belly sick. After he parked his truck next to the sheriff's cruiser, Nick scoped out the landscape. He immediately wondered if the gas station had a surveillance system. There was small sedan being towed away. Nick realized it must belong to the victim. He swallowed down the bile that had started to coat the back of his throat and noticed a wooded area not too far from the gas pumps. He could see several deputies with dogs stomping carefully through the overgrown weeds and grass. Nick hopped out of the truck and stood there for a moment, playing out various scenarios.

The sheriff's gaze connected with Nick's and he tipped his wide brim hat. The sour expression on the sheriff's face concerned Nick.

"We may need your expertise here," the sheriff said as he leaned against his perfectly clean cruiser. He appeared almost unsure of what to do or how to handle this situation. Not everyone was cut out for this life. The dangerous line of duty and being a witness to the heinous things that happened in this world could take a toll on a person.

Some of us should just stay behind a desk.

Nick eyed the ground. The asphalt had a faint, almost undetectable to the naked eye, line that led to the wooded area. He followed it, noticing tiny broken bits of the asphalt strewn from the nearly invisible path. There had definitely been a struggle and the victim had kicked as they were dragged. Nick begged the nauseous waves in his stomach to settle as he approached the victim. A white covering was draped over the body. It stood out harshly against the green-and-brown camouflage of the trees and bushes. Nick inhaled sharply and prayed his coffee didn't make an appearance. He crouched down.

The moist earth gave off a musty scent that caused Nick to gag a bit. He pulled the covering back slowly and discovered the first hint of alabaster skin. He peeled the cloth farther back to reveal a young woman, and Nick noticed deep bruising at her throat. *Strangulation.* Her eyes were open and slightly bugged, her dark hair fanned out like a halo above her head. Deep, round imprints on the front of her throat indicated to him that it was possibly a man who had done this. The thumb-shaped bruises were large and ugly. Nick moved her head carefully with his gloved hand to see if there had been any blunt-force trauma to her head. He couldn't spot a single drop of blood on her. Nick pulled the covering down more to expose more of her cold body. There was nothing to suggest she'd been stabbed or sexually assaulted. This had been a clean kill. His stomach was grateful.

He shook his head and questioned the motive. Back home, this scene could've just as easily been another senseless killing. Nick had seen enough of those during his time as a homicide detective before he'd gone undercover. But he'd been assured that Crescent Lake was about as safe and sound as Mayberry in *The Andy Griffith Show*. It had been the perfect place to transfer — quiet and away from people, where nothing exciting or murderous ever happened. People didn't even speed in this neck of the woods. Would he grow bored of a place like this? More than likely, perhaps after months of nothing happening. Nick hadn't realized he'd be revisiting his homicide roots so soon.

Nick stood as a gurney rolled up to retrieve the corpse. He kept his eyes on the ground for any sign of footprints or any clues that may have been missed by the other detectives on the scene. His instincts were back in full effect. It was as though he'd never left.

"Awful, isn't it?" the sheriff asked as Nick returned to truck empty-handed and no closer to solving this murder.

"I thought you said nothing ever happened here?"

The sheriff shook his head, his thick arms crossed over his pressed uniformed chest. "Not like this. These are good people who live here." Nick tried to ignore the emotional croak in the sheriff's voice.

"So, we think the killer's an outsider?"

"It has to be." The sheriff stared off in the direction of the woods then turned his eyes to Nick. He lifted his hand to shield the sun from his eyes as he said quietly, "I can't imagine one of our own doing something terrible like this."

Nick gave the sheriff a stern look. "I'm going to interview everyone. Right now, we know nothing and everyone is a suspect."

"I knew that girl, Capra. She used to play softball with my oldest granddaughter." The sheriff pinched the bridge of his nose and Nick watched the man lose it. His slumped shoulders shook as he openly cried for the victim.

Nick gently patted the sheriff's back. "I'm sorry you knew her. I know it makes this and what we have to do much harder. You may very well know the killer," Nick calmly explained.

The sheriff shook his head as he tried to regain his composure. Nick knew this wasn't going to be easy. He genuinely felt for this man who had seemed tough as nails the last three months Nick had come to know him. But they had a killer out there. Small town or not, good people or not, someone had wrapped their hands around that woman's throat and squeezed the life out of her.

Nick stood tall and peered over at the convenience store where several people were gathered and watching with horrified curiosity. "I need to talk to the person who found her body."

* * * *

She had just removed all the contents from a paper grocery sack when her phone sang out a delightful little tune. Charley dug into her jean pocket. "Oh, for Pete's sake," she complained loudly as she fumbled with the cell phone. "Hello?" she answered with slight annoyance and without looking to see who the caller was.

"Charley, how are you, dear?" Pamela's voice greeted her politely.

"Just trying to get settled in." Charley eyed her purchases on the counter. She'd bought an array of household-type things and enough snacks to feed an army.

"I'm glad to hear it. Have you met my nephew yet?"

Charley carried her newly purchased shampoo and conditioner into the small single-person bathroom. "Pamela, I could kill you."

Pamela let out an odd laugh. "Why is that?"

Charley went back to the kitchen counter and started to put away her other items that belonged in that room. There was a single shelf and one small cupboard. Charley peered into it and was surprised to find it very clean. She dusted it anyway.

"Oh, I don't know if you're aware or not, but your nephew is gorgeous," Charley replied and was met with another laugh.

"Tucker is my nephew. I witnessed his birth. I suppose I don't quite see him in that light," Pamela explained. "Sure, he's a handsome young man but he's my little Tuck and always will be."

"Well, newsflash... He's hot. You could've warned me."

"Why? You have a book to write. You're not there to check out the dating scene."

"You're kidding, right? You've been to Crescent Lake before, haven't you?"

"I have—plenty of times, in fact. That's why I sent you there. No distractions," she said firmly. "The perfect place for you to get this book done."

"I know," she relented. "But come on. You should have said something."

"Oh, Charley, please focus on what's important here. Besides, that community is mostly filled with retired folks and people on weekend getaways."

Pamela had that right. Tucker was the only good-looking guy she'd come across since she'd arrived, not that she was even remotely interested in hooking up with anyone there. She could imagine what Victoria would think of him. She'd definitely encourage Charley to get to know him a little better. Charley let out a frustrated huff. "You're no fun. You know that?" "Honey, I'm your agent. You don't pay me to be fun," Pamela gently reminded her. "Please tell you've already completed at least a Chapter."

Charley blew out an extra-long breath before she answered, "No. It hasn't even been twenty-four hours. Give me a break." Pamela was quiet on the other end.

Charley was worried she'd lost the connection. "You still there?"

"I am," she finally answered. "You'll be at the cabin for about two months, Charley, and in that time, I expect to receive a rough manuscript in my hot little hands."

"You will get it. I promise." A sharp bite of anxiety attacked Charley's gut. She didn't need this kind of pressure, especially when just this morning she'd felt as though things were finally starting to turn around.

"I'm holding you to it. Now, no more fantasies about my nephew. Get to work, woman."

"No promises about the fantasies… I'm a writer, after all," she teased while stacking boxes of crackers into the freshly cleaned cupboard. Charley added, "You know what they say about all work and no play."
"And do those people have an impending book launch for a book that hasn't even been written yet?" The brief pause caused Charley to swallow hard. "Yeah, I didn't think so. No more playing around. Focus, Charley. I'll check on you in a few days and want a few sample Chapters emailed to me by the end of the week," Pamela ordered and hung up.
Charley removed the phone from her ear and stared at the glossy screen. *No goodbye?* Pamela had never been this short with her or worse, so darned serious. Not that their relationship was ultra-playful, but Pamela hadn't ever been this demanding before. She feared this was far more serious of a situation than she'd originally believed. Her publisher was no doubt breathing down Pamela's neck as well. Pamela could only keep those vultures at bay for so long. Charley desperately needed to get some words down tonight and start hammering out a decent Chapter.

She went back to work putting her groceries away when she heard a knock at the door. Charley only had to move a few feet to reach the door, and when she opened it, Tucker stood there with a sexy grin. *Yeah, so much for no distractions.*

"I hope I'm not bothering you?" he asked as he leaned casually against the door jamb. Just behind him the afternoon sun glow gave the lake a gold shimmer. It was the perfect backdrop.

"No, not at all," she lied. "Actually, I just got off the phone with your aunt."

"Is that so? And what is my lovely Aunt Pam up to?" Tucker motioned for Charley to follow him outside onto the small porch. He lowered himself into one of the canvas chairs and patted the empty seat next to him.

She eased herself down and stared out at the lake nervously. Her heart was racing, and palms grew clammier by the minute. It had been quite a while since a guy had made her react this way. Charley picked at a small tear in her jeans. "She was checking to see if I was all settled in."

"She's a worrywart, that wonderful aunt of mine."

Charley snuck a glance and watched the tanned skin near his eyes crinkle as he laughed. Tucker's blond hair was slightly messy, wind-whipped and bleached by the sun, adding even more sex appeal to his already-handsome features. She darted her eyes away before Tucker caught her studying him.

"That she is," Charley replied. "She has every right to be, though."

His tone deepened. "Why is that?"

"As you probably already know, she's my agent," Charley explained.

"Actually, I didn't know. So, are you an author or something?"

"Definitely more of an 'or something' as of late," Charley joked. She trained her eyes on the lake that moved invitingly. Perhaps it was the warmth of the sun or having Tucker in such close proximity that made Charley want to take a dip in the cool water.

"Well, don't let her get to you. This place is meant for relaxing and recharging your batteries, city girl."

"Not when you have a deadline and have to magically complete an entire manuscript from scratch in a few short months," she rebutted.

Tucker released a heavy sigh as he rose from his seat. "Then I'd better not keep you. I just wanted to see if you needed anything." Disappointment was present in his body language and voice.

"Thanks. I really appreciate that." Charley looked up at him, soaked in his boyish good looks and wished she was only there for vacation.

She'd love to get to know this guy. There was no denying that she was attracted to him. Tucker was definitely her type. He had a lean athletic build, and she knew there had to be one helluva set of abs under the plain gray cotton shirt he wore. His muscular calves were tanned against the long white shorts he wore and covered in a light spray of blond hair. Maybe this was just the push she needed to work a bit faster. What if she were able to have the best of both worlds? She could set certain goals—like completing a Chapter—then reward herself with some playtime with Tucker. She had been single for an eternity and maybe that was part of her problem. Didn't she deserve to have some fun? To live a little?

* * * *

Nick threw the remnants of the cold, stale coffee to the back of his throat and tossed the Styrofoam cup into the wastebasket. The caffeine did little to help keep him focused. It was more out of habit that he even drank coffee. Working all those long and tired hours, it took the edge off his exhaustion…just barely.

He'd been at the station for the remainder of the day, interviewing people and trying to rule out suspects. Nick found it funny how naturally he'd fallen back into the routine of questioning. *Once a cop, always a cop.*

"Capra, can you come in here?" the sheriff called out to him. Nick entered the small office and took a seat when the sheriff motioned for him to sit. The pudgy man was leaned back in his chair and had a thoughtful expression on his face. He seemed older just in these last few hours. This crime had done a number on him. Nick could relate.

"What's going on, sir?" Nick asked politely. He felt on edge and was eager to get back to what he'd been doing. His notes were waiting for him back in the tiny conference room he used as a makeshift office. Nick was hopeful that maybe when he looked them over again, something new, something he'd missed earlier would magically appear.

The sheriff cleared his throat. "Have you introduced yourself to Charlene Vanderberg yet?"

Not this shit again. Nick released an irritated groan. "Sorry. I've been kinda busy today," he replied sarcastically. The sheriff glared harshly at him, a reminder of who was actually in charge here.

"Considering today's event, we need to take some extra precautions."

Nick ran his hand through his hair and argued, "Don't you think we've got bigger fish to fry than babysitting some spoiled celebrity?"

"What if she's a target, son?"

Nick hadn't considered that. His focus was simply on the fact that there'd been a murder in a town that supposedly never experienced an ounce of crime. His thoughts were solely on that they had a killer out there, someone who could very well strike again. Nick was investigating motives for why this had happened.

"Capra, I appreciate your help on this case, more than you really know." The sheriff rubbed his fat chin and continued, "But I need you to turn your attention back on your original assignment and keep an eye on Vanderberg. Is that clear?" His eyes burned into Nick's and left nothing to guess. The sheriff wasn't budging on this issue.

"Crystal." Nick got up from his seat.

Once he'd made his way out of the office and down the hall, Nick slammed his palm against the cream wallpapered hall and hissed a curse word under his breath. *What is so damn important about this writer?* Nick was seething mad. Why invite him to help with a crime scene only to remove him? It made utterly no sense to him.

It was more than apparent to Nick that this hick town had no idea how to handle anything like this. It certainly wasn't wise to take the only detective with any actual homicide experience off a case like this, let alone crown him 'babysitter of the year'. Nick slammed the heavy glass door behind him and went out to his truck. He peeled out and headed for home. It was time to meet this so-called famous author.

* * * *

She decided to take her father's advice and gripped her fishing pole tightly in one hand and in the other, a small sack with snacks and bait. Charley needed to shut her brain off to all the worry and stress about completing a Chapter, let alone an entire manuscript. The cold can of beer she carried in the paper sack might even remedy that or give her some much-needed inspiration.

The walk to the dock was a short one. The sun had begun to dip low in the sky, causing shadows to stand guard around the lake. Bugs hovered just above the surface of the water and Charley heard a fish splash in the distance as it tried to catch its own dinner. She couldn't help but smile. That was exactly what she needed right now, a little time and solitude, a moment of peace to commune with nature a bit.

Charley positioned herself at the end of the weathered but sturdy dock. Her bare legs hung over but kept her feet just above the water. The dock rocked slightly under her as she surveyed the lake. The rounded shoreline had about twenty or so cabins that she counted, all identical to her own tiny home for the next few months. They all appeared to be vacant, but she knew that wouldn't be the case much longer. There was a stillness, almost eerie quiet in the air.

The lodge was to her left, and the massive windows revealed a soft golden glow from the lights inside. If she squinted hard enough, Charley could almost make out the shape of the enormous moose head that was mounted on one wall. It made her shiver. Something about seeing those animals posed like that bothered her. Funny, that coming from a woman who made a living from writing books about gruesome murders.

There was something unsettling to her about preserving a large animal like a moose or an elk. She instantly recalled the bearskin rug inside the lodge. The thought of skinning a bear freaked her out. She'd heard that the muscle structure of a bear resembled that of a human. Charley shook off the heebie-jeebies that tried to take hold of her and turned her mind back to the relaxing task at hand.

Quit thinking so much. Time to shut my brain off.

She rifled through the small sack and pulled out a plastic container. It was cold to the touch as she removed the lid. Charley scrunched up her nose as she bravely plucked out a fat worm from the moist dirt that several worms squirmed in. She baited her hook with the skill of someone who'd been doing it most of her life. Her father had insisted that if she wanted to fish, she'd better learn every aspect there was to know. That didn't just mean casting her line out. It meant every last, gross detail—from baiting a sharp hook with a plump worm, removing the hook from the mouth of a thrashing fish as it gulped its dying breaths, gutting the fish and cleaning it completely. So, why was she perfectly fine with fishing and not the taxidermy of game animals? To her, fishing just seemed different. Maybe it had to do with everyone telling her fish had no feelings. They sure looked like they felt something when their unblinking eyes, full of panic, gazed up at her. Charley mentally slapped herself. Her father's words pierced her overactive brain. She was doing it again—overthinking things.

After she was satisfied with how secure the worm was on the shiny silver hook, Charley expertly whipped her rod back and the line shot out far into the lake. She rested the pole at her side. Now came the fun part, the waiting and time when she could munch on her snacks and let her brain rest. The sky had begun to change from orange sherbet to a soft shade of indigo. This was the best time to fish, that perfect moment when the light was muted and almost gone for the day. Charley popped the tab on the can of beer and swallowed a large gulp of the refreshing cold drink. She could spy her bobber in the water as she let her mind wander in a completely numb state. *Damn, this felt good.*

"Charlene Vanderberg?"

Well, that didn't last long. Charley turned around toward the sound of the voice who'd called out her name. A rather tall man was approaching. He wore dark-wash jeans and a wrinkled black button dress shirt rolled up his forearms. As he came closer, Charley was able to make out more distinct details. His black hair was shaggy and in desperate need of a trim. His square jaw was covered in more than a day's growth of stubble. The light mocha color of his eyes possessed a special but sad light as he stared down at her harshly. There was a simmering anger burning in them. This man, whoever he was, was pissed off. The darkness and hate that emitted from him frightened Charley as she jumped up from her place on the dock. The dock shifted suddenly under her feet and she lost her balance, causing her to fall backward into the water.

Great. He stood there for a moment, not sure exactly what it was he was waiting for, to see if she would drown? Nick watched as she bobbed back up to the surface and paddled back toward the dock. She definitely wasn't the most graceful swimmer. *What if I have to jump in and save her?* That was not part of the plan. He'd come here to confront this prissy broad and was rather shocked to find her out here on the dock — fishing, of all things.

She finally grabbed the splintery edge of the dock. Nick bent down, offering her his hand. She hesitated at first and muttered something under her breath as she accepted it. The second he helped to pull her out of the water, the touch of her cool and wet hand caused him to flinch. He didn't like the immediate charge that coursed through him as they'd touched. Nick quickly released his grasp and stood there, waiting for her to speak.

She was drenched, water dripped onto the dock, creating a large puddle under her. One thing he could tell for sure was that this woman was steaming mad. Wasn't he the one who was angry and ready to battle?

"You shouldn't just come up on people like that, you know?"

"So, you scare easily?" Nick countered as he struggled not to laugh.

He had to admit she was even cuter up close. His binoculars hadn't done her justice the night before. The flecks of red in her blonde hair glittered in the cusp of nightfall. Tiny drops of water hung off her long lashes that framed stunning blue eyes. A light spray of freckles gave her a girlish look that twisted something inside him. He saw an innocence he hadn't expected, but Nick found it staring right up at him with her slightly parted pink lips, still wet from the lake. Nick felt an invisible force tug at him. He needed to feel something good. He closed his eyes for a brief moment and his tired brain fed him visions of the alabaster skin.

"This is your fault," she cried as she stamped her bare foot on the wood. He couldn't help but smile at the sight of her pink painted toenails. Even her feet were cute. Her sweet voice and spitfire tantrum shooed away the awful images from the morning. Nick was grateful for this moment of distraction.

"Hello?" She waved at his face and puffed her cheeks out in anger.

Didn't she know a man had his limits? That he could only handle so much damn cuteness. Nick gathered her to his chest. It didn't matter that she was soaking wet. He needed her. She was nearly a foot a shorter and scowled up at him with pretty irritation. He also needed her to quit looking at him like that. When she bit down on her bottom lip, it proved to be too much for Nick. He swept her up and kissed her hard on the mouth. She tasted like sugar, sweet summertime and everything good and right in the world — nothing like the awful nightmare the world really was.

Charley found herself pinned to this stranger who was kissing the absolute daylights out of her. She struggled for air as her body instinctively molded itself to this man. Confusion had long past set in, and she wondered if she were dreaming this. There was no way this could be real. Her tongue detected a hint of coffee as her mouth continued to be pleasantly assaulted. The man deepened the kiss and pressed Charley closer to him. It was as though she were suspended in time, an odd sensation of not knowing if this was reality or her overstressed brain dousing her in a lust-fueled delusion.

The warmth of the stranger's mouth abandoned her slightly bruised lips. She stared up at him. His eyes were filled with a mix of bewilderment, desire and, strangely, gratitude. Neither of them seemed to have the courage to speak as they attempted to process what had just happened. The man looked at her again and the anger she'd seen earlier had returned. Without a word, he turned around, leaving her there on the dock.

She wanted to call after him but decided that this had to be a dream. Even she couldn't have written a more passionate, impromptu kiss. She moved her fingers over her lips in disbelief as she watched the man disappear inside the cabin next to hers.

Charley bent down and grabbed her pole that was floating on the surface of the water. She reeled the line back and stared out to the other side of the lake. The silhouette of trees against the burnt orange and indigo sky was stunning. She reached the end of the line and saw that the worm had been nibbled off the hook. Charley decided to bait a new one as her mind ran a mile a minute. She desperately tried to concentrate on the simple task but hadn't realized her fingers were shaking terribly as she stabbed the worm onto the hook. Charley yelped when the hook poked her skin and she immediately sucked the blood from her finger. She wiped it on her jean shorts and exhaled loudly. The country girl in her resumed getting that darned worm on the hook and soon, almost on autopilot, Charley cast the line out again without another thought to her finger.

Her mind replayed the kiss, over and over again. *Who is that man?*

Much to her disappointment, the fish weren't biting now. She decided it was best to start packing it up. The temperature had dropped and her clothing was still partially wet. Charley shivered as she reeled in her line but was reluctant to leave the solitude.

"Cold?"

Charley turned around and half-expected to see her mystery kisser but instead, Tucker stood there with a broad grin.

"A little," she admitted as he offered to help her up.

"We better get you back in your cabin and warmed up." He ran his hands sweetly up and down her arms. Charley enjoyed the sensation of his touch, but the reminder of the kiss with the other man was seared into her brain and stained on her lips.

"Hey, Tucker, who is staying in the cabin next to mine?" Charley asked after they began the small trek back toward her cabin.

"Nick Capra. He's a detective from Portland who transferred here a few months back," Tuckered answered nonchalantly.

He's a cop? What business does he think he has kissing me like that? Does he honestly think he can get away with it? Charley fumed inside and planned to pay that creep a visit. *No one is above the law — even the law.*

She clutched her sacks with snacks, bait and pole as Tucker escorted her down the dock. He chatted happily about the upcoming summer season and she tried to focus on what he was saying. Charley wrestled with a torrent of emotions — anger, curiosity and a strange longing. They arrived at her cabin. Tucker fished out a ring of keys and unlocked the door for her.

"You get in there and get warm, okay?" Tucker looked at her with concern but gave her a flirty wink as he left.

Charley smiled sweetly at him as she shut the cabin door. The moment she was alone, her anger worked into a frenzy. The more she thought about the invasion of her privacy, that jerk stealing her precious quiet time, the more Charley wanted nothing more than to wring his neck. Don't even get her started on the kiss! *Hell hath no fury like a soaking wet and pissed off woman.* She changed into dry clothes and decided it was time to confront Nick Capra.

* * * *

What an idiot! What was I thinking, Capra? Nick paced his tiny cabin. Ruger eyed him from the couch as Nick mentally scolded himself. He certainly hadn't had any intention of kissing Charlene Vanderberg. In fact, quite the opposite. Nick had been steaming mad when he'd left the station, but there was something about the way the sunset had hit her hair and those freckles… *Lord, help me.* Add in the factor that today had been his first time back on a gruesome crime scene. *It was too soon.* That kiss helped Nick escape, even if only for a short moment. The rendezvous to somewhere else had almost been worth it.

Nick pulled back the door to the fridge to see if there was anything to drown his problems with. *Nothing.* The racks were barren of anything edible. The carton of leftovers from who-knew-when were questionable, and Nick threw them in wastebasket. He decided to make a quick run to the grocery store and swiftly grabbed his keys and wallet. Nick pulled back the front door of the cabin and, to his surprise, there stood Charlene Vanderberg. Her small hand was raised in a tight ball.

"Planning on doing some damage with that?" Nick asked as he motioned to her fist.

"No, I was getting ready to knock, like a normal person." Her voice was full of sass. Ruger ran to his defense and began to bark loudly.

She moved one step back and crossed her arms defensively. It was obvious she wanted to create some space between them. The small porch light washed over her, bathing her in an angelic glow. She seemed slightly frightened as she glowered down at Ruger, who barked protectively.

"Ruger, come on, boy." Nick tried to calm his pug, who wasn't quite done letting this lady know he meant business. Ruger huffed and finally retreated back to the couch. Nick ran his hand through his hair for more than the hundredth time that day. "Look, Ms. Vanderberg. I'm sorry about earlier."

"Sorry? You've got to be kidding me. What the hell was *that*? Do you normally go up to random strangers and kiss the frigging daylights out of them?" she spouted as she took a step forward and poked him hard in the chest. A fleck of green he hadn't noticed before in her blue eyes teased him.

"No, ma'am." He couldn't hide the grin on his face, no matter how hard he tried. Something about this very angry and feisty female was beginning to do funny things to Nick — things he hadn't felt in a long time and had no business entertaining.

She glared at him hard. "Don't 'ma'am' me."

"You prefer me to call you something else?" Nick was starting to enjoy this little altercation.

"I can think of a few choice words to call you, Nick Capra," she grumbled. He watched as she appeared to bite the inside of her cheek, probably to keep from calling him any of those words.

"I'm sure that wouldn't be a problem for a fancy author like yourself," he shot back and waited for her response. The sparkle in her eyes darkened. Nick was starting to enjoy this confrontation a little too much. It was like taunting a wild animal, seeing how far he could push her.

"Wow, you're really something else, mister," she spat with her hands on her hips. "You and your dog."

"Who you calling mister?" Nick pretended to be offended. "I'd appreciate it you'd leave my pug out of this. He's innocent." It took every ounce of self-control to keep from laughing.

He could see the anger build in her eyes, and if he were truly honest with himself, it was beginning to turn him on. A whole lot of Charlene Vanderberg turned him on, and this posed a huge problem. Was it her petite stature? Her pert breasts that weren't more than a handful perfectly showcased in that thin pink tee? Or the way her hips looked in those tight jeans? Perhaps it was how adorable she looked when she was raging mad? He was pretty damn sure it was the complete package—and the last thing he needed.

Just who does this arrogant ass think he is? I should go complain to Tucker and have this psycho and his damn dog removed from the resort. Charley stayed planted firmly on the porch of the cabin. She didn't understand why he was looking at her the way he was. A hunger and flicker of amusement played in his eyes.

"You had no problem calling me 'ma'am'. I'm not sure I really see the difference," she challenged.

"Well, there is a difference. I was actually being polite. You weren't, now were you?" he countered as he leaned casually against the doorjamb. He was still in the rumpled black dress shirt from earlier and jeans that made his legs look like they were a mile long. *Just how tall was this guy?* The squared-toed boots he wore only added to his outlaw exterior.

Charley's nerves tensed and agitation brewed as he stood there appearing completely confident. She glared at him as she chose her words carefully. Charley could almost see the gears in his mind turn as he studied her. "Do you call what you did earlier *polite*?"

She had him there. He was cornered now. She stared at him and waited for him to come up with some genius excuse to explain his caveman behavior. To her amazement, he just grinned boldly at her, and in what seemed like lightning speed, he was mere inches from her face.

This girl thought she was clever, but Charlene Vanderberg had no idea what she was doing. Hell, if he were completely honest with himself, neither did he. Nick only knew one thing for sure and his brain didn't even try stop him. He covered her mouth with his. Her body went rigid against him but she soon melted into him. *Damn, she's so soft. How is it possible for her to taste even more delicious?* Then Nick felt a sharp sting and opened his eyes to see her face pinched in confusion.

He rubbed his cheek, attempting to ease the burn she had inflicted.

"I can't believe you. I should call the cops," she spouted angrily and began to stomp away.

"Charlene, I am the *cops*," Nick replied smoothly as she shook her head, causing her long ponytail to swish back and forth. He couldn't seem to take his eyes off her as he watched her go. "Ruger, I'm not so sure she likes us."

Maybe babysitting Charlene Vanderberg won't be half-bad after all.

* * * *

She was back in her cabin, riddled with more anger than before when she'd set off to confront Nick Capra. *Where did I go wrong? Why did I allow him to kiss me again?*

Her cell phone chirped loudly and she answered quickly, "Hello?"

"Wow, Charley," Victoria's voice replied, "you sound a little irritated."

"Ugh, that doesn't even begin to cover it."

"What's up? Everything okay?"

Charley plopped onto the couch and sunk into the aging piece of furniture. "Nick Capra is *what*. His stupid little dog too."

"Nick Capra, huh? I gotta admit that sounds like a very sexy name," Victoria purred. "And why do you sound like that wicked witch from *The Wizard of Oz* right now? I thought you liked dogs?"

She countered spitefully, "I do like dogs…just not his." Charley tried to steady her nerves. "That guy is an arrogant ass, Vic."

"Who seems to have you more than a little riled. Tell me more about this arrogant ass. Like for starters, does he have a nice ass? I'm intrigued to find out who has got my girl all hot and bothered." Victoria's laugh lifted her spirits slightly, but she didn't think this was any kind of joke.

"He's apparently some detective here," Charley began to explain.

"Dangerous. Please tell me he's all disheveled and super sexy. Does he wear a uniform? You know those tight ones that show off their very best assets." Victoria went on to describe how much she loved a man in uniform.

Charley suppressed a laugh as she thought of Nick. She closed her eyes and tried to deny the fact that he was indeed incredibly hot and more than a little dangerous. "He's in the cabin next to mine."

"Convenient. And you're going to be neighborly and take over some wine, right? This couldn't be more perfect," Victoria squealed in delight.

"Hardly. Let me bring you up to speed," Charley said as she recounted everything that had happened up to that point. She fetched a can of beer from the fridge and didn't leave out a single detail. Victoria had become rather quiet on the other end. "Crazy, right?" Charley asked nervously.

"You could say that. But how was the kiss?"

"Which one?" Charley found herself giggling. She wasn't sure if it was the beer or the absurdity of the whole situation. "I was stunned by the first one and completely caught off guard by the second. It was just really strange, Vic."

"Okay, I can imagine that. But tell me, what was so weird about it?"

"You mean besides the whole kissing a complete stranger part?" Charley teased. "It's the way I felt in that particular moment on the dock. It was as though nothing else mattered or like, I was stuck somewhere in-between of dreaming and reality," Charley admitted as she nursed her beer.

"Wow, I'd say that was some kiss then. I'm actually a little jealous." Victoria sighed heavily. "You know what? This isn't all that bad, girl."

"Uh, yeah, it is. Strangers—cop or otherwise—should not go around smooching poor innocent people who are just minding their own business."

"Innocent? I'm not so sure about that." Victoria let out a loud giggle. "Maybe it was fate," she offered.

"Oh, come on. You can't possibly believe that."

"You're the writer. You know all about the magic of romance."

Charley hiccupped as she helped herself to another beer. "Do I need to remind you what genre I write? It's definitely not romance."

"But your last book—" Victoria started, to which Charley quickly cut her off.

"Was an utter flop. It's pretty darn clear I don't write the lovey-dovey stuff very well. Now, murders, kidnapping and all that kinda jazz, I've got down pat."

"Do you?" Victoria scoffed.

"You know very well what I mean." Charley took another swig and continued, "It's what I'm good at, not that mushy lovey-dovey crap. I'm pretty good, if I must say so, at writing about people being killed. Doom and gloom are sort of my specialty."

"And have you been writing?" Victoria pressed cautiously.

"I did write a few words but deleted them. I feel like I'm almost back, if that makes any sense. I can see the words, and when I get off the phone with you, I'm going to try to work on a Chapter." She chugged the last bit of beer and silently prayed she could manage to get some words out that night. "I just finished some liquid courage. You know the saying... 'Write drunk, and edit sober.'"

"I know that one well and I'm just glad you're trying," Victoria laughed. "And as for this whole detective thing? Just enjoy it, girl," Victoria advised sweetly.

"Nope, Pamela made it quite clear where my focus needs to be. No distractions."

"What would you call that hottie Tucker you told me all about?"

Charley smiled at the thought of him. "I like to think of Tucker more as a carrot."

"A carrot? Have you lost your mind, girl? What in the hell are you even talking about?"

"A reward system. A motivating cause for me to complete this book. A carrot being dangled in front of me, so to speak."

"I swear only you would think of something that crazy. Is he aware of this ridiculous plan of yours?" Victoria asked with concern.

"Well, no. Of course not."

"Is he even into you?"

Charley felt herself pout and answered truthfully, "I'm not sure about that, either. Quit raining on my parade, Vic."

"Hmm, has he tried kissing you?" Victoria was beginning to kill her slight buzz. *Why is my best friend grilling me about Tucker?*

"Tucker's flirty, and if he's not into me, I need to help him become interested. You can just get the idea of Nick out of your mind right now. He's not my type."

"Since when is tall, dark and sexy not your type? Besides, the man is obviously not afraid to go after something he wants. Very alpha and take charge... I kinda like that."

"Well, I don't."

"You and I both know you're a big fat liar."

They both giggled loudly.

After saying goodbye to Victoria, Charley walked over to her little workstation. The old table where her laptop sat open beckoned her. Tonight, she was going to force herself to write. Those words were closer than they'd been in months, and she planned on snaring them. The hunt and chase were almost over. She would capture those words, even if it killed her. She decided to make herself a mug of motivation. *Coffee.* To some it may seem a little ridiculous to be brewing coffee after ten at night, but to Charley, that was her norm. Writer fuel was a crucial part of her routine of wrangling ghosts and monsters and pinning them to the pages.

Charley gathered a few snacks to munch on and delivered them to the table while her coffee brewed. She placed a few of her favorite notebooks she'd brought next to the laptop. She liked having them handy in case she needed to jot down a few ideas or draw out a rough timeline. Charley fixed the coffee to her taste then settled in front of her laptop.

"You got this," she said as she took a long sip of the hot drink. The warmth traveled down her throat and caused to her hum with delight.

Her fingers hovered over the keys with anticipation. Charley kept her eyes sealed shut. She waited for it...the story. It was like summoning a demon. She needed to conjure up a dark memory. Charley instantly recalled the first murder scene she'd ever written about. It was inspired by a story she'd covered for the newspaper in Seattle early on in her career...a stabbing. It had been an utter blood bath and the most brutal thing she'd ever seen. Charley didn't know a human could inflict that many holes into another person. The knife had been left next to the body, begging detectives to catch the one who'd held it last. The shiny blade had been covered in dry blood and safely tucked into a plastic baggy by the time Charley had seen it.

When she'd retold the story in one of her bestselling novels, the sharp kitchen knife had been used by a housewife, one who'd had enough of being pounded by the angry fists of a man who'd vowed to love and protect her. Somehow it softened the reality of the awful the truth of what she had actually reported. The reality couldn't be further from the words she'd given her readers. The killer who had stabbed a man what seemed like a zillion-and-one times had never been found. He wasn't some pitiful wife who no longer wanted to be a victim, a homemade hero who had ended years of abuse. No, the real killer was just another monster who had been running loose on the streets with all the others.

Think of those monsters now, Charley. And as she did, her fingers began to fly over the keys.

Chapter Five

The sun hasn't quite set but everything is covered in dusty shadows. It's quiet, that evening lull before dusk surrenders to night fall. I've reread every last detail and need her to see how well I've paid attention, to know much it means to me to be helping her this way.

My fingers are tight around the metal handle. It is an extension of my hand now. Isn't that how she described it? She had worded it so eloquently. I recall when I'd read her words for the very first time how they seared my brain, making me fall in love with them. I had never been touched that way before. It was as though she'd written it just for me and me alone. The words seemed so personal and honest. I owed her this.

The trick was to be fast, at least that's what she'd said. I'm operating solely on her words. Her instruction is what plays loudly in my mind. I open the driver's side door and go immediately for his throat, to silence him. He gurgles out thick watery cries for help as confusion illuminates his muddy brown eyes. I try not to look into them. She failed to mention how difficult that part would be. There is blood spraying from him like a sprinkler watering a lawn. It hits my face but I don't dare wipe it off. I plunge into his soft belly and am met with little resistance. I pull back and aim again, and a new piece of flesh is pierced through. Speed is my friend as I race through the skin and meat of my target. My hand is covered in the sticky crimson slickness and I feel the handle slip in my palm.

I work the knife into him again and again. Then I hit bone. It causes me slight pain as the vibrations ricochet down the blade and ruin my rhythm. I reposition my grip and dig deeper into him, twisting the blade with each turn, angry that he has disrupted my work. Sweat is dripping from my brow as I exert myself in the task.

He has quit making any sound. The echo of the knife entering and exiting his body fills the truck cab. My brain records the strange noises of my kill. I'll never forget the sound or the way it feels. I keep my mouth closed as more dark blood splatters my face and onto my arms as I drive the knife farther into his torso. I can smell the sick pungent stench of sweat and the metallic scent of his blood.

This man is nothing more than a pin-cushion now. There are so many holes in his belly as he continues to leak out blood. I should be rattled to the core, disturbed by the gruesomeness before me, but I'm not. I am tempted to lick him, to taste what I smell. I desperately resist the urge because that's not how it's written. That would mess everything up. This isn't for me. It's for her.

There is blood everywhere. The center of my palm aches with the soreness of hard labor. My fingers are tight and demand to be uncurled. Not yet, I'm not done.

I know I must keep going. My lungs burn and I can barely catch my breath. How many times did she say this had been done? I close my eyes and try to see the magic number.

It's truly exhausting. Each stroke devours my energy and strength. I'm worn out and this now feels nothing more than me striking a pillow. Its empty, unmoving and somewhat deflated now. I gaze at his face. His mouth is agape and he's become an ashy pale color. Life has literally drained from him. I stifle a chuckle as I move away.

Dusk has succumbed to the darkness. The sun is resting and the moon is wide awake, shining its dull light all around me and this lonesome truck. The sky is quilted of magnificent stars. I take in the view of pure nothingness and am filled with peace as I hold my sharp weapon to my chest. I feel the vibrations of my heart pounding against the soiled blade. Mountains stand guard and shield the two of us from the rest of the world. As much as I want to remain in this still and perfect moment, I know that is not how her story goes. I have a sense of duty to keep the integrity of her words. This is not the same as before, with the girl and my hands around her throat. That was to let her know I was there for her — to help her through her struggle and that I'm only playing the part of her beloved character. But this time it's different for me. Everything about it. There's a birth of something strange inside me — or maybe it was always there, just dormant and waiting for her to need me. The precise moment for it to be born.

My heartbeat slows to a quiet rhythm, and I feel myself smiling involuntarily at a job well done. I place the knife next to him, exactly as she'd described.

I need to this to be perfect. It's for her. I would do anything for her.

Chapter Six

Nick was refilling his mug when the sheriff joined him. He stood next to Nick and poured the thick liquid into his own mug. "Got a minute, Capra?"

"Sure," Nick answered as he took a sip of the bitter coffee. "We really need better coffee here."

"Not in the budget," the sheriff replied with a smirk. He led them to his office and motioned for Nick to have a seat. He immediately knew what this conversation was going to be about. "Have you introduced yourself yet?"

Nick didn't even bother to hide the grin on his face. "You could say that."

The sheriff gave him a perplexed look. "How'd that go?"

"That depends on how you look at it." Nick was about to go on when the dispatcher rushed in.

"Sheriff, we just got a call." The woman glanced over at Nick and paused as if unsure she should go into detail in front of him. Her dark hair was pulled back too tightly and her uniform was starched and pressed to perfection.

The sheriff turned his attention to her. "What do we have?"

"Another body, sir," she answered. Her gaze shifted to the floor.

Nick shook his head. *Why are they acting so surprised?* They were in law enforcement, and crime was the name of the game — or at least from the neck of the woods where Nick was from. Calls about bodies, missing or found, had been the norm.

"Christ. What is happening here?" he muttered under a strangled breath. The sheriff rose from his chair and straightened the belt on his pants, his overhanging belly jiggling as he moved. Nick studied him and, in many ways, he felt for this man. The sheriff wasn't accustomed to handling any of this. It was apparent as he stood there lost in his troubled thoughts, his forehead furrowed with dread before he waved for Nick to follow him.

The cruiser sped down the stretch of highway and the sheriff didn't say a word. The silence drove Nick crazy. The lack of sound made him nervous. His brain, on the other hand, was too loud with the tornado of thoughts that constantly tormented him.

"What do you think is going on here?"

The sheriff's eyes stayed focused on the road as he quietly answered, "To be honest, I'm not sure."

"Crescent Lake has no history of murder. Now we've got two in one week. Seems pretty damn strange to me," Nick commented as the tires of the cruiser touched gravel. It crunched under them as the sheriff drove slowly down a narrow path in the woods.

Nick could see another cruiser with its lights swirling in the afternoon haze and a medium-sized pick-up. They parked and moved swiftly to meet the other sheriff, who stood near the driver's side of the truck.

"Thompson," the sheriff greeted and tilted his hat. "This is Capra, our new detective here in Crescent Lake."

The man nodded at Nick. "As you know, this property here borders our towns. I figured it was best to call you in on this."

Nick peered into the window and saw blood everywhere. The grisly scene was straight out of a horror movie. The victim was a man who had been savagely stabbed multiple times, including a gaping wound at his throat. The sheriffs moved aside and let Nick examine the scene further. This was his territory of expertise. He heard their muffled whispers as he gloved up and opened the truck door. He peered in and slowly began to examine the scene.

The amount of blood was unreal, and the abdomen and lap of the victim were completely saturated. Nick spied the weapon next to the man and wondered why the murderer would leave it there. Nick wasn't sure if the two murders this week were connected. The first had been so clean, and this was the exact opposite. Nick's brain went into overdrive as he spied the weapon, completely encrusted with dried blood, and left next to the victim. They would run it for any prints and hopefully come closer to finding the killer.

"Well, he left us a present," Nick announced.

* * * *

Charley stretched and yawned as she finally woke. Beads of golden light hit her eyes. *I seriously need to find curtains.* Yesterday's shopping trip had turned up empty when it came to those much-needed window treatments. Charley knew it had to be late afternoon. She had stayed up until after nine in the morning, had written an entire Chapter and outlined what she hoped would become a great book. This breakthrough was a very big deal in her eyes. After months of nothing — no words, no idea where to go — she had finally struck gold the previous night. It was as though something in the universe had shifted, and Charley couldn't be happier, even if the stupid sunlight was blinding her.

After leaving her bed, Charley set about showering as her coffee brewed. Surprisingly the small coffee maker filled the small cabin with the hearty aroma of French roast. Even though she was still slightly exhausted, there was a renewed energy buzzing inside her — mostly in her brain. The creative spark had returned and was burning brightly. The struggle of the last several months had nearly killed her, and Charley welcomed this lovely sensation and burst of thoughts.

As she scrubbed her body with a loofa and delicately scented body wash, her mind was busy writing. Several scenes, plots twists and bits of dialogue played out like a movie in her head. This story was taking form and developing into something different from her other work. The characters, though not entirely attached to Charley yet, were beginning to intrigue her. They had caught her attention and that was definitely a start to forming a relationship with these fictional people. She wanted to know them more, to learn what made them tick. It always started off that way. It wasn't always an instant connection. Sometimes the relationship grew as the story grew. By the time she typed 'The End', they were family and she was met with a bout of sadness when it was time to say goodbye.

Once she was dressed and her wet hair hung loosely, she busied herself with doctoring her coffee. She added extra hazelnut creamer as she mentally planned out her day. She was going to drown her brain in caffeine and focus on getting to know her new characters. Charley made herself a small breakfast of a bagel and banana and hurried to her laptop. She sipped the deliciously sweet drink as she started to reread what she had written the previous night. *Not too shabby.* Charley edited the pages as she went and added more here and there. She was beginning to create the skeleton of her story, good bones that could use some more meat. Trimming the fat would take place during the brutal editing process. Overall, Charley was satisfied with the Chapter and emailed it to Pamela. Her cell phone buzzed almost immediately after.

"Hello?" She stared at a blank new page she had just opened.

"Is this a completed Chapter I have in front of me?" Pamela asked sweetly.

"Yes, ma'am," Charley replied happily as she drank the last sip of her coffee.

"Wow, I'm impressed. I'm excited to read it."

"I think it's a good start and let me know if you like the direction it's headed in."

"It would seem Crescent Lake agrees with you. I won't say it, but…" Pamela began.

"Don't. We both know it."

"Best to not jinx it anyway, I suppose. I'm so thrilled you're writing again, Charley," Pamela said softly.

"Just keep at it and before we know it, we'll have a book there."

"Hopefully a damn good one," Charley added confidently.

"I have no doubt. I better let you get back to it, and thank you for sending this Chapter to me."

Charley smiled as she hung up with her agent. It felt good to be back.

She typed at a rapid pace, words spilling from her brain like a faucet turned on full blast. She was so thick into the scene she was writing that Charley almost did not hear the knock at the door. *Damn. Who is it? Why now?* She reluctantly removed herself from her perch, and her eyes struggled to tear themselves away from the screen as she went to see who was bothering her. Charley had been so completely engrossed in her fictional world that she hadn't realized it was nearly dark outside.

My handsome carrot. "Tucker."

"I'm not interrupting you, am I?" Tucker asked.

"I was writing," she answered and tried her best to ignore the pull she felt to run back to her laptop. She reminded herself that he was her reward for a job well done.

"Oh, I'm so sorry. I should probably let you get back to it." The disappointment was clear in his voice. Charley spied him holding a plastic bag filled with marshmallows.

"Wait. It's fine. I could use a break," she lied. "What do you have there?"

"Oh, these?" Tucker held up the bag. "Just a campfire necessity. Care to join me?"

Hell yes. Charley tried her best to play it cool and nonchalant. "Sure, sounds fun."

Tucker reached for her hand and led her away from the cabin. Her mind kept pestering her. Had she hit the save button before she'd left? She had been known to magically lose Chapters and that was not something she could afford to have happen right now.

"Let me grab a sweater really quick," Charley said and ran back to her cabin. She immediately went to her laptop and saved her work. Charley sighed with relief as she protected those precious words. As she went to leave, she had almost forgot to bring a sweater with her.

"Ready?" Tucker asked as he took her hand in his as he led her toward the shore.

Charley had not realized how late it was. Granted, she had only been awake since midafternoon and had been hard at work on another Chapter. It was easy to lose track of time. But how was it that the stars were already out and the night was alive with the sounds of nature? Insects sang loudly and a breeze swept through the branches of the surrounding trees. She was thankful for the warmth of the fire. Tucker had thoughtfully positioned two chairs in front of the water, the light from the flames reflected beautifully off the dark surface. Could it have been any more romantic? Charley inhaled the smoky scent and licked her sticky marshmallow-covered fingers as she stamped this moment in her memory.

"You want another?" Tucker impaled another fluffy marshmallow onto the long metal fork and turned it slowly in the fire. Charley watched as the flames enveloped the white skin, charring it.

"How can I resist?" Charley answered as he pulled it from the fire and carefully handed it to her.

"So, this book you're writing, what's it about?" Tucker asked as he speared another marshmallow onto the fork. "Is it some kind of cheesy romance novel or something?"

Charley couldn't help but laugh. It was always a little funny having to explain to people what it was she wrote about. No one pegged her for creating these horrific stories and it was kind of neat to watch their reaction when she revealed the truth.

"Not exactly." Charley watched his eyes light up with curiosity.

He leaned back in the canvas chair, the fire illuminating his handsome face. "So, what kind of stories do you write, Ms. Vanderberg?" The way her name melted off his tongue caused her belly to fill with warmth.

"Stories about monsters," she answered slowly.

"Monsters? Like, mythical creatures?" He squinted at her, unsure of her response. "That's cool."

"Human monsters." Charley waited for him to process her words.

"Like, Dracula?" Tucker asked with a confused laugh.

Charley giggled. It was fun having him guess. "No, think more along the lines of Bundy or Dahmer."

His eyebrows rose in surprise. "Wow. So, pretty dark stuff then."

"You could say that." Charley looked up the canopy of stars. She had forgotten there were so many. "It's beautiful out here. You know that?"

"Sorry. I'm still wrapping my head around the fact you write about murderers. You don't seem like someone who would."

"You'd expect me to look more like Stephen King or someone, right?" Charley was near hysterics and couldn't shelter her laughter.

"Kind of. Definitely not a cute blonde." Tucker laughed right along with her.

"I tried writing romance, and let's just say my fans weren't too happy with that novel," Charley explained as she kept her eyes trained on the dancing flames. Her gaze moved up to the brilliant stars above them — tiny burned-out lights that were so many miles away, the beautiful aftermath of something essentially dying.

"Do you really like writing about all that blood and gore? It doesn't bother you?" Tucker asked. "I don't think I could sleep a wink. Honestly, I don't even like watching scary movies."

Charley looked over at Tucker and giggled. A loud pop escaped the fire and echoed in the trees, causing Tucker to shift uncomfortably in his chair. "Someone's afraid of the dark," she teased as she tenderly squeezed his arm. "It's okay. I'll protect you."

Tucker smirked. "Thanks."

They sat together quietly until the fire started to die down. Charley grew anxious, words pounding heavily against her brain, banging loudly on a door that had been sealed shut for far too many months. She was happy to open it and welcome the monsters inside. As lovely as this little date was, she was eager to write. That was also why she didn't have a love life. She spent too much time snuggling with murderers and psychopaths. Her characters were calling for her. Tucker must have sensed her restlessness and offered to walk her back. He seemed slightly frightened after their little chat.

"You sure you don't want me to walk *you* back to the lodge?" she offered sweetly.

* * * *

Charley cradled her mug as she sat outside her cabin. The morning was beautiful. The sun was already shining, the air was perfumed with all the sweet scents of nature, and peace wash over her. That was, until she spied Nick and his pudgy dog walking the shore. Nick would throw a ball and his little pal was quick to retrieve it. The dog would become distracted and start to wander off. His owner would chase after him and seemed to be enjoying this little game of 'catch the pug'.

Nick was casually dressed in shorts and, again, another black tee. The shorts revealed long, muscular legs. She couldn't dismiss the fact that Nick was a good-looking guy and was incredibly fit, but he bothered her. She knew his type—a headstrong alpha who thought the rules didn't apply to him. That annoyed her to no end. She'd been around plenty of cops who had rubbed her the wrong way with their cowboy attitudes. They were in charge of upholding the law and holding citizens accountable. It was kind of hard to do that when they thought they were above the law.

Charley took a sip of her coffee and tried to turn her attention to the beautiful backdrop in front of her. She relaxed and allowed herself to embrace this quiet moment. Her mind began to feed her with ideas for the book. She snatched all the details and locked them away in her memory to write later. Charley was deep in thought, writing in her mind, when she felt something touch her leg. She yelped and looked down to see a wet and sand-covered pug panting at her feet.

"I'm so sorry," Nick apologized as he jogged toward her. "I tried to catch him. I know he doesn't look like it, but he's really fast." Nick attempted to catch his breath. Charley tried to not focus on his very kissable mouth as he spoke. "Come on, boy. Let's go home." The pug laid out flat, his back legs fully extended behind him. His pink tongue was unfolded and he was panting hard.

"Is he okay?" Charley asked. The strange sounds coming from the dog concerned her. He seemed to be guzzling air.

Nick bent down and petted the pug. "I didn't realize they sounded like this either. This is normal, though."

"Well, it's a little disturbing." Charley wiped off the wet sand that clung to leg. This little guy was gross. His snorting and gasping were starting to freak her out.

"Come on, Ruger. You're scaring the author lady." Nick effortlessly scooped up his dog. "Have a good one."

Charley watched as Nick held the pug in his arms like it was baby and heard him cooing affectionately at the pug. She couldn't help but giggle at the comical scene and considered writing that into one of her books.

Charley spent the remainder of the day doing a whole lot of nothing. She mostly lounged around her cabin and even took a few naps. Charley convinced herself this was self-care at its best. In reality, she was procrastinating and knew that novel wasn't going to write itself. She did manage to take inventory of her snack supply and realized she was already running low on coffee. Writer fuel was something she could not go without. It was the very staple of her existence. She reasoned that writing a shopping list was an accomplishment that should be celebrated. Charley enjoyed a beer and watched the sunset from her cabin. Maybe tomorrow she would get some writing done, but tonight would be spent watching a cheesy movie on her laptop and pretending she was on vacation.

* * * *

She finished her second cup of coffee the next morning and found the motivation to start her day. A trip to the store was on the agenda. Just her luck, Charley had picked an awful cart with a squeaky wheel. She cruised the best she could up and down the aisles. One of her favorite oldie tunes played overhead and she couldn't help but sing along. Charley was busy looking at a variety of dish towels when she felt as though someone was watching her. Out of the corner of her eye she spied the new bane of her existence, Detective Nick Capra. She attempted to ignore him as she unfolded another towel to see if it would be large enough to cover her window. Charley settled on a few beach towels that happened to be farther down the aisle but couldn't shake her shadow. Annoyed with the stupid cart, Charley turned around. "Seriously?" The surprised look on his face made her laugh. "Can I help you with something?"

"You work here now?" Nick responded sarcastically.

She bit her tongue and decided he wasn't worth it. Charley hurried down the next aisle a little faster than normal and almost took out a laundry detergent display. Nick was gaining on her as she fled down the cereal aisle. She stopped right at the Cheerios. "Dude, what the hell?"

He reached for the raisin bran and put a box in his cart. "Just doing some shopping," Nick answered casually as he browsed more of the breakfast selection.

"Come on. I'm not stupid. You're totally following me," Charley accused as she grabbed a box of Lucky Charms.

"Lucky Charms?" He eyed with pure adult judgment. "Besides, breakfast is the most important meal of the day." Nick pushed his cart past her.

Charley was a little confused. Was it a consequence that he was following her down what seemed to be every aisle or was he actually shopping? Maybe she just was being paranoid. It was a small town with not a whole lot of shopping options. *The man has to eat, right?* Charley gathered a few more items and found herself in line behind him. She saw that he did actually have a few provisions and felt a tad guilty. He was polite to the checker as she rung up his purchase. Charley could overhear them talking about his damn dog and found herself growing more agitated. Sometimes, Charley would get a little cranky when she was eyeballs-deep in a new story and it was best if she avoided the general public as much as possible. Perhaps she should just stay put in her cabin and steer clear of this guy and his ugly pooch, otherwise she might find herself getting kissed again.

He'd watched as she'd bopped around, dancing to the terrible supermarket music. Nick could see her singing along to Tom Jones' *It's Not Unusual*. She was really starting to get into the song until she paused down the aisle with towels. He knew she'd spotted him and was doing her best to act as though she were ignoring him. When she fled and nearly collided with the detergent, he almost died from laughing. She tried acting so tough, calling him on not being such a good detective.

Maybe he wasn't as slick as he had intended to be. Following little Miss Author-With-an-Attitude wasn't his idea of a good time either, especially when this town now had a killer on its hands. His focus should be on trying to catch that asshole. Instead, he was hanging out at the grocery store and buying crap he didn't need. Nick didn't even like Raisin Bran, and now here he was purchasing a box because he didn't want her to think he was actually following her.

He watched her load her items on the conveyor belt and noticed she was buying towels. Nick couldn't help but wonder if those would soon become new window treatments and also a new obstacle for his surveillance. See? He wasn't that bad of a detective.

"Have a great day, ma'am," he called out to her as he gathered his bags. The annoyed look on her pretty face made him smile, but he made sure to wait until he was outside to do that. Nick didn't want her to see just how much he enjoyed antagonizing her. If he were lucky, she'd complain to the sheriff and he'd be relieved of babysitting duty. This town needed a real cop to solve the murders.

* * * *

She had survived another week in Crescent Lake and it hadn't even been all that bad, minus her shopping trip escapade. Thankfully, she hadn't seen him in nearly a week and had been able to work without interruption. Charley now had seven completed Chapters under her belt to show for it. The first week at Crescent Lake had brought a couple of unexplained kisses she wished she could forget and a few fun late-night visits with Tucker.

The good news was Charley had made it to the first official day of summer. She decided to venture out of the cabin and enjoy the deliciously warm day and celebrate. It finally felt like summer—hot, sticky and scented with the sun's rays. Charley threw on her bathing suit, grabbed a towel and practically danced her way down to the shore. She noticed a few cars had arrived at the resort. There were even a couple of children splashing happily in the lake. They had the same idea she had. *A little fun in the sun.*

Charley stood facing the water with her toes buried deep in the sand. She spotted a boat across the lake. As it glided along the surface, a wake followed and caused mini waves to finally meet the shore. The waves slapped against her calves and the cool contact on her skin felt wonderful. Charley wasn't the best swimmer in the world but she was half-tempted to take a dip. She thought back to nearly a week ago when she'd first met Nick. She often found herself replaying the kisses over in her mind or daydreaming about more kisses, but she dismissed any feelings she thought she might be experiencing. It was Tucker who interested her. There was something sweet and very boy-next-door about him. A simple sexiness in the way he talked that had her heart skipping a few beats.

She decided to stretch out on the towel and let the sun cook her pale skin a little. Charley relished the blanket of warmth and felt incredibly relaxed. As she lay there on the sand, her muscles melted onto the shore and she grew sleepy. If she wasn't mistaken, this felt very much like a vacation.

Damn it's hot. It was the first warm day he had experienced since he had arrived at Crescent Lake. Nick decided to cool off and headed for the beach. Ruger ran to the edge of the lake. Nick didn't blame him. The ground was scorching under his bare feet and he practically ran to the water. Ruger found his prize, a small piece of driftwood, and went to work burying it. Nick was relishing the cool relief of the water when he caught sight of her. Her nearly naked body was tinged pink. The teal bikini beckoned him to join her, so he moved closer to where she was on a towel. He was only a few feet away when he realized she was asleep. Nick inched closer quietly to not disturb her. She looked peaceful, like Sleeping Beauty. Her lashes fanned out on her freckled cheeks. Her delicious lips — lips he had kissed — were parted slightly tempting him to steal another. *This woman is trouble.*

Nick had kept his distance ever since he'd been brought onto the latest murder case. He needed to keep his head in the game and Charlene Vanderberg didn't make that an easy task. Nick had thought about her. *A lot. Too much.* Nothing stopped him from sitting down beside her sleeping body. There was a strange comfort in just being near her. It was a foreign thing he couldn't quite explain and really didn't want to investigate. He'd just let it be for now.

She stirred and flipped over to her side. Ruger was running through the sand when he spotted his new prize. Nick tried to call after him but it was too late. Her eyes suddenly sprang open. They were wide with fear and he waited to hear her let out a scream. He was shocked when she didn't. Ruger began to lick her face and his curly tail went wild. His wet, chubby body shook with pure joy.

"Please get your dog off me!" she growled as she slowly shifted into an upright position and adjusted the top of her bikini. "Crap, I think I got sunburned. I must have fallen asleep," she rambled then glared at him harshly. "How long have you two been here?"

"Not long. Are you always this cranky when you wake up?"

She shrugged. "Wouldn't you like to know."

"I asked, didn't I?" Nick winked at her. Ruger settled down and laid next to her on the towel like he owned it. Nick stared out at the water in front of them and released a heavy sigh.

"What was that for?"

"I feel like we got off on the wrong foot," Nick started carefully. He didn't know why he felt the need to squash whatever it was that was between them, but the apology just rolled out of his mouth. "I shouldn't have kissed you, not that it wasn't nice. I'm sorry, Ms. Vanderberg."

"You can start by *not* calling me 'Ms. Vanderberg' or 'ma'am'," she said. "And to be clear, I'm not sorry for slapping you."

Did he detect a hint of a smile on her pretty face? He studied her for a moment. Her girlish features were pink from too much sun and there was definitely a slight upward curve on those very kissable lips. "Then what do I call you?"

"Charley." To his surprise, she stuck her hand out.

Charley. Now that name fits her perfectly.

Chapter Seven

Charley had been writing nonstop as several days blew past. At this rate, she might very well have the manuscript ready before her deadline. She'd been working hard the last two weeks since her arrival, listening to her characters and writing one helluva story. However, holing up in the cabin was beginning to do a number on her. Talking to oneself or imaginary people was generally frowned upon in society and good cause to be thrown into the looney bin. Charley remembered the adage about all work and no play. *Just look how that turned out for Jack Nicholson's character in* The Shining. What a great movie but an excellent reminder to authors who find themselves getting a little nutty with too much writing. *All work and no play makes Charley a dull girl.*

Funny, only a short time ago Charley would have gladly gone off the deep end to just get a few words out. But with several new Chapters under her belt, she felt as though she had earned a bit of a reprieve. Today she decided to treat herself to lunch, something greasy and full of enough calories to last her a week. The single restaurant in town would have to do. Maybe she would run into that lovely waitress and visit with her for a bit. Charley desperately needed some human interaction — real human, not fictional.

The sun showered the tall pines with gloriously warm rays. Charley paused before getting into her SUV and closed her eyes. In the distance she could hear splashing as children laughed and played at the shore. A mother's warning about not going out too far soon followed. She could faintly make out the sound of the boats on the other side of the lake, a hum that floated in the air. Birds chirped, and there was a distinct clicking noise coming from an insect in the nearby bushes. Charley was keenly aware of her surroundings, and there was a sad tug at her heart. While her characters lived and breathed in the Chapters she had been writing, Charley had forgotten to enjoy herself — to enjoy this, the simple joy of summer.

She released a long sigh as she climbed into her SUV and became lost in her self-reflection. That was the difficult part about being an author, finding that balance in life. It was often difficult being a person who lived in two worlds — one foot in and the other foot in another. It was easy to get the two muddled and forget which one you lived in. There was a sense of playing God in many ways when creating a world — the one you have designed with specific people and all playing the roles you want them to, with hand-sculpted conflict, offering solutions you as the author see fit and deciding how fate will impact their written lives. Then there is the real world, the one that today was sunny and bright, fueled with sugary summer heat and made

Charley long for a dip in the cool water. Granted, Charley was more than grateful that she felt like her old self again, staying up until the wee hours and her fingers flying over the keys of her laptop. But it was easy to fall into the trap of becoming an over-caffeinated hermit, who ironically spent so much time with fictional people. Maybe that was who she was destined to be — alone and yet in the company of people made of words. Charley tried to drown out the feelings by turning on the radio.

The drive to town took only minutes, and soon Charley parked her SUV along the concrete curb with chipped paint. Her cell phone rang loudly in her purse. She dug in the oversized bag and answered cheerfully, "Hey, Mom."

"Well, hello, my sweet girl." The very sound of her mother's voice made her smile. "How's the book coming along?"

"Fantastic. I actually think this book may just be my best one yet." Charley then explained the basic plot and where the story was headed. She did not sugarcoat any of it or leave out much of the gnarly tale she had been working on. Just reciting the words made Charley eager to get back to her little writing cave.

"Wow, that's some story, sweetie. I don't know how you do it."

"Me either. I'm just so glad the words are flowing again."

"Your daddy and I had a silly thought," her mother said with a nervous laugh. "Fourth of July is next weekend and we thought it might be fun if you came home to celebrate, since you weren't able to spend Father's Day here."

Charley chewed on the idea for a moment when a light bulb went off in her mind. "I've got a better idea. How about you all come here? I'm sure I can reserve a cabin from Tucker."

"Who's Tucker?" her mother asked eagerly.

"The owner of the resort here and Pamela's nephew, remember?"

"Good looking?"

"Just a little," Charley giggled.

"Well, I'll see what Daddy thinks about coming to the lake."

"I bet there will be fireworks here, and I know how much you guys love those," Charley attempted to persuade her mother. "The resort is having some kind of BBQ for all the guests too."

"That's neat. I could bring a dish, you know? Maybe my coleslaw," her mother suggested.

"I'll talk to Tucker tonight." Charley heard her phone beep. "Hey, Mom, I've got another call. I'll catch up with you tomorrow, okay?"

"No problem, dear. Love you."

Charley pushed the button to answer the other call. "Hello?"

"Hey, girl," Victoria greeted. "Just checking up on you. You've been super quiet, which makes me think you've been busy. Busy doing what or whom, I'm not sure," she teased.

"Ha-ha. I've just been busy writing. Actually, I've written a ton," Charley was proud to announce.

"That's awesome! Good to know my girl got her mojo back."

"You have no idea how happy I am. I've been in that crappy cabin all week just working my keyboard overtime. My fingers actually a hurt a little bit,"

Charley rambled as she stretched and wiggled her fingers.

"Where are you right now?" Victoria asked.

"Parked outside the only restaurant in this tiny town. Why?"

"Um, no reason." Victoria was an awful liar.

"What's up, Vic?"

"A teensy surprise is all." Victoria was equally terrible at keeping secrets, even her own.

"Out with it, woman," Charley ordered playfully.

"Okay, okay. I just wanted to make sure you hadn't left Crescent Lake or anything."

"Why would I leave? Remember that I'm sort of on house rather cabin arrest by Pamela."

"How would you like a little company this weekend?"

"Please tell me what I think you're trying *not* to tell me."

They both laughed and Victoria confirmed it. "Yep, I'll be there tonight after I finish up some stuff here."

"I can't wait to show you this place," Charley practically squealed into the phone. "Just hurry and get here."

"Yay, a sleepover!" Victoria added, "I'm bringing vodka. Do we need anything else?"

"Yes," Charley quickly supplied. "Sushi. I'm dying for some city food."

"Your wish is my command. You've definitely earned it."

Charley was thrilled with this fun surprise and rather grateful to her assistant. Victoria and she had been friends a long time and, in some ways, were almost as close as sisters. She couldn't wait to show Victoria the lake, not that she had really spent much time enjoying the water. Charley could only imagine what Victoria would say when she saw the cabin. Charley had been cooped up in it for so long that she almost didn't notice the shabby couch or dated décor anymore. Charley wanted more than anything to just to catch up with her friend. "If you get lost, just call me," she reminded her.

"I've got GPS. I'm sure I'll be fine, Mom," Victoria replied sarcastically.

"Drive safe. See ya soon." Charley bounded out of her SUV, even happier.

She entered the restaurant. The enticing smell of charbroiled hamburgers hit her instantly, causing an immediate reaction from her stomach. Charley and her growling stomach knew right away what she wanted for lunch and she quickly slid into a booth. Molly made a beeline to her table.

"Where have you been, missy?" Molly asked enthusiastically.

"I know, I've been meaning to come in but have been so busy writing."

"Well, I suppose I'll let you off the hook then, since that's why you're actually here," Molly chuckled and pulled out her order pad. "What'll it be, darlin'?

The diner was slammed. It seemed like all the residents of Crescent Lake had the same idea. She could hear the orchestra of lunch as forks scraped against plates and glasses clinked together in a near-perfect harmony. Charley barely heard the bell on the front door jingle but saw Molly's eyes move toward it. She looked up and saw Nick enter, along with an older man in a uniform. His eyes found hers instantly. *Great.*

Charley tried to hide behind the laminated menu as she slouched lower in the booth.

"Whatcha doing that for?" Molly whispered.

"Doing what?"

"Honey, it's so obvious."

"Really?" Charley asked as she straightened up in her seat.

"Oh yes. So, I take it you've met our detective. Isn't he delicious?" Molly shamelessly ogled Nick.

"Molly, he's not on the menu," Charley teased playfully. "But I'll take one of those burgers I smelled when I walked in — and a chocolate shake."

"Too bad, I think he'd be a little tastier." They both giggled like schoolgirls, which caused Nick to look in her direction.

Molly snatched Charley's paper shield and winked as she sashayed away. With nothing to hide behind, Charley pretended to turn her attention out of the window but felt his eyes on her. *Just ignore him and maybe he will go away.*

"Mind if I join you?"

Charley peered up to see him standing over her. His scruffy five o'clock shadow was already present and it wasn't even past noon yet. She attempted to look behind him to see if the uniformed man was still with him.

"The sheriff is taking his to-go," Nick answered for her as he swiftly entered the opposite seat. "The burgers are pretty good." He motioned for Molly to take his order.

"I didn't say you could sit here," she hissed in a low breath.

"But I'm already here and it would be rude not to have lunch with a friend," he replied sweetly.

"We're not friends."

"Sure, we are," he argued.

"No, we're neighbors for the time being. That's it," Charley countered firmly.

"Fine, then I guess I'm just being neighborly." Nick gave her a sexy, slanted smile.

"Maybe I should take mine to-go too," Charley said. She was quickly becoming uncomfortable in his presence. There was something about Nick Capra that twisted everything inside her and she didn't like it one bit.

Molly stood there with a broad smile on her face. She was more than delighted to watch Charley squirm. "Have you met Ruger yet, sweetie?"

She almost felt she was being talked to like a child. As if a puppy was going to distract her somehow. Charley nodded. "Yep."

Molly released a dreamy sigh. "Isn't he a darling?"

Charley forced herself to smile. "I was just going to ask if you'd mind wrapping my order up," Charley said politely.

Molly shook her head and completely ignored Charley. "What'll it be today, Nick?"

"What's our writer lady having?" he asked. "Did she get today's special burger, Molly?"

"Yes, sir, and a chocolate shake," Molly provided as she flashed Charley a toothy grin. A smudge of ruby-colored lipstick was on her front tooth again.

"I'll take the same but make my shake a coffee."

"Be right back with your order, honey." Molly bent down to Charley and whispered, "You play nice. You'll thank me later."

Charley exhaled loudly.

"What was that for? God, am I really that awful to be around?" Nick asked. She almost thought for a split second she saw pain flicker in his dark eyes.

"It's not that." Charley felt guilty. "I was just taking a break from working and sort of wanted to be alone."

"You've been hiding in your cabin all week. I don't think I've seen you come out once," Nick commented. "You need a little human interaction."

"You've been watching me?"

Molly returned with a shake and coffee before Nick could answer. Charley repeated her question and Nick avoided her eyes.

"It's actually part of my job," Nick supplied as he held the mug to his lips.

"What does that mean?" Charley was confused.

"The man you saw me with earlier? He's the sheriff," Nick explained.

"What does that have to do with you spying on me?"

"He assigned me to look after you, and please don't raise your voice," Nick replied sweetly as his eyes scanned the restaurant. "People are trying to enjoy their lunch."

Charley inhaled deeply and tried to calm down but there was a storm brewing inside of her. "You were assigned to me? May I ask what in the hell for?"

Nick moved back into his seat and frowned. "Here's the deal... I wasn't all that thrilled at the idea of babysitting some snotty author. Then, with these last two incidents," he began to explain when she cut him off.

"What incidents?"

"Since you've arrived, there have been two murders in a town where literally nothing ever happens." Nick raised his dark brows at her.

"Seriously?" Charley was blindsided by his reveal. How come Molly hadn't mentioned something? Maybe

Nick was just messing with her? Her brain was having a difficult time processing what he had just said.

Nick nodded. "Yes, I've been working the cases but haven't gotten too far. Now the sheriff wants me to keep you company."

"You think I'm a suspect?" she gasped. Her stomach went sour.

He shook his head and swatted the air between them. "No, nothing like that. The sheriff had asked before these crimes happened. Actually, your agent requested the extra security."

"Pamela? She never mentioned it to me." Charley felt betrayed and shuddered at the idea that there had been two murders.

"Look... You're apparently kind of a big deal and she's only looking out for you. She just wanted you to be safe so you could write." Somehow him explaining it that way made her feel slightly better.

Molly arrived with their food, but Charley had completely lost her appetite. It looked like the vodka Victoria was bringing would now serve as lunch *and* dinner.

* * * *

"Can you believe that shit?" Charley had more than a few cocktails as Victoria rolled her perfect smoky eyes at her for what seemed like the twentieth time.

Charley had probably been going on and on way too long about Nick and her being his assignment and was probably boring Victoria to death. Charley was still livid and venting, which only agitated her more. She also told Victoria how there had been two murders and shared her concern whether she was indeed safe there.

Charley grappled with her chopsticks and could not quite secure the piece of sushi. With no patience left, Charley used her fingers to pop the rice-covered fish into her mouth.

"Get over it. I wish a hot detective were assigned to me," Victoria slurred as she poured another drink in her red plastic cup. "Let's go sit outside. I'm camping, remember? This is supposed to be our fun sleepover." Victoria walked a little ungracefully toward the front door and disappeared out onto the small porch.

Charley cruised past the table littered with soy sauce packets and joined Victoria outside. She couldn't entirely shake her sour attitude and was now starting to annoy herself.

"Why would Pamela even ask the police to babysit me?" Charley whined as she sipped on her drink. *Damn, it's strong.* Her throat clenched at the sour liquid, but she managed to swallow it down.

"Because you have a ton of creeps out there, whether you realize it or not," Victoria answered without hesitation. "I don't blame her one bit for wanting to protect her investment."

Charley glared at her. "Her investment?"

Victoria gave her a knowing look that was partially masked with a drunk smile. "Come on. You pay her bills. Hell, you pay mine too." Victoria pointed to the lake. "We should go swimming."

"Now?"

"Yeah, why not?"

"Because we're kinda drunk," Charley explained as she raised her cup. She had to admit the idea on the warm night was rather appealing.

"It'll be fun. Live a little, girl," Victoria urged as she suddenly rose from her seat.

"You know what? You're right. Screw all this bitching and moaning. Let's do it!" Charley sprung up from the chair, causing a bit of her drink to slosh onto to the wooden slats. She stood still for a brief moment and waited for her head to feel a little less dizzy.

Victoria led the way down to the dock, as though she owned the place. Charley was starting to rethink this grand idea of a late-night swim. The resort was quiet, and most of the cabins were dark except for their porch lights. She couldn't help but peek over to Nick's as they walked past it. She didn't notice any lights on inside but wondered if he was watching them.

The dock creaked as they reached the end. The moonlight shone through the trees, casting tall shadows all around them. The lake was a mirror that reflected the brilliant display of stars. The air was warm and still, and there was no breeze or movement on the surface of the water. All was calm and perfect.

"It's so pretty here," Victoria whispered.

"It really is." Charley enjoyed the fuzzy feeling in her head and being there with her bestie.

Victoria chugged the last of her drink and sat the empty cup onto the weathered wood. She didn't bother to remove her pajamas and dove in like an Olympic swimmer with perfect form and a nearly silent splash. She bobbed to the surface. "This feels amazing."

"You sure it's not cold?" Charley stalled, suddenly the idea of getting soaking wet held less appeal.

"Don't be a chicken. Come on." Victoria began doing the backstroke and sliced through the water like a seasoned pro.

Charley swallowed a large gulp of her cocktail, threw caution to the wind and joined Victoria. The moment she hit the water regret filled her. The water was frigid. The cold penetrated Charley to her core, saturating her with its icy embrace.

"You're a liar." Her teeth chattered as she spoke.

"If I had said it was cold, would you have jumped in?" Victoria swam to Charley, who barely kept afloat.

"I hate you." Charley slapped water at Victoria as she tried to ignore how miserable the water felt.

"You know you love me," Victoria shouted as she splashed Charley back. She had to admit this was a lot of fun, despite the feeling that hypothermia might set in soon. The cold sensation numbed her legs and was quickly sobering her up.

Charley saw a flashlight pointed at them and a familiar voice asked, "Don't you think it's a little late for a dip?" It was followed by a bark and the sound of nails tapping on the wood.

"Looks like you can't shake your shadow," Victoria teased as she swam pass Charley. "Is that his cute puppy?"

Nick stood there on the edge of the dock with a crooked grin on his face. He extended his arm out to reach Charley and help her out of the water. What surprised her was the warm fluffy towel he wrapped tightly around her. He stepped to the side and assisted Victoria and handed her a towel.

"She just can't seem to stay out of that lake," he joked. He winked at Victoria, which caused her to release a drunken giggle. His eyes shifted back to Charley. "You guys been drinking?"

"Is that against the law, Detective?" Charley snapped at him.

Nick rubbed his jaw. "Drinking in public kind of is..."

Charley snorted, "Yeah, there are so many people out here right now. Plus, if you add disturbing the peace, I think you may have to arrest us." Charley stumbled slightly.

Nick looked down and paused. "It's also not really safe to be out here right now." His eyes softened as he looked up at her. They both knew what he meant.

Victoria spoke up, "Luckily, she has you looking after her and your adorable little pup. Is he on the K-9 unit?" Victoria bent down and gave the pug some love.

"Well, she seemed less than pleased about that this afternoon," he stated. His eyes never left Charley's.

He couldn't explain the quiet anger that was simmering inside him as they stood there on the dock.

"I'm Victoria, by the way." Her tall friend offered her hand to him.

"Nick," he supplied.

"Oh, I know." Her smile was bright, even in the darkness. She turned to Charley and announced, "I'm going to change into some dry clothes. Meet you back at the cabin." Victoria hurried down the dark dock without another word.

Her mouth hung open slightly as she stepped forward to follow her friend, but Nick stopped her. "Wait," he begged.

"What?" Her voice was quiet as she kept her stare trained on the lake and avoided his.

"I wasn't watching you, if that's what you think. I heard a noise outside my cabin. Ruger and I were about to check it out. I could hear giggling and water splashing, so I brought you two some towels." Nick moved closer to her. He found it hard to keep any distance between them. He was drawn to her like a magnet. "Things aren't safe right now, Charley," he implored.

"We were just having some fun. Maybe we drank a little too much and I know it probably wasn't the smartest idea." She looked up at him and found himself being slightly hypnotized. "I was just mad." Charley's lips quivered from the cold.

"I know." Nick started to run his hands up and down her slender arms to warm her. He couldn't resist touching her. It took everything inside Nick not to kiss her again. That had already done enough damage.

A light blinded Nick's eyes when he heard a voice call out, "Everything okay there?"

Nick shielded himself from the flashlight that was pointed directly at them and he saw the owner of the resort standing there. Ruger gave out a low growl but kept close to Nick.

Tucker lowered the flashlight and eyed Charley with concern. "You sure?"

She nodded and walked away from Nick. Tucker followed close behind her while Nick stayed put. He watched as they disappeared down the path toward her cabin. Nick released a deep sigh. What was it about Charley that had him so tied up in knots? He hardly knew her but felt this magnetic draw, an intense pull that he was beginning to realize was a losing fight.

He didn't deserve to feel anything remotely good like this. He was damaged and broken in too many ways to list. People got hurt around him and he didn't want to inflict anymore harm. Why did their paths have to cross now of all times? He was here at Crescent Lake making a feeble attempt at healing those mental wounds, trying to banish the nightmares that clawed at him every time he closed his eyes. She would never understand. He was alone in this. It was simple. Nick needed to keep his distance from Charley.

"Come on, Ruger. Let's go back to the cabin, bud." Nick and Ruger walked defeatedly down the dock.

* * * *

She woke up with a pounding headache and the harsh sunlight burned her dry eyes. Charley waited for the uneasy waves in her stomach to settle before she ventured out of bed. It was now more apparent than ever to her that she couldn't party the way she used to be able to. As Charley shuffled barefoot toward the kitchen, she saw Victoria seated in front of her laptop.

"There's coffee," Victoria said without looking away from the screen.

"Thank God." She filled a mug of the dark nectar and added a splash of creamer. "How are you even up this early?"

"Girl, it's almost eleven," Victoria replied. "This manuscript is pretty damn good, by the way."

Victoria's eyes remained glued to the screen as Charley pulled a chair up next to her. She laid her head on the table and begged for her headache to go away. "Why did you let me drink so much?" she complained. The sound of her own voice made her ears hurt. She hadn't been this hungover in years.

"You're a big girl and did that all on your own. You didn't need my help. Besides, we didn't drink all that much. The bottle isn't even empty, and that swim should've sobered you right up." Victoria gently patted her shoulder. "Or at least seeing that hunk Nick. Then again, he might have the same effect as booze."

Charley groaned as a wave of nausea washed over her.

"And so, that was infamous Tucker, huh?"

Charley had made quick introductions when he'd walked her back to the cabin the night before. If she hadn't been so pissed off at Nick, Charley would've invited Tucker in. She wanted Victoria to see what she saw in him. Unfortunately, Charley's temper had gotten the best of her but Victoria wasn't blind and had hopefully gotten an eyeful of Tucker.

"Told you he was cute," Charley replied as she managed to lift her head. She massaged her temples and willed the pain to vanish.

"Meh," Victoria responded as she rose from the table and quickly returned with her purse. "Here... This will help," she said as she shook a few aspirins loose from a bottle. "He might be cute, but that Nick? Now that's a man," Victoria added with a smile of appreciation.

"Maybe you just need a better look at Tucker. We need to stop by the lodge today to see about renting a cabin for my parents next weekend." Charley popped the pills into her mouth and washed them down with coffee. She said a silent prayer that her coffee stayed in her stomach.

"Once you feel better, I'd love for you to show me around this place." Victoria was already showered with her bobbed hair blow-dried and makeup expertly applied. *How is she able to look so put together?* They had drunk the same amount, but Charley looked like hell warmed over.

After she showered and felt slightly more human, Charley led the way to the lodge. They were greeted with the same sweet and spicy cinnamon aroma she had smelled the first night she'd arrived. The warm wooden ceilings and rich furniture were inviting. The design throughout was gorgeous, except for the stuffed critters.

"Look at all those heads," Victoria whispered. "It's kinda creepy."

Charley felt their glass eyes stare down at her. "I know, right?"

"I didn't think the day could get any lovelier. I guess I was wrong," Tucker announced as he emerged from his office with a large smile. He wore a robin's-egg-blue polo shirt that played up the color of his eyes. The khaki shorts enhanced the tanned shade of his legs. *How can Victoria not see how hot he is?*

"Hi, Tucker," Charley greeted sweetly, her cheeks heating.

"Everything okay?" He frowned slightly, but even that was sexy.

"Everything's fine. I know this is a long shot, but I was curious if you had any vacant cabins for next weekend?" Charley asked hopefully.

He raised his eyebrows and briefly looked at her like she was out of her mind. "For Fourth of July weekend?" Tucker blew out a breath. "Let me see." He went behind the counter and started to type on the small laptop.

"I was telling my parents about how great this place was and thought it might be a nice a treat for them," Charley explained. "My mom even said she'd bring her famous coleslaw to the barbecue," Charley playfully bribed him. Victoria rolled her eyes in disgust.

Tucker looked up from the computer and grinned. "In that case, we definitely need to find an empty cabin for them." His eyes returned to the screen and he finally said, "Okay, I found one."

"Wonderful," Charley answered as she watched Victoria explore the lodge. She moved about slowly, looking at the taxidermy with a disgusted look on her pretty face.

"So, what are your plans for today? More writing?" Tucker asked kindly.

"Nah, I'm thinking I'll show Victoria around before she leaves tomorrow." Victoria heard her name and smiled tightly in their direction.

"No more night swimming, okay?" Tucker joked as he leaned casually against the counter. Charley giggled and was about to leave when Tucked asked, "I was wondering if you'd like to go out on my boat?"

"Today?" Charley replied.

He shook his head. "I was thinking maybe tomorrow or the day after. Just us." His gaze moved toward Victoria then quickly back to her.

A date. Finally, this guy was showing some interest. *Play it cool, girl.*

"Yeah, that would be fun," Charley answered as casually as she could manage. Her belly become a fluttery mess. "Tucker, thank you again for walking me back to my cabin last night," she added flirtatiously.

"You just be careful. I have heard there's been some pretty bad stuff happening around here. If you need anything, you can count on me." There was genuine concern beaming back at her. Charley nodded and slowly followed Victoria through the large, heavy door.

Once outside, Victoria huddled close to her. "Did he seriously just ask you out?"

"He did. I mean, kinda. He offered to take me out on his boat. That would be considered a date, right?"

"What about Nick?" Victoria countered as they strolled back toward their cabin.

"What about him? I told you, Vic, that I'm not interested in Nick."

"Well, you should be."

"Why? Tucker is a sweet guy and definitely more my type."

Victoria frowned. "I don't know. He's not like Nick."

"Exactly." Charley grinned.

Victoria rolled her eyes. "Why don't you show me around the lake and we forget about both guys."

They found a trail that wrapped around the lake and decided to explore the woods. Charley was pleased to find that Victoria was enjoying herself as they discovered various flowers and insects as they walked together. Though they were shaded by the large trees, she could feel the heat from the summer sun.

"I'm getting hungry. How about you?" Charley asked as she saw her cabin come into sight.

"Actually, I'm starving." Victoria wiped sweat from her forehead. "I could definitely use a cold drink too."

"I know just the place."

Charley and Victoria freshened up back at her cabin then Charley drove them to her favorite place — the diner. They blasted the radio and sang along as they made their way into town.

"How cute is this place?" A flash of wonder sparkled in Victoria's eyes as they entered.

"I love it here," Charley said as she led them to a vacant booth. Molly waved and greeted them with a bright smile.

Molly took their order and left them to chat. They didn't discuss work or either of the guys thankfully. Charley steered the conversation more toward Victoria. She'd felt like an awful friend these past few months and it was nice to catch up on what was going on in her friend's life. Their food arrived and they continued to visit without any interruption. This was nice and something Charley had missed.

"I feel like I've gained ten pounds," Victoria complained as she nibbled on a fry. "And it's completely worth it."

Charley took another bite of her enormous burger and had to admit she was also stuffed. She didn't eat like this back in Seattle, not greasy burgers served with golden fries and tasty ice cream shakes. The way she figured it, she was on vacation and that meant eating whatever the heck she wanted. Today it was a burger and a mountain of crispy fries smothered in an ungodly amount of ketchup.

"I love this funky little place," Charley commented as she slurped her shake. "It's like straight out of a time machine or something."

"Even the waitress," Victoria giggled as she motioned toward Molly.

"Molly's awesome." Charley came quickly to her defense. "Everyone is so nice here too."

"They sure are." Victoria smirked playfully. "A girl could get used to Crescent Lake."

Charley laughed. "Maybe you should hang around a little longer then."

Victoria shook her head. "No can do, girl. I've got to get back to real life."

Victoria might be her assistant but she was also a writer. She had a weekly column at the same newspaper Charley had worked for. It was where they'd met and become fast friends. Victoria loved writing fluff pieces and was thrilled when she had been offered her own little piece of real estate in the Sunday paper. *The Healthy Living and Lifestyle section.* To Charley, it seemed like a death sentence. She'd die of boredom if all she ever wrote about was which shoes to wear when hosting a mommy martini party or which designer teeth-whitening toothpaste worked the best.

Charley wasn't into following trends. She also wasn't exactly the poster child for healthy living and had no fashion sense at all. Victoria, on the other hand was pretty much an expert when it came to what to wear, how to eat right and stay in shape. Victoria played into what readers wanted and, in some ways, Charley supposed she wasn't much different. She'd kept writing all those scary stories, even though she desperately wanted a change of scenery — something light-hearted and romantic with a little less slashing and blood. Victoria was an absolute genius when it came to knowing what readers wanted, but she had encouraged Charley to try something different. When the backlash had happened, Victoria had figured out ways for them to maneuver around it. Victoria had Charley's back. It was as simple as that — and not just in the professional aspect, either. She was constantly pestering Charley to get a life and often pointed out that writing about fictional lives wasn't the same thing.

It was easy to forget. Charley got swallowed into the chaotic lives of her characters and most of the time felt more like an observer in her own life. Maybe that's why she snapped pictures to share on social media. It was a way of seeing her life through her own eyes, capturing moments and memories to stand as proof that she did actually have a life.

Charley pulled out her cell phone and aimed it at the partially empty shake.

"What are you doing?" Victoria asked with annoyance.

"Nothing."

"Didn't we discuss this?"

"Yes, and how good have I been? Not one single picture of the lake or cabin has been posted, has it?" Charley pointed out.

"Thank God. That cabin gives a whole new meaning to *roughing it*."

"It's not that bad," Charley replied defensively.

"It kinda is. Like, how old is that couch?" Victoria arched a perfectly waxed brow.

"It's vintage. Besides, you're just too fancy to truly appreciate it."

"And you're not?" Victoria arched her eyebrows.

"I grew up in the country, remember?"

Victoria let out an obnoxious laugh. "Okay, but be serious here for a minute. How long have you been in Seattle?"

Charley nodded. "True. But you know the saying, *'You can take the girl out of the country but you can't take the country out of the girl.'*"

"Please, you're killing me." Victoria's head tilted back as she let out a contagious laugh.

Charley couldn't help herself. "I'll prove it to you after lunch."

"Why do I feel like that's an actual threat?" Victoria appeared slightly concerned.

"It'll be fun." *At least for me.*

After a quick stop to get a few supplies for the wonderful afternoon Charley had planned, she was eager to show Victoria another side of herself. They had been friends for years but never had they been fishing together. They had traveled to faraway cities together, dined out at fancy restaurants and danced into the wee hours of the morning at some pretty ridiculous clubs. Victoria was her partner-in-crime and Charley wanted to share this very simple experience with her, let her see the real Charley — salt-of-the-earth country girl.

"This is just plain gross." Victoria gagged and pinched her nose. "I thought you said this would be fun," she complained a few hours later as they sat on the dock with a tub of worms between them and her trusty fishing pole.

Charley had finished baiting a hook with a plump and very wiggly worm. "It is fun. Here… Let me show you how to cast out the line."

"No thanks. I'd rather be out there on a boat," Victoria commented as she pointed to a few small boats across the way.

"What do you think they're doing?"

Victoria squinted as she slid her over-sized sunglasses down her nose. "Boating, duh?"

"Those aren't like those fancy yachts or sailboats down at the waterfront in Seattle, Vic. Those folks are out there fishin', the same as us right here."

"How is this supposed to be fun?" Victoria took a swig from her beer.

"It's relaxing," Charley answered as she set the rod down and popped the tab on her own beer. "There's nothing better than drinking a cold beer and waiting for that tug on your line."

"Um, I can think of a few — like, a sale at the downtown Nordstrom's. Now, that is a good time." Victoria winked. "Remember those Christian Louboutin ankle booties I scored?"

"Those were pretty cute," Charley concurred. Despite acting like a bona fide country girl earlier at lunch, Charley had adopted rather sophisticated tastes and appreciated the city life.

The sun had been nearly gobbled up by the lake and the sky was now painted in a hazy tangerine glow. The air was warm and the cold beers they'd drank were refreshing. They hung their bare legs over the dock and let their feet dangle just above the water. Charley felt young again, reliving the simplicity of teenage summers, just being a girl with her best friend, giggling over stupid stuff and not having a care in the world. The beer didn't hurt to help her embark on this trip down memory lane. Her head was happily fuzzy when she felt the familiar pull on her line.

"Oh, I think we got a nibble," she cried joyfully and began the age-old battle of man versus fish. Charley tightened her grasp on the pole and worked the simple reel as she planted herself firmly on the dock. She yanked back when her pole almost slipped out of her hands and she nearly fell into the water. Then the line snapped. She had lost the fish and the battle. "Damn, he got away."

"Okay, I lied," Victoria admitted with a stream of giggles. "This is fun."

"Told ya."

They packed up their fishing gear and walked back to the cabin hand in hand. Charley savored this sense of renewed friendship. Her heart was happy and she realized how isolated she'd allowed herself to become. Back at the cabin, they changed into pajamas and settled in for the evening.

"God, I needed this little escape." Victoria smiled happily. "We need to try to do this more."

"I agree." Charley sipped on her mixed drink.

They were both stretched out on the couch, each with their back resting comfortably on the arm of the couch. Victoria's long, bare legs were next to Charley and hung over the arm.

"I think life just moves too fast back home. This? This is really friggin' awesome," Victoria expressed as they enjoyed each other's company. "I mean, to be fair, I don't know if I could do the whole cabin thing twenty-four hours a day like, all the time. But this is nice." She drew her cup to her lips.

Charley soaked in this simple moment. It was nice just having her friend there, not as her assistant, not talking about the book—just two chicks enjoying drinks, sharing secrets they already knew and laughing more than they had in eons. Soft music played quietly in the background and the scented candles gave off a romantic vibe, which was probably why the conversation shifted into a different direction.

"So, you honestly don't feel anything for Nick?" Victoria asked. "I mean, he even has a cute dog. I kinda want to know the story behind that. Here's this dark and mysterious guy with the cutest dog ever. Aren't dogs supposed to sort of resemble their owners?"

Charley rolled her eyes. "I guess Nick's eyes aren't all that bulgy."

"Oh, come on. Be serious. Nick is hot."

Charley giggled. "Well, so is Tucker."

"Not him again," Victoria groaned. "He's so boy-next-door."

"That's sort of the appeal," Charley noted playfully.

"Maybe like five or ten years ago," Victoria pointed out. "But we're older now and I don't know about you, but I'm looking for man."

"Okay, break it down to me how Tucker isn't a *man*," Charley challenged. "I'm all ears."

Victoria started, "Well, for starters, you'd have to be completely blind not to see the physical difference. Tucker is boyish. Nick is not."

Charley could see what her friend meant. "You saying Nick has a dad bod?" she teased.

"Oh, God, Charley. No, but can you imagine what he must look like without clothes on? Scrumptious is the word that comes to my mind." Victoria fanned herself. "Even with how dark it was, I could totally see that he's got one helluva chest…and those arms? Don't get me started on those. I mean, you gotta figure that since he's a cop. Those guys work out all the time."

"Tucker has a chest too," Charley defended her crush. "And very nice arms too."

"Sorry, not like Nick's. Tucker's just soft-looking in a scrawny kind of way. Like, has he even hit puberty yet?"

"Oh, please. Just because he has that lean, athletic build doesn't mean he's scrawny by any means."

"I think you need to have your eyes checked. Just sayin'." Victoria winked at Charley. "So, are you going to take lover boy up on his offer?"

"I think it'll be fun." Charley lifted her cup to lips and savored the taste of her rum and Coke.

"Just don't let my boy Nick catch you out on that boat," Victoria joked.

"We both know you're Team Nick. Why don't *you* date him?" Charley suggested. A pinch of jealousy hit her as the words left her lips.

Victoria laughed hard. "Don't get me wrong. I would absolutely snag him if he wasn't so into you."

"Yeah, because he's like, supposedly my stupid bodyguard or some shit." Charley swallowed more of her drink.

"Get over that nonsense." Victoria looked her curiously. "Or, on the other hand, remember that Whitney Houston movie?" Victoria's face became animated.

"Jeesh, this isn't like *The Bodyguard* 2.0, Vic," Charley replied with a snicker.

"Uh, it could be if you'd quit being all hung up on Tucker," Victoria explained frankly. "Nick could totally be your Kevin Costner."

"Because I'm just like Whitney, right?" Charley teased then belted out her very best Whitney Houston impression. "And I will always love you," she sang. Uncontrollable laughter followed and the memory of one of the best girls' weekends they'd ever had.

Chapter Eight

Inspiration could hit at any time, day or night. When it does, a writer did not dally. They were a slave to it and answer when they're called. Charley found this to be all too true as she sat typing at an insane speed. It was as though she were possessed by some kind of demon alive inside of her that was snarling and demanding her to write these awful and twisted things. Charley had described one of the most brutal and horrific scenes she'd written to date.

She ended the Chapter with a wicked cliffhanger and trembled in the darkness. It had been an intense ride and she'd barely survived it. How was it possible to be afraid of one's own words? Maybe it had to be from being alone again. Victoria had left earlier that day to beat traffic and Charley found herself itching to write as she waved goodbye to her friend. As much as she'd enjoyed Victoria's company, Charley was there to write this book. She'd spent all afternoon and well into the night spitting out chapters at a supernatural pace.

Pamela will be thrilled.

Charley rose from her chair and stretched her stiff back. She shook out her arms and wiggled her tight fingers in hopes to get the blood flowing again. She needed some air before going to bed. There was no way Charley was going to fall asleep after having written that scene.

Feeling like a naughty child who should be in bed, she tip-toed quietly to the door and snuck out onto the porch. She silently pleaded for her mind to settle. The cool air was moist, night's final kiss to dawn before it surrendered to the light of morning. Her favorite hour was when the darkness clung to stars and fed the hungry shadows. It was magnificently dark except for the dot of lights from all the cabin porches giving off a magic firefly effect. She could hear the haunting hoot of an owl hidden away in a nearby tree. It was as though the owl was asking her why she was still up. Charley was half-tempted to answer him.

Charley studied the glass-like lake, its smooth body black and seeming to go forever. It was a pool of secrets, or was that just her author-mind working overtime, sometimes seeing things that weren't really there? Charley heard a twig snap, possibly a deer moving through the bushes or a killer stalking his prey. She shivered as a chill crawled up her spine and burrowed deep inside her chest. Paranoia had a funny way of visiting her every time she was in the midst of writing something *good…really good*. It was as though her body became ultra-aware of her surroundings and too sensitive to the slightest sound or movement. Charley could only describe it as a near out-of-body experience when she was this deep into a story. Her mind and soul were trapped together in a strange plain that wasn't quite reality. This made it difficult to navigate her way out. Charley stepped carefully between that thin veil as she tried to find her way back to where everything was supposed to make sense…real life. But wasn't that where the nightmarish tales she wrote were derived from?

The hairs on the back of her neck stood on end and goosebumps suddenly appeared on her bare arms. Charley couldn't dismiss the sick feeling in her gut that maybe she was being watched — or hunted. She bravely peeked around the sharp corner of the porch and could've sworn she'd seen a puff of breath that was not her own. Charley froze for a brief second as she searched her brain for a plausible explanation. Her lungs burned as she briefly starved her body of oxygen, a soft floating whisper that quickly dissipated. *Did it just call my name?*

Perhaps it had only been her brain playing tricks on her, self-made hallucinations brought on from being so deep inside her own creative mind? Then a primal survival mechanism kicked in and yelled at her to get back into the safety of the cabin. As Charley ignored the warning, she heard another stick crack loudly in the otherwise-silent space and nearly fell backward. Her mind was kind enough to remind her of the two incidents that had recently occurred in Crescent Lake. Another loud snap. There was no dismissing the thoroughly creeped-out sensation Charley felt as she slunk back toward the entrance of her cabin. The old adage came to mind, *'things that go bump in the night'*. There was definitely something or someone out there.

She instinctively glanced to Nick's cabin, which appeared to have a hint of light glowing inside. *How is he still awake? Well, I don't exactly keep banker hours either.*

Charley didn't bother to fight the urge to go over to his cabin as she hurried toward his dimly lit porch and knocked on his door. Her mind came up with a million reasons why going to Nick was probably the worst idea. For starters, there was the possibility of more confusing kisses. Then there was having to admit to herself that she was more than a little scared. Charley prayed it was only her exhausted brain, but she feared there was something very real out there. Whether it wanted her or not, she didn't know. What she did know was that horrible shit happened all the time to people and that it made perfect sense to go to him. Nick was a cop and wasn't *she* his assignment? Maybe it was time for him to serve and protect.

Why does she have to be standing there looking at me like that? Her eyes were wide with fear but tinted with bravery. Nick moved aside as she entered his cabin. Charley rambled an apology and a creepy tale all yarned together. She was dressed in a soft-looking tee and flannel pajama pants that were bright blue and had donuts and coffee mugs on them. She was the very definition of cute. Nick tried to focus on what she was saying as Ruger ran up to greet her, not a single bark, only his tail wagging like crazy.

"Did you actually see anyone?" he asked impatiently.

"Well, no." Charley paused and looked away briefly as if she doubted what she had seen or heard. "Nick, there was definitely someone out there." Her eyes were not lying and the slight tremble in her voice told the truth—or what she believed was real.

Nick hoped she was wrong, but in the forefront of his mind he knew there was a killer out there. Now whether this killer was outside these cabins was different story.

Charley paced the small floor like a nervous little bird. "You don't believe me, do you? You think I'm making this up, don't you?" she accused in a frustrated breath.

Nick had to fight the urge to sweep her up into his arms and hush all her fears. This constant need to touch her was driving him crazy. *Keep your distance, Capra.*

"Let me check out the perimeter," he offered while he strapped his holster back on.

"You're taking a gun?" she asked with eyes wider than saucers.

"See? I don't think you're lying." He carefully waved the black matte-finish 9mm pistol before holstering it. "You stay here," Nick ordered.

"I don't think so, pal. I'm coming with you," Charley argued. There was that sexy flicker of bravery again. *No damsel in distress here.*

"I'd rather you not," Nick countered firmly. "You came to me, remember?" *Who is protecting who?* "Besides, you can get a little more acquainted with my dear pal over there." Ruger had plopped back onto the couch and almost appeared to be grinning at them. He seemed entertained by their guest.

She huffed and started for the door. Ruger leaped from the couch and Nick managed to reach her before she was able to exit. It would seem they both were trying to protect her. His fingers grazed her shirt and there was that shock of electricity again as he touched her. "Look... If there is someone out there and it's the same person who has been committing these murders, I don't think it's wise for you to go out there by yourself." He watched as a flash of fear lit up her gorgeous eyes. She parted her lips to speak and she swallowed her words.

She was his to protect, and in this very moment, no matter how much he tried to ignore it, it felt more than a job. He wanted to keep her safe.

The moment they'd made contact, she'd felt it. Like the strike of a match, it was sudden and hot — an intense burn and completely unexpected. She hushed the feelings that sprang alive inside her. His eyes were rich with warmth and concern, and she saw a glint of humor. *Does he actually find this funny?*

"You're something else, you know that?" Nick said as he stepped in front of her and blocked Charley from leaving.

"I'm sorry. This was a mistake," she said as she began to doubt herself again. Charley felt like an idiot coming to Nick.

"No, it wasn't. It was the smart thing to do, Charley." His words held a lot of weight. Nick's jaw was tight as he explained, "There have been two murders here. I can't even begin to tell you how important it is to speak up when you think you may've seen something. Even if it turns out to be nothing, we need all eyes and ears open." Nick opened the door and reached for Charley 's hand. "Stay close," he ordered. She'd be a liar if she didn't admit it was a relief to have this man protecting her from those scary noises. "Ruger, you hold down the fort," Nick ordered as the pug raced back to his favorite spot on the couch.

Everything was cloaked in shadowy darkness as they stalked their way back to her cabin. Charley tried to pick up any sounds as she kept next to Nick. Charley felt the tension leave her body once they reached the porch. Nick went inside first and checked out every square inch of the cabin. Once he was satisfied, Nick asked her to lock the door while he went outside. Charley peered out of the small windows and kept her own watchful eyes on Nick as he rounded each corner carefully. Charley couldn't deny that it was sort of sexy to see him step with trained precision and his gun out. *Honestly, what in the hell is wrong with me? This shouldn't be a turn-on. There could very well be a killer outside this very moment and here I am wondering what else he's packing.*

Nick rapped on the door as Charley waited eagerly for him. She opened and quickly shut it behind her after he came inside.

"Your cabin is a lot nicer than mine," he joked. "Sort of. Looks like we both got a crappy couch." Nick motioned toward the ugly sofa.

"So, you didn't find anything out there?"

He shook his head. "Nothing." Nick stared at where her laptop sat. "You were writing, huh?"

"Yeah, I was," she answered and closed the computer. She watched him frown. "Maybe I'm being paranoid, Nick. Sometimes when I write, I get so wrapped up in the story."

"Even so, I'm glad you came to me."

They both stood there awkwardly, neither of them sure what to do next. Charley didn't know how to play this. *Do I offer to make coffee or just bid him goodnight?* In many ways, it would have been easier had Nick stumbled across something — anything — out there. *This is just plain uncomfortable.*

"Well, I guess I'll let you go to bed. Keep the door locked, and if you need anything, you know where to find me and my guard pug," Nick finally said as he let himself out.

"Thank you," Charley said softly and turned the lock. She kept her back against the wooden door and felt like a paranoid idiot. She also felt something else…disappointment. It was rather strange, almost as if she had expected Nick to do what he'd done every other time they had come in contact. *Kiss.* Charley licked her lips and could faintly recall the feel of Nick's on hers. There was no doubt she was going to bed hungry, starving for more of those unsettling kisses.

Chapter Nine

That was too close. It is my fault. I needed to see her. I could almost smell her fear. I tucked myself back against the cedar frame of her dwelling, the small cabin with no curtains. I cannot help but smile at the thought that she may have seen me or felt my presence. In many ways, I want her to know I am here. That I am the one steering her back on course. I want her to become inspired. Maybe if she remembers, that's all it will take for her to find those words she's been missing.

I reluctantly move past my beautiful distraction and step carefully through the pine-needle-littered path. There is a red glow of a cigarette and dirty smoke fills my nostrils as I approach. I am disgusted and feel justified as I slink tightly against the wooden slats of the cabin. She is alone. An ear-splitting screech of an owl almost alerts the woman that I am there in the shadows, hunting and waiting for just the precise moment to strike.

Then it comes. I see her shadowy figure bend down to smother her cigarette out on the ground. I raise the heavy chunk of wood I have been carrying and connect with her skull. She drops to the ground and squirms in spastic movements. Her feet scrape against the floor. I slam the wood down again to ensure she will not wake up. The noise, the cracking sound as the wood meets bone fills my ears. I can feel it bend and shape inside of me and I almost vomit. The weakened wood splinters into pieces, and I toss the broken remains into the nearby holly bushes.

I lean against the building and catch my breath. I take in the impossibly perfect view. The moonlight drips onto the lake and sits on top of the unmoving black surface. There is no sound, no air, just a vacuumed space. I soak it in and cherish this moment of complete blankness.

I know there is still work to be done, the figure at my feet needs to be dealt with. I am relieved that there is not much blood this time but oddly, I miss the smell. There is a new hunger that has developed inside me. It has locked itself within this human cage as I do her bidding.

I hoist the woman's body over my shoulder and begin the trek to the water's edge. As I near the shore, I hear the water as it slaps against the rocky sand in muted waves. I drop the woman down onto the ground, and her limp body makes a loud thud. I stare down at her, and with the help of the moonlight, I make out dirty blonde hair and overly tanned skin. She is old and her skin has lost its firmness. She is ugly and will not be missed by this world. *Or will she?* She was alone.

I pull the white nylon rope from the pocket of my shorts and begin to bind her ankles and wrists together when her eyes suddenly spring open. Her screams are quickly silenced with the thick dishtowel I cram almost to the back of her throat. I couldn't have her making any sounds and alarming anyone of our little rendezvous. She begins to gag and tears glisten against the shadows of her cheeks.

"You should've stayed asleep, dear," I scold and wag my finger at her. I scan the immediate shore for a large stone but stop when I realize that is not how this is written. I release an irritated sigh as I gather more of the rope from my pocket. There isn't much time left, but enough to do what must come next.

I crouch down next to her. My knees touch the cool, wet sand. It's rough against my skin as they sink in. I wind the rope around her saggy throat and yank the two ends to meet. Her skin folds over the thick nylon. She wiggles under me, thrashing about with the best of her ability. Her limbs are bound and there is no point in resisting. I pull the ropes tight in my palms, and they cut and burn through my skin. She has stopped moving. I hate when they don't close their eyes and I have to fight the uncontrollable urge to shut them. But that is how it is written. Those swollen blue eyes with thick mascara-slathered eyelashes need to be looking up at the heavens. I can see light emerging through the clouds in the east and morning will soon give me away if I do not leave now.

The next part is essential. I extract a sleek silver tube of ruby-red lipstick from my back pocket and smash it onto my lips. The foul taste somehow manages to touch my tongue and I spit onto the sand. *Stay focused. She needs you. She cannot have distractions and neither can you.* I power through the awful texture that is smeared upon my lips and smooth the woman's hair away from her brow. I gingerly place my lips to her warm skin and press my mouth down hard onto her flesh. I lean back and admire the perfect print of my lips in red. The mark that will tell her this is hers. I dip my hand in the water and rid my mouth of the color.

This she will see. This will show her. This is what she wrote.

In the light, Charlene Vanderberg will see what happens in these small hours.

Chapter Ten

Charley woke up cranky and irritated at some distant noise that had interrupted her sleep, not that she had even slept well. Between fighting the morning light and thoughts of Nick, she had struggled to get any real sleep at all. Charley flipped onto her belly and tried to cover her head with the pillow. All hopes of blocking out the sound were further dashed when there was another knock at her door. Charley growled a curse word under her breath and stomped to answer it.

Nick stood there with a solemn expression on his face. His hair was tousled and she couldn't dismiss the bags under his eyes. *Looks like someone else didn't get much sleep either.* "You were right."

"About?" Her brain was fuzzy and slow at processing anything he said.

"There's been another one." His voice was gravelly and rough with regret.

"Oh, shit. Are you serious?" The realization of his words finally compounded into the raw sense of what he meant, and Charley went to pass Nick.

He stopped her. "You did hear someone and I just wanted you to know that you weren't just being paranoid or having an overactive imagination."

"I actually really appreciate that," Charley replied as she wrapped her arms around her body. She was filled with a sudden chill. "Where was the murder at?"

She studied Nick, and saw the hesitation as he answered, "Here."

"What? *Here*?" She immediately felt as though someone had punched her hard in the gut.

"I don't know what's happening in this town, but I intend to catch this creep," Nick hissed and started to retreat away from her.

"Where are you going?" Charley followed him. She didn't care that she was barefoot or only wore pajamas. A ferocious need clawed inside of her. Charley had to see the body for herself.

Why did I even tell her there was a body? Nick had been asking himself a lot of questions lately and coming up short on answers. Now this girl was following him to a gnarly scene she had no business seeing. He knew there was no point in arguing with her, no telling her to stay put. Charley Vanderberg might be small and seem delicate, but she was a mighty force of nature.

They hadn't come to retrieve the body yet when Nick and Charley were at the shore. He wanted to spare Charley from having to see this. He expected to her to vomit or act repulsed but she didn't. She stood there like a statue—her eyes trained on the body as the cold morning lake water washed over the gray skin of the strangled woman. Charley didn't move. It was as though she were mentally taking notes and digesting what was in front of her. Shock maybe? Nick wished she would have stayed in the cabin. It was his fault for alerting her.

Charley wore a curious expression on her face as she peered down at the woman who was bound at her wrists and ankles. *Poor Charley.* Nick instantly became consumed with guilt. She had probably never seen a dead body up close. Nick wanted nothing more than to whisk Charley away and tuck her safely back inside the cabin. There was a monster on the loose, who very well could have been right next to Charley last night and the thought that this could have been her on the sand made Nick sick and seeping with a silent rage.

The sheriff stood near the corpse and frowned at Nick. His eyes were angry as he glanced over at Charley. "Capra, you got a minute?" It was more of an order than a question. They walked a few paces away from where yellow tape whipped violently in the morning wind. "Why in the hell did you bring Vanderberg here?"

"It wasn't my intent. Last night, Charley came to my cabin with concerns that someone was outside. I checked it out and made sure she was safe," Nick explained. His eyes stayed on Charley. Her strawberry-blonde hair blew around her sad face. "I didn't want her to see this, but she'd thought it was her imagination."

"It would've been better to have kept it that way," the sheriff replied. "We've got a serious problem on our hands. Fourth of July is this weekend and one of our busiest times of the year. This situation is getting out of control."

"I know, and we aren't getting any closer to figuring this out either," Nick added. He ran his hands through his wind-tangled hair, and his fingers snagged as he combed them through in frustration. Each murder had been different. This woman had some trauma to the back side of her head but it was the strangulation that had killed her and all though the first murder was a strangulation as well, that woman had not been tied up or left the way this one had been. It was as though whoever did this wanted to put the body on display, for it to be seen. *And what was with the lipstick on the poor woman's forehead?* Nick hadn't quite figured that part out yet. The second murder had been a male and one of the messiest scenes Nick had witnessed in a long time, except the killer had done a phenomenal job of hiding all traces of prints and clues. All three cases seemed unconnected except that they had happened here—a place where nothing ever happened. Somehow, Nick felt there was a link, something that would eventually tie them together. He had racked his tired brain all morning, trying desperately to make the pieces fit the puzzle.

"You need to get her out of here, Capra." The sheriff wore a grim expression as he gazed at Charley, who was kneeling next to the body. "You make sure you keep a close eye on Vanderberg. Be her shadow, and we'll handle this investigation."

"Shouldn't this be an all-hands-on-deck situation?" Nick asked. "We've had three murders so close together now. We need to stop this psycho."

"Nick," Charley called out.

He jogged over to her. "What is it?" Nick asked as he saw a new awareness and alarm fill her face.

"The kiss on her forehead," she pointed out.

"Yeah, I know. It's strange."

"No, it's more than that. I wrote about that," she seemed to confess. It was obvious Charley was more than a little shaken up by this entire scene.

"Let me take you back to your cabin," Nick soothed as he tried to usher her away from the body. He felt the sheriff's eyes on him and wanted to deescalate this before it got out of hand.

"No, Nick, I'm serious. I think whoever did this read my book."

"I think it's time to go," he whispered close to her ear. She could feel the sharpness as his stubble grazed her skin.

Nick attempted to pull her away from the group of cabin dwellers who had gathered on the shore. She managed to free herself from his grasp and knelt next to the woman. Her eyes were open wide with the fear still trapped inside them but absent of any light. It was as though she were seeing what she had written come to life. Charley eyed where the rope had cut into the woman's skin, the same as she had described it in that Chapter. Charley was not just imagining it. She remembered writing about the cherry-stained kiss on her victim's forehead. The difference was in the way she had told the story — the fictional body of the woman who was found under a bridge, away from these staring eyes. This poor woman had been left out in the open to be gawked at.

Where is the coroner? Why hadn't they covered her body yet? Charley was consumed with anger but could not tear her own eyes away. The vibrant print of lips on the pale flesh seared into Charley 's brain and her stomach squeezed with a wave of nausea. She grew dizzy as she reread the scene in her head — a scene she had written years ago in a novel that had quickly become a bestseller and Hollywood blockbuster hit. Charley drowned in the overwhelming sensations that churned inside of her. Why didn't he believe her? Some monster did this because they had read her book and was trying to get back at her somehow. Victoria was right about the creeps who had been emailing threats. This was all her fault. A woman was dead because of one of her books. Charley jumped up from the sand and raced through the crowd toward her cabin. This had to be a nightmare. There was no way this was real. She just needed to get back into bed and wake up. It would all be okay then.

He trailed after her. This was entirely his fault. As Nick watched the small cedar door slam shut, he heard a truck pull up and saw the resort's owner, Tucker, hop out with a happy smile glued on his face. Nick knew that was not going to last long once he learned what had happened on his lake.

Nick was torn. He wanted to comfort her, to make sure she would be okay. He also wanted to have a few words with Tucker. Nick approached quickly and saw Tucker removing plastic bags from the bed of the truck.

"Good morning, Nick," Tucker greeted politely.

"Morning." Nick eyed him curiously. "We got a call this morning. Did the sheriff contact you?"

Tucker shook his head. "No. I was out gathering supplies for this weekend. We're having that huge barbecue. You really should join the rest of the guests."

Nick nodded. "One of your renters called the police this morning after they found a body," he spilled out.

Tucker's mouth dropped. "Are you serious?"

Because the cruiser, yellow tape and coroner van that just rolled up weren't a dead giveaway, dumbass. Nick didn't like how Tucker was acting. Something seemed off. His senses were dialing in on Tucker's expressions and awkwardly casual movements.

"Last night, Charley came to my cabin," Nick started to re-tell the encounter and Tucker's face twitched with irritation.

"She wasn't writing? Why did she go to *your* cabin?" Tucker asked as anger deepened on his brow.

He wasn't sure why he felt the need to defend himself. Nick instantly tried to explain, "Hey, man, it's not like that." *Or was it, Nick?* "Charley came to me because she thought she heard someone outside and was frightened." Nick pointed to the shore. "Charley was right, and the killer left a little present."

Tucker's eyes remained trained on Nick. "Where is Charley now? Does she know?"

"She's back at her cabin. I told her what happened."

"God, did she see the body?" Tucker asked impatiently, almost with eager anticipation.

Nick felt the onslaught of guilt hit him again. "Yes."

"For Christ sake, that poor girl. I'm going to check on her," Tucker said as he dropped the bags back into the truck bed.

Nick's guilt shifted quickly into jealousy. He couldn't explain the dire need to protect Charley and the very thought that Tucker would be comforting her when it should be him caused a wicked storm inside him, a conflict of emotions he feared would emerge. Nick knew he should have kept his distance. *A little late now.*

She heard the knock but wasn't sure she wanted to answer it. Hiding in bed was her solution to this awful nightmare. Charley rolled over and wiped away the tears. She had been crying since she'd returned to her cabin. Charley couldn't get the woman's swollen face or bulging eyes out of her mind. But it was the lipstick on her forehead that made Charley's heart break into pieces. She was somehow responsible for that woman's death. Her words had played a vital part and there was no escaping that reality. This wasn't a coincidence, a random killing that by chance had carried with it the same sick act as her story. This had been done intentionally. No one could convince her otherwise.

The knock persisted and Charley moved at a snail's pace to answer it. She expected Nick but was surprised to find Tucker there, his face ashen with concern.

"Are you okay?" Tucker's voice was low.

"Yes," she lied. "No, I'm not actually," Charley admitted as Tucker entered.

"The detective said you heard something last night."

Charley inhaled the air between them. "Yes, I think I did. I went to Nick's cabin because apparently, he's been assigned to babysit me, thanks to your aunt. I just figured…"

"You could've come to me." Charley detected disappointment in his voice. "I'm sorry you had to see that."

"It's not the first I've seen," Charley joked. "But I'm hoping it's my last."

Tucker frowned. "No one should have to see anything so awful." He stepped forward and pulled her to him. "I'm just so glad you're safe," he whispered into her hair.

Charley snuggled into his chest and breathed in his fresh laundry scent. Her mind slipped a vision of Nick to her. She needed to keep her distance from that man.

"I have an idea," Tucker started as he peered down at Charley. "Have dinner with me tonight."

"I'm not sure I'm up to it, Tucker." Charley wanted to cheer on the inside at the opportunity, but the heaviness of the woman's death smothered any excitement.

"Look… I know that was a lot to take in."

"Understatement. I just feel responsible."

Tucker cocked his head to the side. "How so?"

Charley felt the tears return and swatted them away as she tucked herself back into his embrace. "This is going to sound crazy. Nick didn't believe me when I tried to tell him."

"You can tell me. I won't think you're crazy. I promise," he soothed as his fingers combed through her hair. "That guy has got a lot of problems. It is probably for the best you keep your distance and steer clear of him. To be perfectly honest, I don't trust him."

There was no doubt that there was something strange and mysterious about Nick. He probably did have a slew of problems and Charley was sure him being a cop wasn't making them any easier. "I would probably think I was crazy too," she argued playfully.

"Nope. You're intelligent and creative. Did Nick make you feel like this is somehow your fault?"

"Not at all," she quickly replied. "I'm not sure staying here is a good idea anymore." Charley stepped back.

"And miss the barbecue? What about your parents?" Tucker tried to appeal to her senses.

"Is it even safe to be here? I mean, Tucker, there's a killer on the loose." A shiver nipped at her spine.

"Let Nick and the other cops do their job. They will catch whoever did this. I will not let this creep ruin our big Fourth of July celebration. But you?" Tucker searched her eyes as he said each word slowly, "You need to be working on that book. My aunt had you come here for a reason and she knows you are safe here with me." Tucker looped his fingers through hers and squeezed her hand gently with reassurance.

This would be so much easier if there had not been a body outside her cabin only moments ago. Charley wanted to believe him and go back to pretending everything was fine and dandy. Did it really matter if she stayed or left? Murder happened everywhere. It was an unfortunate reminder of the monsters who lived alongside them. There was no running away or hiding from it. Charley closed her eyes as she debated what to do next. She saw the ruby-red lips again and said a silent prayer for the woman.

* * * *

She purposely avoided the spot where only hours earlier a woman had lain on the shore, lifeless and ruined. Charley carved her way through a wooded trail that seemed undisturbed by humans and only used by animals. The pines gave off a deliciously sweet scent as she stepped carefully over broken branches and fallen limbs. She could feel the warmth of the sun even through the thickness of the forest but couldn't escape the chill that had settled into her bones. Seeing that woman discarded on the sand had bothered Charley more than she'd realized. It probably wasn't the wisest idea to be wandering about, but she needed to distance herself and try to wrap her head around things. The solitude would hopefully give her the answers her brain so desperately needed. Charley said a prayer as she set off on the trail and convinced herself she wasn't trying to sacrifice herself. *Just don't venture too deep into the woods or your mind.*

She had called Pamela after Tucker had left her cabin that morning. Pamela had been shocked and absolutely horrified. She also acknowledged that she had asked the local police to keep a protective eye on Charley. Pamela explained that the publisher had informed her they'd received some unusual hate mail and even a few threats. Pamela felt it was better to be safe than sorry but didn't want to burden Charley with the trouble. They both knew what was really at stake.

Charley wasn't completely sold on the idea of staying at Crescent Lake for the remainder of the manuscript, but Pamela had assured her that she was more than safe and to think of all the progress that had been made. Unsettled and guilt-ridden, Charley had contacted her mother, who'd immediately suggested she come home. Her father had gotten on the phone and offered to come get her. Charley promised she would be fine. They reminded her that they'd be leaving the next morning for the lake. Her father had assured her they'd be there bright and early and that she had better get her pole ready. It was comforting to know her family would be visiting and that the sad happenings of the morning would hopefully be replaced with fond memories. Guilt nipped at her once again. How could she possibly even think of staying there and pretending to enjoy what should be a happy celebration? Charley felt like a fraud in so many ways.

The trail dumped her out near the largest dock of the resort where several boats were anchored. They gently rocked on the surface of the inviting water. Charley could feel the heat of the scorching ground through her flip-flops as she continued to where several rows of white plastic loungers were. Most of the loungers were occupied with sun worshipers who were busy relaxing and working on their tans. It was as if nothing horrible had taken place that morning. Charley moved past the vacationers and caught a glimpse of Tucker. He was stretched out on a lounger, his chiseled abs and chest on full golden display. She could think of worst distractions.

"Any good?" she asked. A paperback was opened on his trim waist.

"Not sure. I fell asleep," he teased. "Join me," Tucker said as he patted the empty lounger next to him.

Charley lowered herself onto the hot, plastic seat. She winced as her body was burned but it adjusted quickly. She found herself beginning to relax for the first time that day and felt incredibly guilty. "What were you reading before you passed out from all the excitement?" In her opinion, there wasn't anything sexier than a hot man reading a book. Tucker handed her the worn paperback. She examined the dog-eared pages and cringed. There were two kinds of people — those who cherished the pages of a book and had the decency to use a bookmark and those were monsters who dog-eared their place. Charley fought the urge to smooth out the bent pages as she read the back blurb. It was a well-known author and held all the trappings of a good lazy afternoon read.

"I'm not much of a reader." He grinned as she handed him back the book.

"I've always loved books," Charley explained. "I read all the time as a kid and just fell in love with stories. The ability to go on as many adventures as you wanted right from the comfort of wherever you were seated? Fantastic. Books definitely hold a lot of appeal, especially if one wants to escape reality."

"Which explains why you write them," Tucker said as he lowered his sunglasses.

"I suppose you're right."

"So, where is it that Charlene Vanderberg is trying to run off to?"

Charley laughed. "I'm not really sure. My stories are a lot different than the ones I read as a kid."

"Just a grown-up version of *Alice in Wonderland*, right? Rabbit holes and wacky characters."

If only he'd read any of her books. He would soon learn that her characters were anything but wacky. Tucker sat up on the lounger and the muscles of his stomach rippled. His swim trunks hung low on his hips and seemed to tease Charley with the view of more tanned skin. *Lord, help me.*

"So, you reconsider having dinner with me yet?" He gave her a sexy grin that caused her to giggle like a schoolgirl.

Fully embarrassed and with her cheeks on fire, Charley replied, "I'm thinking about it. What did you have in mind?"

Tucker motioned toward the line of boats. "You like to fish, don't you?"

"I love it actually. I even brought my old pole from my childhood with me."

Tucker laughed. "Really? That's pretty cool."

"Hey, my dad was adamant that I bait my own hooks," Charley added flirtatiously. "I even gut and clean my catch."

"I don't believe you. I guess you'll have to show me," Tucker said with a teasing light amusement in his voice.

"I'd be happy to clean our catch. The cooking it part is not really my strong suit," Charley remarked.

"Well, I happen to be a damn good cook, thanks to my bachelor lifestyle."

"I'm not so sure I believe you. I guess you'll have to show me."

"I think that can be arranged. So, I guess this evening will be our first date." Tucker winked flirtatiously.

The butterflies took flight her stomach. Wouldn't it be nice if things worked out between Tucker and her? Charley could get used to this—to spend lazy days in the sun, reading books and napping by the lake—pretending people didn't get murdered here. She closed her eyes for a moment and the smeared lipstick kiss on pale skin flashed back at her. She nearly bolted up from the chair and feigned a calm exit, despite seeing ghosts she had created.

"See you later," she managed.

It didn't matter who was interested in her. Romance had a way of keeping its distance from Charley. The realization was the monsters were the ones who held her. They had tethered themselves to her and she wasn't sure she would ever be allowed to just love someone.

* * * *

Charley fumbled through the clothes she had brought along with her. Nothing jumped out at her as terribly cute or date-worthy. *That's because you're supposed to be writing or getting the hell outta this place, you idiot.* She hushed her brain and tried to put together an ensemble that was a perfect mix of sexy and casual. Charley didn't want to come off as desperate or too eager. She was out of practice when it came to the whole dating scene. Her last relationship had been eons ago, and even then, it hadn't been ultra-serious. Charley had accepted her fate. She was probably destined to roam this ugly planet alone. That didn't mean a girl didn't want to get laid once in a while. Maybe things would change one day, but for now she'd settle for a fun excursion and mental distraction with a cute guy.

She applied a light coat of gloss on her lips when her cell phone rang. "Hello?" Charley answered.

"Why didn't you call me?" Victoria's voice was riddled with anger.

"I'm sorry. I was going to call, but everything is okay now." Charley felt like a liar. She was still busy pretending that her brain wasn't still traumatized by the scene from earlier.

"Uh, no, it's not. A lady got murdered right outside your doorstep," Victoria countered. "You need to come home now." It wasn't as though Charley had forgotten, but she wanted to remove herself from thinking about it, to erase the image and guilt that was infecting her heart.

"Vic, don't think for second I didn't consider leaving immediately. Tucker says it wouldn't help matters if I did, and Pamela urged me to stay as well." Charley felt almost dizzy as her brain once again replayed the horrific images. "My parents are headed here tomorrow, if that makes you feel any better," she explained softly.

"What does Tucker know? Someone was killed at *his* resort. As far as I'm concerned, he should be held responsible," Victoria unleashed onto her. "What does Nick say? He's the one you should be listening to."

Nick. She hadn't seen him since that morning and would prefer to keep him out of her head. It was time to put that notion to rest. "Look... I'm not interested in Nick and have no desire to pursue anything with him."

"That's such a load of crap and you know it."

"Tucker says he's got a bunch of issues and I should stay away from him. I mean if we really look back at how my initial encounter was with him," Charley explained but as the words fell from her tongue, she instantly thought of the kisses they'd shared and how turned on she had been the night before. Charley had always considered herself an honest person, and today she had lied more times than she could count.

"Again, why are you listening to Tucker? Even Pamela is all wrong on this."

Charley exhaled sharply and didn't want to argue with Victoria. "Who called you?"

"Your mom, and it's only a matter of time before it's all over the news."

"I'm sorry she called and worried you."

"Stop right there. *You* should've called me right away," Victoria stated firmly. "I'm not only your assistant, Charley, but I'm also your best friend. It makes me sick knowing you're still there."

"It's awful, but this kind of stuff happens in Seattle all the time."

Victoria grew quiet. "This is a little too close for comfort, if you ask me."

"You have no idea," Charley muttered.

"What do you mean?" Victoria pressed. Charley shouldn't have said anything.

"Nothing. It's crazy and besides, your pal Nick didn't believe me anyway," Charley added as she slipped her feet into pretty sandals.

"What are you talking about?"

Charley debated for a half of a second if she should tell Victoria. Maybe it was all in her head.

"Spill it," Victoria pressed.

She started slowly as if summoning the nerve. "The woman today? There was lipstick on her forehead. Just little markers that were kind of creepy, to say the least."

It didn't take long for Victoria to catch on. "Oh shit. Like, in the book. Okay, and why are you still there? That was obviously meant for you to see. You do realize that, don't you?"

"I know. That's sort of what I thought too. It's kind of strange," she concurred, her nerves tightened at the thought of how much this involved her.

"Just a little." The irritation and worry were evident in Victoria's voice. "This could be the work of some delusional fan and you're not the least bit worried about staying there? I think you've been holed up in that stupid cabin for too long and have lost all rationality."

Charley heard a soft knock at her door. "Someone is here. I'll call you later. Vic, I'm really sorry about not calling you right away."

"I just worry. Please be safe and call me back."

"I will." Charley ended the call. She shoved the phone in the back pocket of her jeans. Charley hurried to the door and discovered Nick. He looked worn and utterly exhausted. The fine lines on his face seemed deeper, the bags under his eyes heavier. *Poor guy.*

"I wanted to check up on you," Nick said. "Are you doing okay?"

"I'm good, thanks. You don't need to worry about me, Nick," she replied coolly.

"I feel really terrible about this morning. I just felt like you needed to know."

"I appreciate that, seriously, I do." Charley tucked her hair behind her ear and it became tangled with a long silver earring.

"Were you headed out?" Nick asked with slight confusion as he reached to help her. She felt his fingers work the hair free of the jewelry. The tips of his fingers were warm as they skimmed the surface of her cheek.

She backed away awkwardly as she smoothed her sweaty palms down her jean-clad thighs nervously and tried to gather her thoughts. "Yeah, Tucker invited me to go fishing."

"Well, I better not keep you then." Nick looked wounded and dejected.

"Nick," she called to him as he stepped off the porch. He turned and the hopeful longing in his face almost did her in. Why was it that every time she was near this man the world seemed to stop moving? "Thanks for checking on me." Why did she also have this sudden urge to hug him? He waved and walked toward his cabin. Her eyes followed him until he disappeared inside.

She shook off any weird feelings their little interaction had caused and reminded herself she had a date with some fish and a very handsome man on a boat. Charley grabbed her pole and practically skipped down to the large dock.

"Permission to come aboard, Captain," she hollered to Tucker. Charley squinted through the bright sunset and saw Tucker untying large, heavy ropes.

"Granted," Tucker replied with a laugh as he helped her onto the small boat. "I see you brought the pole."

"You thought I was kidding?" She held it up proudly.

"Okay, maybe a little," Tucker admitted. "I haven't met a girl who actually liked fishing."

"Well, now you have," Charley flirted as Tucker steered them carefully away from the dock.

"There's a cooler over there with some drinks. Help yourself." Tucker pointed to the large red-and-white container. Charley snatched an ice-cold can of beer and offered one to Tucker, which he happily accepted.

Charley popped the tab on her can and tried to steady her wild nerves. She surveyed the view that surrounded them as they glided over the water. It was a completely different perspective. The tall pines looked like a wall protecting the resort from the rest of the world. This private lake with its curvy shore was quite stunning, a sheltered little piece of paradise. The cabins grew smaller as they sailed farther away, and they soon disappeared altogether. Charley didn't realize how large and eerie this lake truly was. It sent a slight tremor down her nearly naked spine. She suddenly wished she had worn a sweater with her bathing suit. Even though the sun was beating down upon them, her thoughts were chilly and it was starting to grow dark.

"Have you heard any more about the woman they discovered?" Charley asked as they cruised farther out into the lake. She rubbed her bare legs, hoping to warm them.

He eyed her with a curious expression. "Are you really cold? It's so hot out here." Tucker shrugged his shoulders in the pale blue polo shirt. "She was a guest here and had come alone. I think the police notified whatever family she has. I prefer not getting involved. It's best to leave it to the professionals, you know?"

"It's just awful to think about what happened. I can't seem to fully get it out of my mind."

"Well, you need to. It's not good to dwell on terrible things like that," Tucker countered with an odd, carefree tone.

"Kinda hard not to when you feel partially responsible," Charley argued. She felt a slight spray of water hit her as Tucker sped up.

"It wasn't your fault. It's not like you killed her...unless you're holding a dirty little secret out on me," he teased over the roar of the powerful engine. Tucker slowed when they were almost on the opposite side of the lake. "Here's a good spot." He killed the engine and dropped anchor.

Charley peered over the shiny silver rail, looked down into the dark depths of the water and tried to ignore his stupid comment. The sun didn't pierce through the seemingly endless blackness. Charley almost felt herself being drawn in. She nearly had to fight the urge to toss herself to fall overboard and sink to the bottom.

Get out of your head.

While Tucker set up his rod and dug through a simple tackle box, Charley tried desperately to turn her attention back to what mattered in the moment. She tore her eyes away from the water and watched him.

He was rather quiet while he worked. Maybe he regretted bringing her out there. Charley couldn't help but build up some ridiculous speculation. The slight breeze played with his hair and there was that delicious smile he kept tossing her way. It would be easy to fall for a guy like him. He waved at Charley to prepare her hook. She quickly showed him a trick or two and he was pretty darn impressed. This lighthearted distraction was what Charley had needed. She was able to dismiss his comment and odd behavior for the time being.

"So, tell me more about the mysterious Charlene Vanderberg—the girl who can not only bait her own hook but who is also drop-dead gorgeous," Tucker said as he plopped down next to her. He snapped the top off another beer and she watched his throat as he swallowed. Never had she felt so thirsty. The simple movement of muscles on his tanned skin sent her into lust-filled tizzy.

Charley struggled to find her words and fought with her hair as the wind suddenly picked up. "The hook part I get. The drop-dead gorgeous part? Not so much."

"I think you are," Tucker answered slowly, causing Charley to draw in a breath. He reached for that pesky strand of hair that had been whipping her cheek and tucked it behind her ear. She licked her lips and leaned in seductively to kiss him. She expected to feel his lips on her, but he retreated just out of reach. *Awkward.* Perhaps she had somehow misread his signals. She could have sworn that he was into her. Maybe he had wanted to make the first move. Some guys didn't like when girls were the aggressor. He pulled back farther and put the beer bottle to his lips. He gazed out into the distance. "How's the book coming along?"

She tried to mentally shake off her embarrassment. "Really good, actually. I haven't written this much in months," Charley admitted as she rose from her seat and went to her pole. She fiddled with the rod and tried to dismiss her disappointment in the miscalculated romantic moment. "By the way, my parents will be here tomorrow. They seem pretty excited, despite everything that has happened. I know they're eager to see this place and make sure I'm okay."

"And you told them that you're fine and busy writing the next bestseller, right?" Tucker smiled widely, his teeth bright and obnoxiously perfect. "This weekend is going to be great. You'll see." Tucker leaned back casually and stared in her direction. His sunglasses had slipped lower on the bridge of his nose as he continued to sip his beer. It was as though he didn't have a care in the world. She was almost envious.

"You don't seem too troubled by that woman's death," she commented as she cast out her line. She couldn't help herself from asking. It was rather odd that Tucker seemed so unfazed. Charley let out a happy sigh when she heard the distinct plop as it landed in the water.

"It's not that. I just don't really see the point in rehashing it. What's done is done, you know?"

His blasé attitude kind of rubbed her the wrong way. It seemed to Charley there should be more concern, some sadness, just something that honored that poor woman. Maybe Charley was a bit overly sensitive because she'd seen so many similar murders and found the injustice or disregard for human life utterly disgusting. That was why she wrote about it. It was in many ways her attempt at righting these wrongs. Suddenly, she wasn't exactly feeling this date — or Tucker, for that matter. She turned her full attention to trying to catch a fish and didn't realize that Tucker was now next to her.

"I'm not trying to upset you. I know today bothered you. But people live and die every day," he said softly.

"But they don't deserve to be tortured like she was. They should live to be old and die of natural causes, not at the hands of a monster," Charley spat.

"I agree. It just doesn't do us, the living, any good discussing it. We're here to catch fish, aren't we?" Tucker was close to Charley but kept enough space so they weren't touching. It was almost like a game, a tease of coming so close in contact with her. Maybe it was his plan, doing things his way.

The sun was sinking low in the sky as purple clouds emerged. A couple of stars had greeted them and Charley hadn't realized how long they'd actually been out on the water. Her thoughts were all over the place. It had been an emotionally draining day, and perhaps this outing hadn't been the best idea. She didn't want her mood to taint the possibility of anything special happening between her and Tucker. In the back of her mind, she feared she might be pushing for something that wasn't even there. Maybe Victoria was right.

It was dark and the lights from the boat cast an eerie glow on the water. He helped Charley off the boat after they docked. He suggested a nightcap back at the lodge but Charley feigned a yawn and asked for a raincheck. After stumbling over a few more apologies along the way back to her cabin, Charley said goodnight.

Once inside and all alone, she eyed her laptop and questioned if she should write. Charley knew she wasn't in the right head space to even try. She was overly emotional, and it would come out in whatever words she would type. There had to be the right mix of emotions to sculpt her words perfectly for her readers. She released an exaggerated sigh. Bed… That was where she needed to go, to put the day to rest. Charley washed her hands in the small sink and peered out of the window. Nick's cabin was in her view, and she could see a soft glow through his dusty windows. She hoped he got some sleep. He had looked awful earlier and she probably didn't look much better. This day had taken its toll on them. She was glad it was finally over.

Chapter Eleven

"There's my girl." Charley welcomed the strong feel of her dad's burly arms wrapped tightly around her. She might not be bright-eyed and bushy-tailed this early in the morning but it felt amazing having her parents there.

"You eat breakfast yet?" Her mother asked sweetly as she fluttered about the cabin. The woman couldn't help herself. She was already busy tidying up the small space. It just wasn't in her nature to stay still. Then there was also the fact that a murder had happened only several yards away. They were all pretending that things were hunky-dory.

Charley stifled a yawn. "The restaurant you drove by is about the only place to get a meal."

Her mother eyed her with concern. "Are you having trouble sleeping? You don't look well."

"I'm fine. I promise." Charley picked at the invisible lint on her shirt and avoided her mother's stare.

Her mother didn't appear convinced. "Is the diner any good?"

"They make some mean biscuits and gravy. The burgers are pretty tasty, and the waitress Molly is incredibly sweet."

"Good. I'm starved," her father added. "Your mother fed me one of those cardboard granola bars she raves about."

"You poor man," her mother cooed as she hugged him. "You're so malnourished."

Charley giggled as she watched her parents. She secretly hoped that one day she found someone she could be like that with. "Did you guys check in at the lodge yet?"

"No, we wanted to see you first." Her mother's pretty face scrunched with worry. "You doing okay, sweetheart? You know, we don't have to stay here. You can come home with us." Her gaze darted past Charley.

Her father shook his head. "Nonsense. We're here now and you saw that lake when we got here, right? How are those fish, Charley?"

"I haven't caught a single one."

"Well, see, honey? We got some fishing to do while we're here." He turned to her mother and gave her a small peck.

"When is that barbecue supposed to be?" her mother asked. "I went ahead and made the coleslaw. It's in your fridge. Do you think they need anything else? I think I saw a grocery store."

"I think tomorrow afternoon. Mom, I'm sure Tucker's got everything under control," Charley tried to reassure her mother.

"Does he?" Her mother looked doubtful. "I'm rather shocked that he is still hosting a barbecue. It seems a little ridiculous, if you ask me. I would think he'd consider shutting down the resort after that incident."

"This is the season when towns like this make any type of living, dear," her father added.

"Victoria mentioned you have a cop staying next door. That really made us feel a little better about things," her mother said as she finally seemed to be less agitated.

"Thanks for calling her, by the way."

"Sweetie, she was so terrified after I told her," her mother explained.

"Victoria freaks out easily, Mom. That's sort of why I wanted to wait until I was calm enough to discuss it with her."

"I'm sorry. Victoria is like family. I thought she should know." Her mother shrugged defensively.

"It's okay. Your heart was in the right place." Charley stood next to her father, who looked much too large for the cabin.

"Well, we're here now," her father chimed in. Charley smiled at him. He was right. "Your old man will protect you."

Today was a new day and she intended to make every attempt to enjoy this weekend with her parents. Her heart ached for the family of the woman who was killed, but she was in a better place now. At least that's what Charley liked to think. It's what she had been raised to believe, and there was a blanket of comfort in imagining that all the victims were hanging out with angels and smiling down upon them. She'd never really delved too deeply into the afterlife in her books because she wasn't sure she believed that they actually went anywhere. It was the sheer terror of death she understood. Charley knew what the families experienced. She'd interviewed enough mothers, fathers and siblings to understand the suffering they endured when they learned someone they loved had been killed. Charley had never experienced it on a personal level and selfishly hoped she never did.

They rode together in her SUV and her mother chatted on nervously about how lovely the area was. It was her mother's way of coping with the reality of the ugliness of what had happened in this quaint little town. It didn't matter how peaceful or beautiful it seemed, there had been a dead woman discarded like garbage yesterday and there was nothing pretty about that. Charley spared her mother the knowledge of the other two murders Nick had mentioned. Charley didn't know or want to know any of the details of those. She couldn't help but wonder if any of the others had telltale signs from her books.

Molly smiled at Charley the second they entered the diner. "These must be your parents. Wow, you look just like them. You have your father's eyes," Molly went on to describe as she led them to an empty booth, "and your mother's smile."

Charley's mother grinned happily and thanked Molly. Molly handed them a few laminated menus and left to bring back coffee.

"She seems quite nice," her mother commented politely to Charley as she studied the menu.

"Told you." Charley smiled as Molly quickly returned, masterfully balancing a tray of three mugs.

Molly rattled off a few breakfast specials and everyone decided on pancakes and eggs. Molly hurried to place their order with the cook and Charley added a few small plastic containers of creamer into her coffee. The color changed from a deep black to a milky beige.

"You're ruining it," her father teased as he motioned at his unaltered mug. He sat across from her and her mother.

"Wait until I add the sugar," Charley shot back playfully. She grabbed the glass container and made it snow into her mug.

"Gosh, it's so nice being here with you, sweetie," her mother added as she squeezed Charley in a side hug. "So, what's the game plan for this weekend?"

Charley stirred the small mug. "Well, there's the barbecue tomorrow and I'm sure there will be fireworks. I would think the resort will have games and that kind of stuff. But I'm thinking we can just relax, maybe get a little fishing in." Charley winked at her father, who sat across from her. "I would love to just hang out."

"I was hoping I could read some of what you wrote while the two of you try to catch the biggest fish in the lake," her mother nonchalantly suggested as she sipped her coffee.

"Yeah, that would be great, Mom. Pamela likes the direction and overall feel of the story. Victoria read a few Chapters when she came last weekend." Charley had relied on her mother's input in the past with other manuscripts or articles she'd written. She valued her honest feedback. Her mother might be supportive, but she didn't sugarcoat her opinion when it came to Charley's work. There was only one time her mother had steered her wrong, her last novel. Her mother had loved it. She had found it romantic and a sweet breath of fresh air from Charley's other work. But it had tanked and now here Charley was, trying to recapture the magic of her successful novels.

Molly brought their plates, which were towering with fluffy pancakes. The sweet scent spurred Charley's appetite. Being here with her parents and enjoying this breakfast with them reminded her of a simpler time. In the past when Charley didn't know of the horrors that lived in the real world, she just knew she was safe and protected. The timing couldn't have been better for their arrival. She needed this...this shroud of normalcy. It would hopefully reset the off-balance emotions Charley had wrestled with.

She heard the familiar jingle of the tiny bell on the front door and looked up to see Nick had entered the diner. There would be no hiding under the table or behind a menu this time. Molly grinned at Charley as she refilled their coffee. "Looks like your friend is here."

Nick stopped at their table on his way to the empty one behind them. He wore a devilish grin that made her tummy do somersaults. "Good morning, Charley," he greeted her sweetly. He immediately stuck out his hand to her father. "You must be Mr. Vanderberg."

Charley's father lit up. "Yes, I am," he answered proudly.

"I'm Detective Capra. Nick," he struggled with his introduction. "Mrs. Vanderberg, it's a pleasure to meet you."

Charley studied her mom's reaction. Did her mother really just blush? *Good grief!* Her mother elbowed her ribs. She knew exactly what her mother was trying to do and it wasn't happening. *Nope.* Then she poked Charley with a little more force. She glared at her mother from the side. There was no getting out of this one. *Damn.*

"Nick, would you care to join us?" Charley offered reluctantly.

"I wouldn't want to interrupt your breakfast. It's nice you're spending time with your family." Nick stood there awkwardly as if he wasn't sure what to do. He avoided Charley's eyes but there was a definite hint of a smile on his lips.

"Son, you can sit by me," her father quickly offered as he slid closer to the window, making room for Nick. "Charley won't mind if her friend joins us."

"Dad, he's not my..." she started when another sneaky nudge to her ribs happened. She rubbed her side and said, "It's fine, Nick."

He sat and Molly took his order. She returned with a mug for him and topped off their cups.

"Not adding any of that crap, are ya?"

"No, sir. Why fix something when it's not broke?" Nick chuckled along with her father but his eyes stayed on her.

"Maybe I like a little coffee with my creamer," Charley defended herself playfully and they all shook their heads and laughed. The weirdness melted away.

She had to admit that it was actually quite fun with all of them sitting there eating breakfast. There had been some great childhood stories shared and the conversation moved naturally between Nick and her parents. Nick and her father seemed to enjoy one another's company, much to her mother's obvious delight.

Charley happily survived breakfast and the countless refills of coffee. Her bladder had about all it could hold.

"I need to use the restroom," her mother whispered. Charley nodded in agreement and scooted out of the booth.

The bathroom was small, just two stalls and an ancient-looking Formica vanity. Charley locked herself inside a stall and sighed at the relief as she emptied her bladder.

"So, that's Nick," her mother commented loudly from the other stall.

"Yep."

"You two have something going on?"

Charley rolled her eyes. "Nope."

"There should be," her mother stated before the loud sound of the toilet flushing drowned out whatever else her mother was saying. Charley was tempted to stay in the stall, with its awful piss-yellow metal door and dated brown-tile floor. Anywhere was safer than being out there with her matchmaking mother.

"I think he's rather handsome in a scruffy sort of way," her mother continued as the water from the sink ran.

"Wait until you meet Tucker, Mom." Charley met her mother at the sink and waited for the water to turn hot.

"Is there something going on with that guy?"

"I don't know. I'm supposed to be working on this book." Charley dried her hands on a rough brown paper towel that wasn't much better than a grocery sack.

"Victoria likes Nick too," her mother supplied sweetly.

"Then maybe she should date him," Charley offered with a mocked innocence.

"Why must you be so stubborn when it comes to this sort of thing?"

Charley released a heavy sigh. "I'm not trying to be. My life is back in Seattle and my focus needs to be finishing this manuscript. Maybe when it's done, I can start thinking of dating again, okay?"

Her mother shook her head. It was obvious she was annoyed with her. "We better get back before they send out a search party."

Charley followed her mother back to the table. It was cleared of the dirty dishes and her father and Nick were standing.

"I need to get to the station. It was great having breakfast with you both," Nick spoke gently to her mother who gave him a motherly hug. Nick shook her father's hand again. "Let me walk you folks out to your car."

Molly waved at Charley as they exited the diner. Nick's hand was on the small of her back as he protectively steered her toward the SUV. He said goodbye again and hopped into his truck that was parked a few spots in front of them.

"Now, honey, that's a nice man for ya," her father announced once they started the SUV and pulled away.

"That's what I tried telling her, dear," her mother chimed in.

"I'm glad you guys like him," Charley replied as she drove back toward the lake. "We should probably get your cabin and you can meet Tucker."

"Tucker is the owner of the resort, dear. I think she likes him," her mother supplied.

"Mom, I'm like, right here."

"What's he like?" Her father gave her a curious glance.

"He's nice. Now, would you two quit trying to marry me off?" Charley demanded playfully.

Her father patted her arm. "Honey, we're not trying to do that. Just be thankful arranged marriages aren't something we practice." Charley couldn't help but laugh.

As they pulled up to the lodge, Charley spotted Tucker on a ladder securing a festive and very patriotic banner to the building. There were streamers and white star-shaped lights hung above several picnic tables. Red-and-white gingham tablecloths were draped over the tables. If this wasn't a picturesque scene of Americana, Charley didn't know what was.

"Well, this couldn't be lovelier," her mother commented as they made their way closer.

"Check out the size of that barbecue," her father pointed out.

"Let me have you guys meet Tucker," Charley said as she saw him step off the ladder and walk toward them.

"You must be the Vandenbergs." Tucker shook her parents' hands then began to give them the tour.

He didn't miss a beat as he shared with them all the festivities he had planned—food, games and fireworks each night of the long weekend. But to cap it off, there was going to be a fishing tournament. Charley warmed at the smile that never left her father's face. She was suddenly glad that she hadn't fled yesterday. Nothing terrible would happen now that her parents were there.

Tucker finally led them inside the lodge. She could feel her mother's discomfort as the creepy stuffed critters looked at them.

"This is some place you've got here," her father commented as his eyes traveled the room.

"You hunt?" Tucker asked as he situated himself behind the counter and started to type on the small laptop.

"No. Just fish."

Tucker nodded as he checked in her parents. "I did the best I could, but you're not going to be right next door to Charley. Just a few cabins down. But you have the shortest path to the dock to fish."

Charley glanced at her mother, who frowned, and she squeezed her hand. "I'm just grateful there was a vacancy."

"This is our busiest season, and a lot of the cabins are usually reserved almost a year in advance," Tucker explained as he handed her father the keys. "We'll see you at the barbecue tomorrow."

"Mom brought her famous coleslaw," Charley added as she ushered her parents out. She waved goodbye to Tucker. "Well, let's get you guys all settled and kick this weekend off," she said cheerfully.

"Do you think Nick likes to fish?" her father asked as they passed her cabin on the way towards theirs.

"I'm not sure, Dad. But you're going to be too busy fishing with me," Charley joked.

Her father grabbed her hand and winked. "The more the merrier, pumpkin."

* * * *

After a brief nap, Charley felt refreshed as she headed over to her parents' cabin. She knocked twice and was greeted by her father. He wore a smile on his face, but it was stiff. She could tell they must have been having one their grown-up chats before she had arrived. She could sense the tension in the small space and tried to grin her way through it.

"I brought stuff to make sandwiches," her mother announced from the small kitchen. She began opening a loaf of bread. "You hungry, sweetie?"

"Sure, Mom," Charley answered as her father ushered her back outside to the small porch. "So, what do you think of this place?"

Her father nodded. "I think we're about to get in some good fishing."

"I sure hope so. I swear I've had the worst luck since I got here."

He turned to her; the worry was obvious in his eyes. "You sure have. You doing okay with everything that happened?"

"Dad, you don't have to worry about me. You know the kind of stuff I've seen." He seemed quieter than he was earlier. "You also know what I write about. But it does go without saying that what happened here was a little too close for comfort."

"I'm allowed to be concerned, just so you know," he reminded her. "What if that had been you?"

"I know, Dad." The heaviness of his words bothered her. "But it wasn't. We're here together and I plan to enjoy every second of it with you guys."

After her mother served them simple turkey sandwiches, Charley desperately wanted to cheer up her father, whose mood hadn't improved much since she'd arrived at their cabin. Maybe the reality of the situation had finally settled in. She wouldn't be surprised if her parents made her pack her bags and go home with them.

"You ready to see what those fish are up to?" Charley wiped her mouth and dusted herself free of any crumbs.

"I'll get my pole," he answered happily. Maybe while they were on the dock, she could convince him that she was really okay.

The air was lovely, not too hot but warm enough. Charley savored the delightful feel of it on her skin.

"I think this is my favorite part of the day here," Charley stated as she cast her line out again. "Or maybe that's just because you're here." Her father extended his arm and launched his line out farther. Charley gazed in awe. "Gosh, I don't know how you get it out that far."

"I remember when you were a little thing. You would always ask me to cast out your line. You remember that?" He expertly maneuvered the rod and reel, almost showing off on purpose.

"That was because the best fish are way out there. Maybe I need you cast mine for me." Charley stared up at him and she reeled her line back in and prepared to send it out. He'd always been one of her heroes. He was incredibly mild-mannered and always joking. He found pleasure in the simplest of things and didn't borrow trouble. Charley sometimes wished she were more like him. Being here with him reminded her just how much she missed him. His very presence was calming. It also broke her heart knowing how very worried he was about her. He had always encouraged to do things on her own, to be independent and brave.

"Looks like we got one," he announced happily as he began to reel it in.

"Dang, you're good. See? All the best fish are way out there," she playfully pouted.

"It's all in the wrist, sweetie," he explained as he cast the line out again with ease.

Charley practiced casting her line out but was certain she'd never be as good as her father. She wished they had more opportunities such as this. A quiet setting with conversation that flowed easily. A girl could learn a lot from her father. He kept things simple, all the while making her feel as though this memory would live on as one of her most important.

Hours went by without much notice. They were low on bait and had finished their last beer.

"Your mother is going to send out a search party soon if we don't head back," her father said as he reeled his line back in.

"You're probably right." Charley began to gather her fishing gear.

"I bet dinner is about ready and she's got everything ready for game night," he added cheerfully.

Charley had almost forgot about their plans for the evening. One of her favorite family traditions was game night. They often played card games and spent the time reminiscing. She loved hearing stories from her childhood and learning more about her parents.

The walk back to the cabin was a quick one. She hugged her father and promised to return to their cabin shortly. Charley jogged back to her own and got ready for the fun night ahead.

After a quick shower and change of clothes, she headed over to her parents' cabin.

"I'm here," she announced. "Let the games begin!" And so they did.

Someone produced the deck of cards and they'd gone through several hands, mock accusations, finger pointing and hooting over supposed cheating keeping spirits high.

"I win again," Charley cheered playfully. Her cheeks actually hurt from smiling and laughing.

"I think your father let you win, dear," her mother teased, and she laid her cards down in defeat. "Me? I'm just terrible at this darn game."

It didn't matter if he did or not. This was some of the most fun Charley had in ages. Playing cards and sipping wine with her parents in the small cabin, nothing quite beat this moment.

"You guys want anything?" Her mother got up from the table in search of snacks. "I brought popcorn."

"Oh, that sounds good." Charley shuffled the worn deck of cards. She felt relaxed and truly happy. Her legs were tucked under her and her hands worked the cards. The sound of the cards running together and the simple movement was a great way to numb one's mind. Her father announced that was going to take a practice nap. Charley wasn't quite sure how late it was but she wasn't quite ready to call it a night just yet. She peeked out of the window and it wasn't completely dark yet. That didn't mean much in the Pacific Northwest. Summer nights stayed light late and it could easily be after ten.

"Mom, you want any help?" Charley offered as she dealt out the cards. A knock at the door caused her to lose count.

"You can get the door for me," her mother answered over the sound of corn popping. The aroma filled the cabin and brought back many happy memories of past game nights with her family.

Charley reluctantly moved off the floor and made her way to the cabin door. She paused before opening it. In all honesty, Charley didn't want to have an intruder ruin her impromptu game-night with her parents. She selfishly wanted them all to herself. Another soft knock echoed inside.

"Aren't you going to see who it is? On second thought, maybe your father should answer it," her mother said swiftly.

Charley moved aside as her father slowly made his way to the door. *My true protector.*

"Hey, Nick," her father greeted after he opened the heavy door.

"Sorry to bother you folks. I noticed Charley's cabin seemed very quiet and I just wanted to make sure she was with you," he explained, his eyes trained on her. *My hired protector.*

"Oh, is that Nick? Invite him in, sweetie," her mother instructed as she carried a large plastic bowl filled to the brim with popcorn.

"Come on in, son. We're just playing cards." Her father led the way back to the small living room area.

Ruger nudged his way past Nick's legs and entered the cabin. "I really don't want to intrude, but obviously Ruger has no manners," Nick said politely. "I just wanted to make sure Charley was okay."

"We really appreciate that more than you truly know, Nick," her mother said sweetly. "My goodness, how cute is this little guy?" She bent down and greeted Ruger, who was eating up the attention. He snorted and his breathing grew louder as he wiggled his short body.

"Well, as you can tell, I'm right as rain. Just hanging out with my parents," Charley added but felt ignored.

"Join us, Nick, I just made popcorn."

"It smells wonderful." Nick stood awkwardly and waited for Charley's approval.

"Mom, I'm sure Nick has stuff to do." She turned to Nick. "Thanks for checking up on me. As you can see, I'm safe and sound."

"Charley," her mother hissed, "we'll deal Nick in. Let's move this game to the kitchen table."

They all took a seat around the weathered table and Nick accepted the offer of popcorn her mother continued to bombard him with. It didn't take long at all before Charley was in hysterics and her sides hurt from all the storytelling and joking. She wasn't sure why she had hesitated having Nick join them. Much like when they had been at the diner, they were genuinely having a nice time. Maybe she'd just wanted her time with her parents—to be secure in her nest, being the precious baby bird with her parents' protection. She knew it seemed silly. Nick wasn't trying to impose on her good time, and he had only meant to ease his mind with where she was. She could see that he genuinely wanted to make sure she was okay.

"I need a refill. Do you need anything, Nick?" Charley offered casually after he beat her fair and square at the last hand.

"Sure, let me help," he replied.

"Sweetie, I'll have some more," her mother said as she handed Charley her empty cup.

Charley caught her mother giving her father a gentle nudge. She rolled her eyes and shook her head at her parents.

"I'll take a beer," her father asked sweetly, as he spoiled Ruger with attention. "This little fella is just so darn cute. See if we have any lunch meat to give him, will you?"

Alone in the tiny kitchen, Charley fussed with the cork on a bottle of wine.

"Here… Let me help." Nick maneuvered the corkscrew into the cork and gently eased it out of the bottle. He poured the pretty pink liquid into the two plastic cups. "I'll grab a beer for your dad and me."

"Thanks." Charley took a sip and couldn't take her eyes off Nick. He seemed the most relaxed he had been since she had met him. "You having fun?"

"A lot, thanks." He snapped the cap off his bottle. "I really didn't mean to ruin your night with your parents."

Charley waved at him. "Nah, it's fine. I kept winning anyway. I needed a little competition."

He hadn't felt this relaxed and what was the word he was looking for? *Happy*. There wasn't anything spectacular about hanging out in this cabin, playing cards and drinking with Charley and her parents, but it was exactly what he'd needed. The simple moments provided a sense of normalcy. Nick's mind couldn't help but venture off into a direction he knew it shouldn't.

The *what ifs*. What if he and Charley could be something? A couple who spent nights like this with her parents and family? He seemed to fit in with them so effortlessly. Nick listened to her parents share stories of her childhood and he couldn't help but grow more intrigued with who she truly was. She put up this tough-cookie façade, but he was able to see her for the sweet, loving and playful person she worked so hard at hiding from him. Her laugh was infectious, and he found himself mesmerized by her beautiful eyes — the way they sparkled and the blue tones danced with surprised when her parents told an embarrassing story about her and her siblings.

In this kitchen, with her parents only a few feet away, he wanted nothing more than to pull her to him and kiss her — to get lost in all that was good and happy, to claim her as his.

Charley watched him as opened the wine, a smiled stayed planted on her pretty mouth. How could a woman be this sexy without even trying? The slight blush in her cheeks, was it from too much wine or her wanting to kiss him too?

"Hey, you guys coming back sometime tonight?" her father called out, interrupting the moment when Nick planned to steal a kiss.

Nick shook loose all the fantasies that played in his mind. "We better get these drinks back to them. Plus, I gotta beat you at least one more time before we call it a night."

Charley giggled and playfully punched him in the arm. "Oh, buddy, we'll see about that."

* * * *

The scene was straight out of a book, and Charley couldn't have written it any better. The happy laughter coming from the campers and their children with popsicle-stained clothing and faces. Music spilled from an unknown location and set the cheerful mood. The star-shaped lights were beginning to twinkle in the dusk. The inviting aroma of charcoal still hung in the air, even though it had been an hour or longer since the last patty had been grilled. There were countless plastic containers containing a variety of salads, all nearly empty now. Her mother's coleslaw had been one of the first to be cleaned out. The sun had started to dip into the lake and soon it would be time for explosive beauty followed by *oohs* and *ahhs*. All in all, the celebration had been nice, but Charley was exhausted.

After playing cards late into the previous night and having such a great time with Nick and her parents, she'd decided to write. She had been inspired, her mind finally at ease, and the words literally poured from her. She'd written two Chapters and knew they were pure gold. The bad news was that she had been expected to be up early to fish with her father. The quality time with her dad was precious and Charley wanted to soak up every minute that she could. They had even managed to catch a few fish before it was time to get ready for the barbecue. Charley had tried to nap before the late lunch but found herself just lying on her bed and staring up at her ceiling. Now she was paying the price for not having rested.

Charley sat at one of the picnic tables and observed the occasion in full swing. Her belly was comfortably full, which caused her to become even more sleepy. She covered a yawn that she'd been working hard to resist as she watched as her parents mingle with other guests, one in particular. They seemed especially fond of *Nick.* He was kind and respectful but was able to joke and be genuine with her parents. Nick was attentive to both of them but didn't make it obvious. It was all very organic. She watched as Nick tossed a horseshoe at the metal pole sticking up from the ground. Her mother clapped with appreciation and her father patted his shoulder.

They got along so well that a twinge of jealousy bit at Charley. It made Charley happy that her parents were enjoying themselves. They looked in love, holding hands and hugging when they thought no one was looking. But here she was grumpy and tired, feeling like a party pooper when her father had asked her to join them. She waved at them and politely declined. Charley was focused on the slice of apple pie in front of her. The perfectly baked crust, with its cinnamon and sugar, glittered in the evening sun. She moved a fat slice of apple around the paper plate, completely lost in her thoughts.

"Having fun?" Charley looked up to see Nick standing over her. He was dressed casually in jeans and a black cotton tee that stretched across his chest—one that she could see was well-defined. *Does the man own anything that isn't black?* Charley had to admit he did pull off the whole dark and mysterious thing pretty damn well. She nodded as he handed her a bottled beer. "Thought you could use this."

"Thanks." She accepted it and smiled at the thoughtfulness. Nick sat down next to her as she put the cold glass against her forehead. It felt fantastic.

"Nice little party," he commented.

"It is."

"So, why do you look like you'd rather be anywhere else but here?"

Charley laughed. "It's not that. I'm just tired."

"You doing okay?" The caramel color of his eyes intensified, and flecks of espresso black glowed with concern.

Charley shifted uncomfortably as she found herself becoming hypnotized. "I think so. How about you? Any leads on the case?"

Nick shook his head and gradually took the bottle to his lips. "None."

"It's crazy, isn't it?" Charley took in the sight of everyone. The jovial atmosphere proved that life did not look back. It simply moved on—perpetual and unforgiving, giving no time to grieve or pause to assess the new absence.

"What is?" Nick asked.

"No one here acts like anything happened. I guess burgers and pie bring on a false sense of security." It bothered Charley. No matter how much she tried to ignore the disturbing feelings, she hadn't been able to fully push them away. After writing as much as she had the night before, Charley was back to mentally wading in the dark again. "I can't stop seeing her."

Nick wrapped his arm around her, and the moment she felt the weight of him her body tensed then relaxed. Charley sensed someone was watching them and half-expected her parents to be staring, but it was Tucker. He stood with a few men, laughing while his eyes stayed on her. She didn't quite know how she felt about him anymore since their fishing date. She toyed with the idea that it was just *her* being weird. He had been polite this afternoon but hadn't tried to talk to her much. He kept his distance, and she took that to mean that he wasn't interested in her. But the intense way he was looking at her made Charley uncomfortable.

"I'm really sorry you had to see her. I never meant for you to follow me back to the shore," Nick apologized, bringing Charley back from her thoughts.

"I had to see. Like, hearing wasn't enough, you know? I needed proof or something." Charley found herself leaning into him. There was a gentle warmth that moved between them and it made her sleepy and content. Charley rested her head on his shoulder.

"Your parents are really great people," he added softly.

"Yeah, I kinda like them." Charley yawned again. "What about your family?" Charley realized she knew next to nothing about Nick. They had spent the last day with her parents and sharing her past. She was surprised her mother hadn't interrogated Nick.

"My mom lives in Spokane and my dad passed away a few years ago." His words were matter-of-fact, with no hint of anything more.

"I'm sorry," Charley offered.

"Don't be." Nick didn't explain any further and Charley itched with curiosity but decided not to press him for more information. Not everyone was an open book.

Tucker announced that fireworks were about to start soon and for everyone to gather near the lake. Nick grabbed her hand and led her toward her parents. She saw a glimmer of surprise in her father's eyes as they approached. Her mother wore an appreciative smile as she looped her arm through her husband's.

"Nice of you two to join us," her mother said.

Nick frowned. "Actually, I need to go, but I wanted to make sure she was in safe hands," Nick answered as he handed her off to her parents.

Where does he have to suddenly go? Charley felt oddly disappointed.

"Goodnight," he whispered near her cheek, his lips grazed her skin softly.

Nick walked away with a definite purpose in each step. Charley watched him until he disappeared.

"You two seem to be getting along," her father commented. Charley was about to answer when a large glittery red explosion filled the sky. The loud boom and crackle of another series of light reflected over the water. Her parents smiled each time the fireworks spread their colorful rays. Smoke hovered over the lake and the strong scent of gunpower made her nose itch. Charley couldn't shake the sadness she felt consuming her and let them know she was headed to bed. Charley faked an exaggerated yawn as they hugged her goodnight. They quickly turned their attention back to the magnificent display.

Charley hurried to the cabin, her feet quick on the dirt path as growing shadows and darkness crept into the camp. Fear tickled her spine, causing her to turn her steps into a jog. It was still too fresh and too close for comfort. Victoria was right. It wasn't normal to think it was okay to be here. It was wonderful seeing her parents have a great time, but Charley felt as though she wore a mask, constantly smiling to reassure her family that she was fine when she was anything but. Charley had never felt quite like this. It was a strange mix of feelings. The images of that woman were now permanently burned into her brain. Any notion of tranquility or relaxation was sadly replaced with itching anxiety and uneasiness. It wasn't as if she'd never seen death close-up. Truth be told, she was spooked to her core.

She stared up at the cedar ceiling, and the pale glow of the moon spilled into the room through the tiny window. Charley could see the character in the wood, the natural burned circles and varied shades of striped red and honey tones. She tossed and turned for hours. The energy spent kicking the covers off and flipping her pillow over a million times could have been put to better use. *Like writing.* Charley let out an annoyed huff and threw back the covers for what was probably the hundredth time. The humidity of the cabin made her skin damp and sticky. She would have normally kept the windows open but thought better of it. The idea of being plucked from her bed and dragged out into the forest to meet her demise hadn't strayed far from her mind. Having a writer's brain wasn't always a good thing.

Admitting defeat, Charley padded barefoot to her makeshift workspace and plopped down. She stared at the opened laptop and clicked the mouse. The screen came to life and illuminated the dark space in a technological blue hue. She opened her manuscript and read over the text. The sentences strung together to create perfectly orchestrated paragraphs. There was a rhythm to the way her words moved to tell the story. As her eyes feasted on her own writing a chill buried itself inside her chest. This book was different than all the others before it and Charley wasn't certain if that was a good thing or not.

She perched on the edge of her seat and contemplated which words to add next. The sound of cracking her knuckles echoed inside the cabin as the gears in her mind turned. Charley hovered her fingers above the keys, and she waited for the words to spill from them when a knock at the door almost caused her to fall from her seat. She moved slowly to answer it and almost chose to ignore the next knock. The fear that had already taken residence inside her peaked as she placed her hand on the wooden door. She swallowed a deep breath and cracked the door open slowly. Nick, looking devilishly handsome in a disheveled kind of way, stood there. His messy hair and shadow of a beard caused her to lick her lips. The slightly wrinkled shirt he had most definitely been sleeping in stirred something inside Charley. Fear had a funny way of masking other feelings.

"Nick," she managed.

His eyes shone in the dim light as Nick spoke softly. "We saw you were up." Ruger rushed past her and made his way onto her couch like he owned the place.

"Just make yourself comfy, Ruger." Charley let out a nervous laugh. "Keeping tabs on me, are we?" Charley moved to the side and invited him in. "Writers don't exactly keep banker's hours," she explained as she shut the door behind them.

"Neither do detectives." His slanted smile filled her belly with a flirty warmth.

"So, what's up?" Charley stood straight and attempted to act casual.

Nick paced the small area and she could feel the anxiousness waft from him like a dense fog. She grew concerned and dizzy as she tried to keep her eyes trained on him.

"It's this case, just everything surrounding it," he answered. As his words spilled openly, her heart dropped. Had she been hoping he was going to say something else? Of course, this was all because of the murders. Hadn't that been the very same reason why she was up at this hour?

"I have just the solution," she replied more perkily than she intended. Charley walked over to one of the small cupboards mounted onto the wall near the sink. She retrieved a glass bottle and smiled. "Rum. It pretty much solves everything—or at least helps us forget for a while."

Nick smirked as she grabbed two plastic cups. "Alcohol is definitely a solution."

"Exactly," Charley replied as she poured the amber colored liquid into the red and white plastic cups. "I can't tell you how many of my author buddies refer to whiskey as writer's tears. I prefer rum. All the best writers are pretty much shameless drunks," she added. Charley handed Nick one of the cups and clinked carefully against the plastic. "Cheers."

They both took a sip and stood there awkwardly. Charley could feel the liquid coat her throat in a pleasant burn.

Nick silently wandered over to the couch that was only a few feet from them. He plopped down next to Ruger, who seemed less than pleased. Nick released a long, heavy sigh. Charley joined him and matched his sigh in perfect harmony.

"We're quite the pair, aren't we?" Nick asked as he held the cup to his lips.

Charley nodded and swallowed down a large gulp of the rich liquor.

"So, you were writing, huh?" He motioned to the open laptop.

"Yeah, trying to, anyway."

"Writer's block?" Nick shifted on the couch.

"It started it out that way. That's actually the whole reason why I'm here. My agent sent me," she explained and paused to take another sip. Her cheeks felt like they were on fire. "I found my words again after having not written for months. Then all this crazy shit happened."

Nick nodded but his mind seemed occupied.

Charley continued, "It's not like I'm not used to murder and menace, you know."

Nick turned his attention to her. "How so?"

Charley swallowed another sip of the rum and felt it burn. "I used to be a reporter back in Seattle. I covered the homicide beat for years."

Nick's dark brows raised in surprise. "Really? I never would have guessed."

"I know I look more like I write advice columns or cheesy romances, right?"

"Maybe a little," he teased. "So, what kind of books do you write?"

"Redrum," she impersonated the little boy from *The Shining*. Nick gave her a confused look. "Murder," Charley said confidently.

Nick coughed and rum sprayed slightly from his mouth. "What?"

Charley laughed. "Don't worry. That's everyone's reaction."

"So, why exactly did your agent send you here of all places? This is definitely like a scene from a Stephen King novel," Nick observed as he recovered from his visible shock and seemed captured by her. His body was now turned attentively toward her as he listened.

"See? That's exactly what I said," she exclaimed. "She wanted me to have zero distractions and figured this place was as good as any to hide out."

"Well, that didn't go exactly as planned. How did you get into writing those kinds of stories?" Nick moved closer, he seemed to be trying to figure her out and she almost laughed out loud.

"Oh, where do I begin? I have written some pretty gruesome books, all thanks to seeing the stuff I did when I was a reporter. Well, those books did very well, and some were even made into movies," she explained and eyed Nick's reaction.

"Whoa. So, you're definitely a big deal then?"

Charley shrugged casually. "I don't know. I guess maybe a little." She grew nervous and used her plastic cup as a mask. When she felt brave enough, she continued, "Well, my last book didn't do so great. I guess I developed writer's block. I've never had an issue before, but it was as though all my words were gone."

Nick frowned. "And that's how you ended up here."

Charley nodded. "You got it." Charley relaxed as she explained, "This place is like a lost episode of *The Andy Griffith Show* or something—all Mayberry and perfect." She felt her words slur slightly as the rum made its way to her head.

"That's why we came here. I thought it would be all nice and boring." Nick petted the pug's head.

"But now we're both seeing it's more like *Twin Peaks* or something." Charley wanted to find out more about the man who sat next to her on this ugly couch. She tucked her leg under her and moved into a more comfortable position. She welcomed the drink's calming effect as she studied his features in the dim light. Charley imagined how she would describe him if he were one of her characters. She couldn't have created Nick any better. The man was the perfect rendition of any sleep-deprived-detective-running-from-his-demons character she could possibly come up with.

"So, how did you end up with this ugly dog?"

Nick laughed as he covered Ruger's ears. "Don't let him hear you say that. You'll give him a complex. Haven't you heard of something being so ugly that it's cute?"

"My apologies. But seriously, you gotta admit that you guys don't exactly seem like the stereotypical pair."

"True. Actually, he was given to me by my partner. It started off as a joke really. A Ruger 9mm is my gun of choice. Well, my partner told me he got me a Ruger and said how great it was and that I was going to love it. He built it up big time. Well, this was the Ruger he had for me. He was right, though. I do love it." Nick smiled lovingly at the pug.

Charley giggled. "That's funny and a rather cute story. I guess you guys do look alike in the sense you always were black, and his fur is black," she pointed out.

"I wear black shirts because of this little monster. Pugs can shed like crazy."

"I suppose he's pretty cute." Charley reached over and stroked Ruger gently.

Nick grew quiet and his aura darkened. Charley could almost see her reflection in his eyes and felt as though a magnet was tugging her to him. She wasn't sure if she wanted to kiss him or brush away that stubborn strand of hair that kept falling near his eyes. Charley attempted to distract herself by taking another sip. Her eyes kept finding their way to Nick's as he stared off again, lost in his own thoughts. She could practically see the worry and inflection working in his mind. *What is he thinking?*

He turned toward her and in one fluid sudden move revealed exactly what had been going on in his mind. Nick's warm lips were on hers and she could taste the sweetness of the rum as he deepened the kiss. Her brain grew alive with sensations she had almost forgotten existed. In the back of her mind, that reasonable dark corner, she knew this was wrong, but it felt so incredibly right. She wrapped her arms around his neck and pulled him with her as she fell back on the couch.

Charley wanted to forget everything — the past few months when she had been crippled with no words, the last couple weeks of being lost in her own fictional world and the past few days where she'd witnessed more of the ugly truths of humanity. Charley absorbed every bit that Nick offered. The weight of him, that closeness they shared brought back memories of making out with boyfriends on her parents' couch. It was funny how this replayed back to her like yellowed photographs she had stored in a shoe box, reminders of fumbling hands and lips from the past, boys who turned into skilled men. That naughty thrill of not wanting to get caught by her parents coursed through her. Charley arched her body as Nick explored with his hands over her clothes. She expected them to be rough as he kneaded her breasts through her thin tank, but instead they were gentle as he toyed with her nipples. He traveled his fingers down the length of her ribs.

The kisses grew more desperate and hungrier, adding more fuel to the growing fire of want and need. Charley erased any pestering thoughts of reason and escaped into that familiar sense of floating with Nick. She had experienced this with him before back on the dock and couldn't quite explain how odd it had been. But now more than ever, Charley realized it was everything she needed. Time had a strange way of holding still, as if allowing the two of them a moment to just breathe. Charley pulled Nick's head closer and nipped at his neck, the throbbing ache between her legs begged for mercy. The scent of his aftershave suddenly became her favorite smell in all the world. She wanted to devour this man—a stranger, a neighbor, her protector. Her Nick.

Then, without any warning, Nick froze. He tucked his head into the crook of her neck, and she could feel the warmth of his breath as he released a heavy sigh. Nick moved off her and immediately she missed him.

"Time flies when you're having rum," he awkwardly joked and rose from the couch. His voice was gravelly, and he darted his gaze toward the door. She didn't have time to stop him as he made a mad dash out of the cabin, and just like that, he was gone.

What happened? Did I dream the whole encounter? The tingling throughout her body begged to differ.

He was grateful that Ruger, his trusty wingman, had followed him back to the cabin. The thought of having to go back to fetch his dog was terrifying. The flurry of feelings that moved inside him proved to be too much for him to handle. It had felt so right at first — the perfect way Charley fit beneath him, the sweet taste of rum as he drank her in. The compulsion to take her right there on the couch had been intense. Then reason shone brightly in his numb brain and woke him up as to how very wrong it would be.

Nick had waded through more sick emotions in the last several months than he had ever dealt with in all his life. As complicated as things with Charley might seem, he knew one thing. She was sweet and innocent in all of this. Those were the ones who often were victims. Nick slammed his cabin door as his brain pelted him with the blinding reminders of all the hurt. He could almost feel a physical ache, but he wasn't certain if it was from leaving what could be a warm comfort or the loneliness that was his existence. Nick didn't want another person to get hurt because of him. He couldn't bear the thought of something happening to Charley. The idea of having to tell her family that he'd failed her, failed them. Things would be better off if Ruger and Nick just stuck together. No one else needed to die because of him.

Chapter Twelve

The early morning fog is creeping in slowly, making its way closer to me like a specter dancing on glass — cold and misty, a faint body but nothing tangible to grip and hold. Haunted moss-covered trees shelter me as I stare out into the direction where I know a lake sits, still and calm.

In a sweet, twisted version of *she loves me, she loves me not*, I absentmindedly pluck the eyelashes from the blank eyes staring up at me. I am filled with a quiet storm that is brewing deep inside my chest. It has been tearing away at my nerves and battering any peace I may have believed I possessed. It is her fault. All of this was her fault. She is far too demanding. I shift because of the uncomfortable weight across my legs. I feel a cramp begin to torture my calves and needle its way into my feet. I look down at her, strewn across my bottom half in a poetry-spun lover's pose, an empty expression and lifeless like all the rest. With my thumb and finger, I pull another set of thickly mascara-coated lashes from the rim of hazel eyes. I feel the oily black composition of bullshit beauty between my fingers. I wipe my fingers against her cheek and the black smudges her perfect cool skin.

Her brown hair is matted, and I can see bits of bone and brain. I manage to pick out a dull white piece of skull, no bigger than a pebble, and examine it closer — the hard and rough feel of it as I mash it between my fingers. How easily it had crumpled against the blow I struck her with when God should've been watching her.

Her skull had failed to protect her precious brain, weak and no match for what I had done. I look up toward the heavens and smirk at the white abyss. I feel a surge of power. It's becoming more familiar as I view myself as a god, sitting with my sacrifice. This is almost becoming too easy. I inhale the frigid dawn air. It burns as it fills my lungs. I am beginning to wonder what will become of my darling. Will I hurt her? I picture Charlene's perfectly demented brain conjuring up stories. I feel the storm growing even stronger inside me. I wonder if the storm wants me to hurt her, to make her pay — an ironic plot twist to our own story. The battle to keep from wanting to is nearly impossible to ignore.

My mind races as a vision flickers across — one where it's Charlene, lifeless and beautifully punished. I have laid her to waste and suddenly bile crawls up my throat and sprays from my mouth. The thought is so intense and sickening that I choke on the fantasy. The angry clouds in my mind thrash inside me. She is my darkness, the one who compels me to do the evil I have done and can never undo. It has and has always been for her. If she can't see that I'm helping her and doesn't do her part soon in all of this, it has been for nothing. These lives claimed were for nothing. But I can't give up on her just yet. She needs to see the lengths I will go through to help her. She cannot be distracted from her task. I will do whatever it takes to protect her, even from herself.

Chapter Thirteen

The silence between them was comfortable and familiar, the kind that takes years to perfect. The last twenty minutes or more were free of any words, but a new memory had been made and would be cherished for years to come. There was an unseasonable chill in the air, the sun hidden behind a mask of clouds, and Charley shivered as she cradled her mug of coffee. Her fingers were curled around the mug, stealing any warmth it might still have left. The coffee inside the mug was nearly finished and she waited desperately for the caffeine to kick in.

"Not really biting this morning."

Charley agreed. "Maybe it's too cold?"

"Fish or no fish, I'm just happy to out here with my gorgeous girl," her father commented sweetly as he threw his line out into the still water.

"Me too." Charley snuggled closer to him. "I'm so glad you and Mom came."

"It was either that or drag you back home, honey." He frowned. "You know, when we heard about that poor soul, it took everything for me to not hop in my truck and come get you."

"Oh, Dad."

"After meeting Nick, I feel a whole lot better about things here."

Great. It was much too early to have this conversation, especially with how things had gotten weird between her and Nick the night before.

Her father reeled his line back in, the steady clicking sounds of it spinning filling the space between them. "I know you don't want to talk about dating, especially with your old man. But one day the right man is going to come along."

"Dad, I want to meet someone, just not right now," Charley replied kindly. She knew her father's heart was in the right place. Hell, he might even be right about Nick. Last night there had been that spark that kept teasing them. Whether it was just two battered souls coming together to find peace or some sort of love connection, though, it didn't matter. She had her deadline and other future projects were already coming alive in her mind.

"A dad just gets a feeling about things, sweetie. You say you like that Tucker fella, but I'm not sure he's the right guy for you."

"And why is that?" Charley eyed him curiously. It wasn't entirely like her father to open up and discuss matters of the heart with her. She trusted whatever his gut was telling him.

"I just don't see it, I guess," he answered without looking at her. "But with Nick, he annoys you and you light up like a little firefly." He chuckled. "I used to bug your mom, and she was convinced I was the not the *one*."

Charley smiled. "But you were."

He nodded and turned his gaze to her. "You darn right I was. I knew it all long. It was her who needed the convincing."

She exhaled. "Nick definitely annoys me. That's for sure."

Her father draped his arm over her shoulders and pulled her close to him. "Well, you're a lot like your mother, and it might just take some time for you to realize. Nick needs to do the convincing, though I'm happy to help," he offered.

"Oh, Dad," Charley laughed and snuggled against him. "I love you, and thanks for being such a great father."

"Thanks for being such a great daughter." He gently kissed the top of her head.

* * * *

His boots crunched over the pine needles that littered the path. The sky was still gray as morning gave way to afternoon. There was an ominous sense of doom in the air, and Nick had felt it the moment his phone rang. *Another one?* Here he was again, the sheriff looking older than ever, shaking his head as he approached Nick.

"I can't make heads or tails from this, Capra."

Nick walked with him as he led them down a narrow path. It was obvious that mostly wild game traveled through here, not a trail that humans would frequent. "Who called this one in?" Nick asked as they entered a small clearing, possibly where deer would bed down. The tall grass was flattened, the area tucked away, a safe place to hide out.

Unlike the crime scenes, there was no other law enforcement there. On the ground, a woman was on her side, her bare legs twisted together unnaturally. Nick could see her scalp was bloody and there were specks of white and tissue. He bent down to take a closer look.

"An anonymous caller phoned in the tip," the sheriff answered gruffly.

"Anonymous, huh?" Nick gently moved the woman's face with his gloved hand. Her eyes peered up at him. The whites were a grayish color, matching the rest of her skin. Something struck him as odd, as if her bashed-in skull was normal. He saw it then. Her eyelashes…they were gone. A few small hairs clung to her cheekbones, which were streaked with an oily black smear. It dawned on Nick that it was mascara. The killer had plucked the eyelashes from this woman. "I wonder if that was our killer who had called in," Nick commented as he continued to examine the body.

"Possibly." The sheriff paced nervously. "I didn't want to send any deputies out here. We need to get a handle on this. I know I asked you to focus your attention on Vanderberg, but I need your help, Capra."

A sick sense of relief washed over Nick. After the previous night's failed rendezvous, Nick wanted to keep as far away from Charley as possible. "So, I'm relieved of babysitting duty?"

"Not quite," the sheriff answered. "It seems funny to me that this killing spree started right as Vanderberg arrived here," he explained.

"True. But I think it's safe to say Charley isn't the one out here doing this." Nick couldn't help but defend her.

"Charley?" A confused scowl traveled across the sheriff's plump face. "Never mind. I don't think Vanderberg is a suspect. I just find it extremely odd that these murders started after she got here. Her agent said folks weren't real keen on Vanderberg and that there had been some threats."

"Wouldn't they target her as instead of these random victims?" Nick searched for any more evidence on the victim. If only there was a clue that would tie everything together and point them in the direction of this nutjob.

"I agree. Why would the killer go after these people? How are all of these connected?" the sheriff asked as squatted down next to Nick.

"Maybe it's a coincidence, maybe not," Nick offered as he sent a silent prayer for her, not that he was even on speaking terms these days with the Big Guy upstairs. Whoever this killer was could very well be after her. Nick remembered how freaked out Charley had been when she'd told him about the lipstick on the last victim. A part of him wished she were here to spot anything else that may have been copy-catted from one of her books, anything he wasn't catching.

It wasn't out of the realm of possibility that some weirdo was imitating scenes from her books. As much as Nick might want to avoid Charley and all the emotions he was experiencing, he knew he had to protect her. He couldn't live with himself if he got the call that it was her body they'd found. A nauseous wave slammed him, his heart began to beat faster and anger unexpectedly tore through him. He couldn't let anything happen to her.

"We need to find this asshole before we've got a dead celebrity on our hands, Sheriff."

* * * *

"This is really good," her mother exclaimed with muted surprise as she sat at Charley's makeshift workspace. "There's an intensity to it that's different than your other stories."

Her father was stretched out on the ugly couch, his long legs hung over one side and his snores filled the small cabin. Charley had been checking emails on her phone as her mother read the manuscript.

Charley looked up from her phone. She'd been pretending to be engrossed in social media but was mentally biting her fingernails as her mother read her work. "It's weird. As I was writing it, it just felt different than all the times before."

Her mother removed her reading glasses and leaned back in her chair. "Don't get me wrong. You're a fantastic writer, sweetie. This is just a little disturbing."

"Mom, pretty much all of my books are," Charley countered as she scoffed.

Her mother shook her head in disagreement. "This one is chock-full of some kind darkness I haven't seen from you before. Usually in your work, there's a sense of balance, light and darkness. We always know which one will win. In this one, I feel all tangled up with these characters. I'm conflicted and not even sure if the good guys are even good in this one."

"So, how do you think my readers will respond?" Charley suddenly feared another reaction like her last release. She couldn't bear the thought of them hating it then another bout of writer's block visiting her again. She didn't think she could survive any of that. If this book failed, Charley would hang up the towel and retire.

"Oh, honey, stop with that kind of nonsense." Her mother rose from her seat and came over to where Charley sat. "This book is going to be phenomenal, and we're not even close to the ending. I can't wait to see how you tie this all together. It's pure magic, sweetie."

"You're sure about that?" Charley wasn't entirely convinced now as self-doubt reared its ugly head once again.

"Baby, your writer's block is definitely gone. That" — she paused and pointed at the laptop — "is some of the best writing I've ever read. Your words have a way of stamping themselves on a readers' soul, and these words are going to haunt people, Charley." The serious tone and expression on her mother's face didn't lie.

Charley smiled. *I'm definitely back.*

* * * *

It was another night of celebration. Children held sparklers and one could easily see the delight in their young eyes. *The magic of summer.* Charley sat on the wood picnic table with her parents and enjoyed the perfectly grilled burger. She wouldn't be shocked if she'd gained ten pounds or more by the end of this weekend.

"Have you seen my buddy?" her father asked playfully as he worked on his second burger of the evening.

"Nick or Ruger?" Her father had fallen hopelessly in love with the little black pug when they'd all played cards. Who knew big men were softies for tiny dogs?

Her dad laughed. "You know which one."

She shook her head. "I haven't seen him all day." Her parents both frowned. His absence was definitely felt.

"I was hoping to get in another game of horseshoes," her father said as he seemed to be scouring the vicinity for Nick.

"It's a shame to miss out on all this fun. I'm sure he's busy working on that case," her mother added. "Any leads on that?"

"Not really." Charley pushed her plate away. "I mean, how does something like that happen in a place like this?"

"No rhyme or reason, I suppose. There are horrible people everywhere, people who want to make other people hurt," her father explained. "I sometimes think maybe a lot of these folks were hurt themselves. Either way, they'll answer to God one day."

"I always feel so bad for the families," her mother added. "I don't know how you worked for that paper in Seattle for so long. Honestly, I'll never understand how you can write the stories you do."

"I feel like she's honoring those folks," her father defended her. "Those poor souls. Charley finds a way to make sure the bastard who killed them pays. She gives their families some closure." She'd never heard father's take on her work before. It warmed her heart to hear the passion in his words.

"Thanks, Dad. I feel like you really get what it is I'm trying to do."

"It has to be that. I can't imagine my daughter writing all that crazy nonsense for no good reason."

"We're lucky to have such a talented daughter. I just wish you would reconsider writing more of that sweet romance stuff," her mother suggested. "That was one of the nicest books I have ever read. The writing was still wonderful, dear. I loved how cute the story was."

"Mom, my readers hated that novel. They want the murder and suspense."

"Oh, they're definitely getting that in this new one." Her eyes were wide as she continued, "Maybe you need different readers."

"Those readers have afforded me this life," Charley countered as the sky lit up with the first firework of the evening. She found the interruption fitting.

"Time to watch the fireworks, ladies," her father said happily.

Charley reached across the picnic table and patted her mother's hand. She smiled at her through the dusky light. They both knew that she meant well. What mother wouldn't want their author child to write stories about love and happy things? Charley wondered. How did Stephen King's mom feel about his work? Did she ever tell him to be a nice boy and write something a little more like Nicholas Sparks?

* * * *

Charley chewed the inside of her cheek as she reread the paragraph she'd written. She had redone it what seemed like a million times. As she sat there and studied the black words, she couldn't help but feel as though something about them wasn't quite right. Perhaps it was the mounted pressure from her mother's review. She wanted to more than live up to the expectation and fly over the bar she had set for herself.

"Maybe I've been staring at this for too long," she said out loud and rubbed her eyes. She'd been up since the crack of dawn to fish with her dad then spent the rest of the day hanging out with her parents. They would be leaving soon and she wanted to get in as much time as possible with them.

After dinner and fireworks, they had parted ways. Charley had found herself anxious to write. After discussing the manuscript with her parents, she had new ideas she had wanted to add. Her mother would be proud of some the new additions she had in mind. Charley plopped herself down and got to work. The light emitting from the screen of her laptop illuminated the small cabin. Charley hadn't gotten up from her spot in hours and could feel her butt and legs going numb. She had been working in the dark and had no real idea what time it was but knew it had to be late. Charley moved her head in small circles, her best attempt at relieving the tension in her neck. Why was she having so much difficulty with this Chapter? She debated whether or not to call it a night when there was a soft knock at her door. The unexpected noise startled her.

Charley moved carefully to the door and was about to ask who it was when she heard Nick speak. "Charley, you here?" he asked through the wooden door.

She cracked the door open just enough to get a glimpse of Nick, the dim glow from the porch light washing over his handsome features. Charley felt a surge of happiness course through her, which was quickly replaced by irritation. "What are you doing here?"

He looked down then back at her. "I'm not entirely sure." Something appeared to be bothering him.

"Everything okay?" Charley asked as she opened the door wider. He ran his hand through his messy hair. The movement was rough and almost caused Charley to wince. "Come inside," she ordered softly.

"I'm sorry for coming over here, especially this late," Nick rambled an awkward apology as he went straight for the couch. "I hope I didn't wake you."

"You do realize who you're talking to, right?" Charley attempted to be playful and lighten the mood as she followed Nick. "As you can see, I was working. Well, trying to, anyway." She pointed at the open laptop and joined him on the couch. "So, what's up?"

He exhaled and looked up at the ceiling. Charley watched as he mulled over his thoughts and chose his words carefully.

"I'm not even sure where to start." She could see the lines near his mouth bend. He looked older and even more exhausted since she'd seen him last.

She couldn't resist the urge to touch him and patted his arm. "Well, the beginning is usually a good place." She saw him crack a smile and it warmed her heart. What was it about Nick that got to her? She didn't want to like him, but with him looking a little like a broken baby bird, he pulled at her heart strings and ignited her protective instincts.

"I suppose you're right." Nick released a quiet breath. "I guess I wanted to say I'm sorry for last night."

"Hey, I get it, Nick. Emotions are high from all this stuff going on, then you meeting my parents, which is kind of weird and all," Charley nervously rambled. "And there was the rum," Charley added.

"Yeah, but I shouldn't be kissing you." It looked to Charley like Nick was doing everything possible not to do just that. He cleared his throat and shoved his hands into the pockets of his jeans. "I really am sorry."

"Okay, I forgive you." Charley studied him. He wasn't there just to apologize for locking lips. There was something else he needed to say — something that seemed far darker. "But would you like to tell me the real reason why you're here?"

"There's been another one." Nick spilled the words out without any more hesitation then went on to explain the grisly scene he had been invited to by the sheriff that morning.

Charley could tell he was holding back on the details or perhaps it was just the writer in her who knew the scene could be described with a little more finesse. She closed her eyes and tried to imagine herself standing there. What did the air smell like? Was there any noise in the trees? What was she wearing? Was her skin that frozen white or a grayish blue that may have matched the surrounding clouds?

Charley's brain moved in hyper speed as she tried to process all that Nick was saying. Her mind began to itch, and she wanted to rewrite all his words. As the gears in her busy mind turned, Charley could feel his eyes on her. The moment she looked over at Nick, she saw the regret in them.

"I have been trying to follow up on some leads the entire day. I figured maybe you'd have a little insight."

"Like, if I had anything to do with these?" Charley gasped at the unexpected turn of the conversation. *Does he actually think I'm the killer?*

Nick moved closer to her. "No, nothing like that. Like, the one murder. You mentioned there had been something from one of your books done to the body, right?"

"Yes. I tried telling you that morning." She grew slightly agitated as she recalled the way he'd ignored her. Charley continued, "As I stood there staring at her, it hit me. The lipstick kiss on her forehead." As she recounted the horrific image of the oily crimson smudge on the gray skin, she rubbed her own forehead as if it were possible to remove the lip stain. No matter how hard she tried, Charley wouldn't be erasing that image from her mind anytime soon. "Now, after hearing about these others, I sort of wish I had seen the crime scenes...to see if maybe there were any other things that would stick out to me."

Nick nodded. "See? I've been telling the sheriff somehow these are all connected. I just haven't figured out exactly how. My gut says this is about you in some way." He looked at her in a way that caused a chill to travel down her spine and spread through her entire body.

"Me?" Charley asked cautiously as she wrapped her arms around herself. She couldn't bear the thought that she was responsible for these poor souls in this sleepy little town being butchered because of her. What had she done to piss someone off so badly that they wanted to mimic her stories and inflict that kind of pain on innocent people? She had hoped maybe the murder at the resort was some kind of fluke, and that was the end of it. Charley swatted away tears and tried to swallow down the hard lump that had formed in the back of her throat.

Nick pulled her to him and tucked her close to his chest. Charley instantly felt the chill leave her. He held her in the perfect tightness — a mix of protective tenderness. Charley could get used to this, if she'd just allow herself — or maybe if things had been different and there weren't dead bodies involved.

Why was he always touching her any time he had the opportunity? Wasn't the plan to steer clear of Charley? Yet, here he was with her against his chest, all delicate and frightened. He'd shared with her the other murder cases and regretted it instantly. The sheer look of sadness in her beautiful eyes told him how much this affected her. It also told Nick there was more to this girl in his arms.

Fate had brought them together whether Nick liked it or not. In the beginning, the idea of playing bodyguard to Charley had royally pissed him off. Then seeing those bodies and knowing someone was out there and that they might be after her had done something inside him. He knew what type of evil existed and, obviously, so did she. Nick smoothed her hair, and the golden strands felt like spun silk and pure magic. He groaned as quietly as possible. *This woman.*

He couldn't ignore how he felt about her. Nick wondered if maybe he had suffered enough and this sweet angel of a woman who pretended to be annoyed by him was his reward. Maybe he'd gotten it all wrong, believing he had deserved severe punishment for his partner dying and everything going to hell back in Portland. He figured the penance he had to pay for the bloodshed could take years, if not his entire life. Never would he think that maybe he had suffered enough. Could he keep her safe? If anything happened to her, he would be in an even darker and deeper pit of despair. His throat closed as he nearly choked back tears.

"Nick," she whispered with concern.

Could she tell he was a thread away from coming completely undone? Nick straightened his back and shelved the demons for another moment when he was alone. He allowed himself to enjoy her touch. "Yes?"

"When do you think you're going to catch this creep?" Charley looked up at him. Her eyes were starting to fill with tears.

"I'm working on it. Trust me." He wished they could just stay there snuggled on the couch without a worry and that the circumstances of them being there together were different.

"Maybe you need to turn all your attention on this and not focus on babysitting me," she offered. "I could talk to the sheriff and let him know I'm a big girl and can take care of myself," Charley said firmly.

"Look... I know you don't like the idea of me to babysit you about as much I don't," he lied. He wanted nothing more than to be around her, to look after Charley's wellbeing. "But considering what's happening here, and until we know more, I think it's for the best if we work together on this, okay?" he pleaded with her as Charley moved away from him. "No more fighting about whether or not you can take care of yourself."

"I really don't need a babysitter, Nick," Charley rebutted sassily. Her tone was laced with defensive ice, but Nick could see through her. She was scared. Hell, he was scared.

"You got any more of that rum?" he asked with a wicked grin that was met with an annoyed sapphire eyeroll and the hint of a flirty smile.

* * * *

He knocked lightly on the door and waited patiently. The cardboard cups of coffee were getting colder by the second. Why hadn't she answered the door? Panic swept through Nick as he immediately envisioned the worst. At the moment he was about to kick down the door, Charley opened it. She looked less than amused at his early morning visit. Nick found her utterly adorable in pink fuzzy pajama shorts that gave him an ample view of her beautiful legs. She was barefoot with painted toenails, his new favorite shade of pink. Nick was beginning to notice everything about her. The tide had definitely changed. He felt more alive and awake than he had in months, which would greatly explain why he couldn't wait to see her this morning.

"Really?" she huffed.

Nick held up the coffee. "I brought coffee." There was that sexy eyeroll again.

She groaned and let him inside. "What time is it?"

"Almost eight," he answered. "I figured maybe we could go over some of your books for clues...maybe talk to your assistant." He handed her one of the cups.

"You think Vic is the killer now?" Charley scowled as she took her first sip.

Nick almost laughed at the notion. "I highly doubt she's a killer. She might break a nail or something," he teased

"Very funny, Nick."

"I just wonder if she's got any hate mail we can look at." Nick drank his coffee and waited for her to answer.

Charley cradled her coffee in both hands and leaned against the small kitchen counter. She was quiet, which was unusual for her. Since he'd met her, Charley had had a lot to say and it concerned him that she wasn't running her pretty mouth.

"Charley?" Nick prodded gently.

She looked up at him. He saw the worry in her gorgeous eyes, and he also noticed they were slightly puffy. Had she been crying? Last night after he'd suggested rum, Charley had countered with him going home. Nick had kept guard all night, not that she would ever know. Truth be told, he'd actually never been to bed. He was running on a new kind of high that wasn't caffeine or nightmare-induced. Nick buzzed with the idea that there were feelings he wanted to explore with this woman. She might not realize yet, but she was probably busy as hell fighting her own feelings for him. *Been there, done that, even got the T-shirt.*

Her sweet voice croaked, "Do you think this person would hurt Vic or any of my family?"

Nick sat his coffee down and took her cup from her. He towered over her. It took more willpower than Nick thought he possessed not to kiss away her fears. Instead, Nick brought her close to him. He was surprised to find Charley wrap her arms around his waist. He wanted nothing more than to banish her fears and protect her from the monsters of the world, even the ones she wrote about.

"Don't worry about that right now and just take one thing at a time, okay? But you aren't being paranoid. You as well I know what people are capable of." He wanted to validate her and not dismiss any notions that she had.

"Oh, Nick, what have I done?" she asked as uncontrollable sobs took over.

Nick squeezed her then pushed her slightly away from him. "You didn't do anything. Believe me, babe. We're going to catch this asshole," he growled through clenched teeth.

She cried into his chest. "I don't want anyone else to die."

She pulled herself together when she heard a knock at her door. Nick was slow to release her. Even Charley wanted him to keep holding her, but as another knock echoed in the cabin, she reluctantly said, "I need to see who that is."

Why is Nick acting like this now? He didn't even seem like the same guy she'd met when she'd first arrived. Was she even the same girl now? She ran her fingers through her tangled hair and used her palms to smooth away any leftover tears. After taking a few deep breaths, she carefully opened it.

"Good morning, sweetie." Her mother and father stood with happy smiles fixed on their faces. "We thought maybe you'd like to go to breakfast before we leave." She saw her mother's eyes wander past her then back at Charley. "Oh, I see you have company," she whispered.

Charley let her parents inside and the already small cabin felt even tighter with all of them in there. She needed some air but knew her parents would know something was wrong.

She felt him behind her. "Good morning, Mr. and Mrs. Vanderberg," Nick greeted them politely, but in a casual manner that was comfortable and natural.

"Nick, we'll be heading home today and wanted to take our girl here out to breakfast. Care to join us, Nick?" her father offered as he wrapped Charley in a strong side hug.

Nick searched her face for approval. She shrugged in defeat, more for show in front of her parents, but her heart was happy that he would be joining them. "Let me get dressed."

Charley shooed them out of her way then began the task of trying to get ready. The lack of sleep from last night wasn't doing her any favors. She fumbled with the buttons on her jeans and she'd dropped her brush a few times. If she were honest with herself, she could admit that her nerves were more than a little on edge.

After she'd sent Nick home the previous night, Charley couldn't write a single word. That didn't mean she'd actually gone to bed like a normal person. Instead, she'd found herself sucked into the vortex of social media. Charley had cruised around her site, visited all the links to her accounts where she interacted with fans. Charley answered delightful messages and emails filled with encouragement and support from her readers. They missed her and were concerned about her lack of posts.

Charley had been immediately consumed with guilt, something that was starting to become an ongoing problem for her. She couldn't help herself and posted a few pictures of her laptop. She teased her readers about all the magic that was coming out of her well-loved and overly abused computer. She even snuck a late-night picture of a cup of coffee. Charley knew Victoria was going to pitch a fit, but a part of her had missed this. It was a distraction from everything else that was happening. Oddly, after all the likes and comments, Charley didn't feel any better. What if she had just fed the troll who was doing all these heinous things? Maybe she secretly had been hoping to snare him? Charley went to bed with a heavy heart and endured a restless night's sleep.

"You almost ready?" Nick called through the door.

Charley grabbed her purse and sighed in frustration. Why couldn't life be anything like the sweet romance she'd written? Simple boy meets girl, boy irritates girl until she falls hopelessly in love with him then they live happily ever after. Instead, life was like the gruesome novels that had made her a celebrity, and somehow that made Charley sick to her stomach. She had become wealthy from corpses. Her bank account was plump from writing stories about people who were robbed of their life. Their families weren't any richer. It was like a twisted version of *Robin Hood*. It didn't matter how much money Charley donated to various victims' organizations, she was making one helluva profit from stories derived from loss and suffering. It was moments such as this when Charley truly wished her readers had accepted her sappy love story. She would've been content writing those happily-ever-after stories for the rest of her career.

She tried to focus on the road and cancel out the lively conversation. Charley would catch a glimpse of Nick in the rearview mirror every now and again. Their eyes would meet and it was as though he could read her mind. She saw the sympathy in his rich, dark eyes and knew that his attempt at keeping up the conversation with her father was for her benefit. She appreciated it more than he knew.

"Nick, you make sure this girl gets in some more fishing, you hear?" her father said joyfully as they drove into town. "I don't want her holed up in that cabin."

"Dad, I have a book to finish," Charley argued softly without much conviction.

"From what Mom said, it sounds like you're about done," he countered with a wink. "Looks like you'll have some time to enjoy this place a little."

Charley looked at Nick, who frowned. She was relieved when she spotted the restaurant and found a space to park. "We're here."

"Great, I'm starved. I'm thinking of getting some more of those pancakes — not that they even stand up to your mom's." She heard her mother giggle and funny thought crossed her mind. *Would Nick ever cause me to giggle like that?*

Molly greeted them with a large smile. "Howdy, folks." Her gaze traveled from Charley to Nick and back again with a questioning stare. Charley shook her head as they were led to a booth. The seating arrangement was different than before. This time, Charley and her mother were both pinned next to the window. Nick sat beside Charley and her father next to her mother. Molly quickly returned with coffee and menus. Charley could tell Molly was dying to inquire about this little breakfast double date.

There was no awkward silence. Her parents weren't people who could enjoy a quiet breakfast. Charley wasn't in the mood to talk and again, guilt nipped at her. Her parents would soon be on the road and Charley didn't know when she'd see them next. Considering the awful things currently happening, there was also the chance she might never see them again if the killer ever decided to go after her. Charley wanted nothing more than to be cheerful and enjoy this precious time with them. Having Nick next to her felt odd but strangely right. He kept the conversation going and answered all the questions both of her parents kept batting his way. *Bless his heart.*

Molly returned with her trusty order pad and curiosity filling her overly made-up eyes. "What'll it be?"

Nick motioned for her father to order first. She knew her dad was just eating up this whole respect thing and was probably trying to figure out a way to marry her off to Nick. Not that her mother was any better. She kept slipping Charley looks of appreciation and seemed quite taken with Nick. The last couple of days had almost seemed like when the typical daughter-brings-home-the-boyfriend scenario. The only thing was Nick was not her boyfriend. She questioned whether his new behavior was based more on his role as bodyguard or did he actually have feelings for her? She couldn't deny how much closer they had grown in such a short time, but trauma would do that to a people.

Molly was just about finished taking their orders when Tucker entered. He removed his visor and sunglasses. He noticed Charley and gave her a smile. His gaze quickly moved to Nick and his face soured. Tucker looked away and took an empty seat at the counter. She felt Nick stiffen next to her and under the table he reached for her hand. Why did Charley feel all of a sudden like she was either part of a lover's triangle or back in junior high?

Charley had a mouthful of pancakes when Tucker appeared at their table. "Shouldn't you be writing?" he joked with a light chuckle. "Good morning," Tucker said to her parents with a professional coolness. "I hope you folks enjoyed your stay here."

Her father nodded as he quickly swallowed his own mouthful of food. "Yes, that's quite a resort you've got."

"Thank you for making accommodations for us so late," her mother added.

Tucker ignored Nick's agitated glare and his eyes had a way of constantly finding Charley, causing her to squirm in her seat. "It was no trouble at all. Anything for Charley." Tucker winked.

Did she still have feelings for Tucker? There was no doubt there was chemistry and attraction. He was good-looking guy, borderline gorgeous. Nick ignited feelings that, truthfully, she was terrified of. They were real and raw. She found herself just wanting to hold him and to hush any monsters that might be lurking inside him. He had this way of calming her and pissing her off, all at the same time. Maybe their demons would play really well together.

She didn't know what lurked inside Tucker. He gave off this carefree and fun spirit but there was strange stillness about him if she looked closely. His reaction to the murder was flat and somewhat callous. Nick, on the other hand, was almost too absorbed in them. She imagined he had his cabin set up like a headquarters, with yellow Post-it notes pinned to a board and red yarn spider-webbed across the pictures of possible suspects — the stuff people saw in movies to show how close the detective was to solving the crime.

That probably wasn't the case at all, but Charley wouldn't be surprised. The cases were eating him alive, chipping away at his soul. But was that much different than all the murders Charley had written about? Hadn't they nearly destroyed her? That was exactly why Charley avoided love. It was messy, confusing and not something she'd ever been exactly great at. Love was suicide. Should she cut her losses and just get the hell out of town? She wanted to bang her head on the table but that might cause too much of scene.

Nick's gaze was unwavering from Tucker. Tucker glared right back at Nick. Neither wanted to break eye contact and show any sign of weakness. This dominance bullshit was getting old really quick. The tension built and grew uncomfortable. She was tempted to tell them both to knock off their crap. She looked to her father, who seemed to be rooting for team Nick.

"We also felt incredibly safe having Nick so close by," her mother added sweetly but with full intent to let Tucker know who she was siding with. *Another member of Team Nick.*

"He's been taking excellent care of our sweet girl," her father said genuinely, though the undertone spoke volumes of which team he was on.

Tucker smiled tightly at her parents and Charley could detect his annoyance. She wasn't the only one. Nick seemed like he was waiting for Tucker to slip up and say the wrong thing. She wanted to de-escalate this before things got out of hand.

"Thanks again, Tucker. We need to really finish breakfast so they can beat the traffic," Charley explained behind the mug of her coffee. Why did she have to play peacemaker with these two right now? She was going through enough and wanted nothing more than hide back inside her cabin. It wasn't like she even wanted to write, but she could at least let her demons duke it out in private. Charley needed to sort out her feelings and figure out what she was going to do about this manuscript. Maybe this was the tipping point, the signal to just pull the plug. She released a heavy sigh.

"We even talked about maybe coming back next summer." She wanted to soften the goodbye somehow.

He nodded politely. "Have a safe trip back home." Tucker went back to the counter in defeat and kept his back to them until he received his order. He gave Charley another glance before leaving. He almost looked rejected, hurt that she hadn't invited him to join them. He seemed somewhat sad that he was not the one sitting there with her folks.

"Do you mind letting me out? I need to visit the ladies' room," her mother announced. She eyed Charley to follow her.

"Can you let me out as well?"

Nick nodded and scooched to let Charley work her way out of the vinyl booth.

Once inside the bathroom, her mother stared hard at her.

"What, Mom?"

"Nothing. I just had to pee," she answered as she headed into an empty stall.

Charley leaned again the wall as she waited for her mother. There was no way her mother wasn't about to comment on what just happened. "Come on, Mom. Just say it."

"I'm not sure I care for that Tucker."

"Yeah, I don't know really what to say on that front, Mom." Charley started the faucet and splashed cold water on her face. The bags under her eyes were awful. She began to wonder why either guy would be attracted to her.

Her mother flushed and joined her at the sink. "I know you don't appreciate your father and I getting involved in your love life." She scrubbed her hands with the liquid soap, taking her time so that they could have this little mother-daughter chat. "But considering your history in that department, I would think you'd appreciate a little insight from this old married lady."

"Not really. I'm not looking to engaged or married anytime soon. I don't even want to date right now," Charley groaned.

"I know. You've got that book to finish. But Nick is a keeper."

"He's a nice guy." Charley didn't really know him and had only scratched the surface of that tough exterior. He had no idea what a total disaster she was either. "Maybe if things were different."

Her mother looked a little sad. "Is it wrong for a mother to want to see her baby happy? You haven't been for a very long time, dear." The truth in her mother's eyes and the words coming from her mouth were not anything that she didn't already know. Something inside gave way, like a dam that had been holding back a tremendous amount of water and broke. "Oh, baby."

Charley didn't even realize she was crying. Her mother wiped away the tears as Charley stood there frozen. It had been too much. Just running from herself, making excuses, the writer's block… It was exhausting. Pile on the guilt she felt and it was only a matter of time before it bubbled to the surface. She just wished it had been when she was alone.

"I just want you to have what your father and I have. It's special, but it takes work. Don't think for one second that man doesn't drive me crazy. That's how you know it's real." Her mother wrapped her arms around Charley and tightly squeezed her. "I don't want you to miss out on an opportunity to be happy with someone. I think Nick might be that someone."

Charley couldn't even get out the words she longed to say — to admit that she might not be worth loving, that this might be the cost of her fame and career.

"Just please don't shut out the possibility."

Charley could only nod. The embrace broke when another patron entered the restroom. Charley awkwardly wiped her face and blew her runny nose. As she stared at herself in the mirror, she poked at the swollen bags under her eyes, they were like triple the size they had been before her little meltdown.

Fanfriggintastic.

What Nick would give to punch Tucker's teeth to the back of his throat. That arrogant asshole fired Nick up. He had seen them having a nice breakfast and still felt the need to horn his way in. *Fuck that guy.*

"Nick, I need you to promise me something," her father said sternly.

Nick nodded. Her father didn't need to ask him to watch out for his precious daughter. It was an unsaid request and one that Nick would fulfill with his life if he had to. "I promise to keep her safe."

The older man with Charley's eyes shook his head. "I already know you'll do that." Nick was confused and waited for him to continue. "Have you figured out yet that you love Charley?" Now he was nervous and didn't know how to exactly answer that. He put his hand up to stop Nick. "I can see it. My wife sees it. It's the ones in love who don't." He took a quick sip of his coffee and continued, "Please be patient with that stubborn girl of mine. She's a lot like her mother. But trust me, she'll come around." He chuckled.

"Charley is an amazing young woman," Nick stated. "She's unlike anyone I've ever met."

"You don't need to convince me, son." He studied Nick thoughtfully. "Charley thinks she isn't worthy of love. I get the sense you two aren't all that much different."

Nicked blinked hard as he took in what her father was telling him. "I mean, I don't want her to get hurt," he opened up honestly.

"You think you're going to break her heart? Newsflash, son... We are all capable of getting hurt. I think she could hurt you even more."

"I'm not scared of Charley hurting me," Nick admitted.

"Then what?"

"I feel responsible to keep people safe. It's literally my job." Nick paused and took a long sip of coffee to compose his thoughts. "Well, I wasn't able to that a few months ago, and people I cared about were murdered because of my mistakes. My partner and his son were killed right in front of me. I had to tell his wife and daughter." Nick almost felt himself come undone with this impromptu confession.

"I'm so sorry, son."

"So, you can imagine with all this happening," he explained, "I could never forgive myself if anything were to happen to Charley." Nick swallowed hard against the lump that had formed in this throat.

"See? There it is again. That look on your face." He pointed at Nick. "You do love her."

Chapter Fourteen

It was late or early, depending on your definition of the day. Charley rubbed her eyes and yawned loudly. Blurry words stared back at her as she tried to blink away the exhaustion. She was tempted to hit the delete button again for what seemed like the hundredth time that night. Something about the words were all wrong. The feeling—or lack thereof—pissed Charley off. Maybe it was just her rotten mood. After her parents had left that morning, her heart was heavy, and she felt a little lost. She missed them but was strangely grateful they were gone.

Her meltdown in the bathroom at the diner sure hadn't helped matters. When her mother and she had returned to the table, Nick and her father had been deep in conversation. She knew they had been talking about her. Maybe she was over-analyzing everything and still reeling from her breakdown in the bathroom, but Charley felt as though she had little control in her life.

Her agent was pushing her to finish a book she wasn't even sure she wanted to write anymore, Nick was helicoptering and causing so many weird emotions inside her, and her parents were trying to marry her off. She'd honestly had enough—and now her words were beginning to disappear again. Charley wanted to scream. She thought she had overcome that obstacle, but here it was once again rearing its ugly head, taunting her and shaking any confidence she had regained. Charley was her own worst enemy. She reread the last Chapter she had written. Charley felt so detached from the words. They were strange and didn't feel like they had come from her fingers. Something had changed inside her and she was terrified.

* * * *

Nick lay on the couch, unable to sleep. Charley was on his mind. She had taken up permanent residency there. He replayed his conversation with her father over and over again. *Love.* Was he actually in love with a woman he'd only known for a few short weeks? Nick smiled as he pictured her on the dock—wet, angry and breathtakingly beautiful. She was this magical creature, a siren who was luring him to a new depth he didn't know existed. Sure, he'd been in lust and would even go as far as to say he'd thought he was in love in the past. This was entirely different. He had convinced himself he would never experience love in any shape or form again. Yet, here he was.

He gently moved his sleeping pug aside and grabbed his phone off the coffee table next to him. Was she up? Would it be weird if he messaged at this hour? She was the one who said writers didn't keep banker's hours. Nick went with his gut and wrote a short message, nothing over-the-top or too lovey-dovey. He just wanted her to know he was thinking about her. Nick stared back at his words and instantly regretted sending the message. He could tell she wasn't her usual feisty and cheerful self when they had left the diner that morning. He'd written it off to her parents leaving, but he began to wonder if any of it had to do with him. Was he starting to come on too strong? Nick waited for her to respond. He was hopeful she was up, thinking about him.

Curiosity got the best of him and he started to do a little research. He wanted a better look into her life. Nick logged into his nearly forgotten social media accounts. It only took a half-dozen tries to remember his username and passwords, but he managed to get in. Nick went into full-on detective mode but felt more like a stalker as he viewed her posts. He feared it would show him another side of her, that she was indeed a spoiled celebrity and someone he should steer clear of. But instead, most of her posts were funny and sweet...like Charley. There were more pictures of coffee and food than he could count, a seemingly endless stream of witty memes and quotes from famous dead people. There weren't many selfies, and he found himself oddly happy about that. It was one thing to post pictures of jumbo-sized coffee mugs and cinnamon rolls, but the few selfies she did post reflected the real Charley — the private layer of Charley that she worked so hard to keep locked away from the world.

Nick was shocked by the number of people following her across social media. A picture of her laptop on the cabin table seemed incredibly popular.

Her fans were practically drooling over the idea of a new book coming soon. There was something about the picture that struck Nick, this solitary instrument of creation and torture. That was where her heart and soul lived and caused her so much suffering. The picture spoke volumes. He found himself beyond fascinated with her online life. He read her responses to comments from readers. She took the time to answer each one in such a friendly and kind manner that was truly Charley. She seemed more like their friend than the famous author they were obsessed with.

Nick became more enamored with her and wanted to read her work. He wanted to feel what these readers felt and decided to purchase one of her books, not something he did often. Truth be told, Nick wasn't much of a reader. He liked movies well enough, but really just enjoyed peace and quiet when he could steal it. Being here at Crescent Lake was turning out to be one of the best decisions he'd made. Nick silently prayed that whoever was behind these murders would be caught and he could focus on matters of the heart.

Nick downloaded some app that would allow him to read her book on his phone. He waited patiently and kept peeking to see if she had responded to his message. Maybe she was actually asleep or writing — probably the latter. It must be such an odd profession. Nick couldn't imagine planting himself in front of a computer for hours. His back ached at the very thought. He didn't know how it was possible to create these tales that moved people so much. From the reviews of her books, fans seemed so taken by her work. They loved her storytelling ability and couldn't get enough.

Nick smiled as he read comments claiming her to be one of the best authors of their generation. He'd truly had no idea she was this famous or gifted. He knew Charley was special, but he didn't see her in the same light as her fans. Charlene Vanderberg seemed like a fictional character. The search engine produced tons of facts on her but that wasn't his Charley. He found out that she'd donated quite a hefty sum of money to charities for victims' families. Just when Nick had thought it wasn't possible to like her more, he'd stumble on a news article singing her praises. Charley was a good person.

Nick decided to start a pot of coffee. Ruger whined to go outside. Nick needed a breath of fresh air and joined his dog. He was actually excited to start the book but couldn't shake the slight disappointment that Charley hadn't yet responded to his message. When Nick returned, he inhaled the aroma of freshly brewed coffee and eagerly poured a mug full of the dark liquid. He planted himself back on the couch as he opened the app. He feasted on the heavy words that hit him right away. The first paragraph didn't ease him into the story. No, it kidnapped him. Her words sharply described a scene he had visited too many times, and the detective in him felt like he was right there. She had this magical power of transporting him, and now he was bound to the main character. He had no idea that Charley, the pretty-girl-next-door had it in her to write such chilling and captivating words.

Hours later, with a pug snuggling on his lap, Nick gasped out loud when he came across a passage. It wasn't just like he was there. Nick *had* been there. He had seen the brutally stabbed victim firsthand. Her words described everything in perfect detail. He kept reading and there was another scene where the victim's eyelashes had been plucked. Nick had to stop reading for a moment and process everything. Whoever was behind the murders in Crescent Lake had definitely read her books and wanted her to know.

Charley had been right.

* * * *

She had finally slept, not the best, but it was better than nothing. Charley woke up starving and her stomach growled loudly, announcing the already known fact. She'd managed to find the motivation to remove herself from the bed when her phone rang.

"Hello," she answered. Her throat was dry and she cleared it and replied again. She grabbed a bottle of water from the fridge and chugged it down.

"You sound awful. Are you seriously just waking up?"

"Yes, what time is it?"

"A little after five," Victoria said. Charley could picture her rolling her eyes. "You must have been up late writing."

"I was up late."

"And the writing part?"

"Not so much," Charley answered honestly.

"Oh no."

"Yep. It would seem my writer's block might be making its grand return," Charley announced with sarcasm.

"That's not good. But let's be positive. To be fair, you've had a shit ton of stuff going on."

Charley cradled the phone in the crook of her neck as she wandered into the small bathroom. "I guess. I don't what's wrong this time. I was making progress but my heart just wasn't feeling it last night."

"Pamela emailed me this morning," Victoria started slowly.

"And?" Charley wiped and flushed. She washed her hands and gazed at herself in the mirror. The skin under her eyes was still slightly swollen from crying but she looked rested, which surprised her.

"Let me forward it to you." Charley could hear her typing on the other end. "Basically, she's wanting to go over marketing for the new book. She said the publisher is pushing for an earlier release now."

"Seriously?" Charley groaned. "Well, that's awesome. Perfect timing for the words to go missing again."

"I know. I didn't even want to tell you. I can try to reach out to her and see if we can ask for an extension," Victoria suggested.

"They won't give one. I would just like to know why they're wanting to release it earlier than agreed upon. I still have a little over a month or so to turn it in to the editor."

"Do you want to come home and we can work on this book together?" Victoria offered. "I could come there? I want to help you see this through."

"No, I need to figure it all out. Maybe last night was just a fluke, a little hiccup." Charley milled around the cabin nervously. Why would the publisher move the date? Was this some kind of a cruel joke?

"Don't worry. I have complete faith that you can get this done." Victoria was quiet for a few minutes. "How was the visit with your folks? They left yesterday, right? Maybe you're just a wee bit worn out from the visit."

"Maybe." Charley felt tears surfacing. "Vic, I feel like my emotions are all over the place these days."

"Uh, for good reason. Shit seriously hit the fan there not more than a few days ago."

Charley acknowledged that it hadn't even been a week since that poor woman was found on the shore. It felt like so much time had passed with the visit from her parents and things with Nick.

"Channel all that emotion, and use it to write this book," Victoria advised. "I'm here if you need to talk. If you want me to come out there, I will."

"You're right. I need to just focus on the task at hand. I've been under worse time constraints and survived." Charley bit at her nails as worry started to fill her.

"I think you need to get some food and just relax. Don't get inside your head."

"Food would be good." Her stomach growled again. "God, Vic, I just want life to be back to normal." Her voice cracked.

"Oh, babe. Normal isn't what all it's cracked up to be. I do know I'd rather you be back here instead of in that crappy place. The only good things there are Nick and that diner."

"True. I could go for a burger," she admitted.

"And Nick?" Victoria prodded playfully. "Granted, those milkshakes are amazing."

"Ugh. I just don't know about this whole Nick situation. He and my folks totally hit it off," Charley explained. "You know, maybe if things were different."

"Or maybe this is fate's way of bringing someone into your life. You deserve to be happy."

"My mom said the very same thing yesterday. In fact, she informed me that I'm not happy."

"Well, you are and you aren't. I'm just being honest with you. I'm not saying a man is what it takes to make a girl happy."

"Exactly... I don't need a man to be happy."

"Your mom isn't saying that. You've just kind of self-isolated yourself in life — and especially in love. A little romance could do you some good. She wants you to be happy."

"More like married and having kids," Charley countered. "I have a career to consider."

"That's all you've been focused on for years. Right now, even your career isn't bringing you much joy," Victoria pointed out. "Maybe after this book you can reevaluate things. You definitely don't need pressure from anyone. You've got a lot on your plate, but your mom means well."

"I know she does. Nick isn't half bad," Charley answered. "My dad even likes him."

"Wow, that speaks volumes." Victoria laughed. "Let's just tackle one thing at a time. First, go get food."

"Yes, ma'am." Charley appreciated Victoria. She was her little calm voice of reason.

"Call me later."

"I will. I promise." Charley ended the call and dressed quickly.

She hung up and noticed there was a text message from Nick.

I just wanted you to know I was thinking about you. Hope you can get some writing done or at least some much-needed sleep. Thanks for letting me spend time with you and your parents.

His words were thoughtful and caused the butterflies to take flight again. Charley couldn't help but smile.

Charley relished the new-found positive feelings as she got ready to go to the diner. Her mind focused on what Victoria had said and perhaps after this novel was done she could take a little time for herself. The possibility of starting an actual relationship with Nick made her equally nervous and excited. Charley grabbed her purse and set off. The sun was already low in the sky but the air was still warm from the hot summer day. Charley released a happy sigh. Her stomach growled as she daydreamed about what her new life could be like. Lost in thought, she almost drove past her destination.

The diner was busy with the dinner rush. The noise of silverware clanking against dishes, conversations at the counter and the sizzle from the grill was happy music to Charley. She was greeted by another waitress and led to her favorite booth. Molly appeared out of nowhere and plopped down across from her.

"Sweetie, your parents are lovely," Molly said as she reached for her hands across the table.

"Thank you. They thought you were great too."

"Did they?" Molly blushed.

"I told them you were pretty much my only friend here," she casually complimented.

Molly cocked her head to the side. "Is that so?"

Charley was a tad confused. "What do you mean?"

"Come on. A bright cookie like yourself knows exactly what I'm talking about — or rather who."

Charley groaned. "Okay, he's a friend too."

"So, that's what the kids are calling it these days? I'd say he's more in the boyfriend zone rather than friend zone, sweetie," Molly countered. "You two looked adorable with your folks."

"They really seem to like my *friend* Nick," she emphasized. "But we're just friends."

"I'm not sure if Nick got the memo. You should see the way he looks at you." Molly sighed happily. "He's the happiest I've seen him since he arrived here. I know he comes off as moody as all get out, but Nick is a good one."

"He's a nice guy and all. I just need to focus on this stupid book," Charley said in frustration.

"Stupid book? Yikes, still having trouble with the writing?" Molly's eyes darkened with concern.

"Just had some trouble last night. This afternoon Victoria told me my publisher wants the book sooner than we agreed."

"Can they even do that? I mean, is it legal?"

"I'm sure their fine team of lawyers will make sure it is," Charley teased. "But I'm sure everything will work out once I get some food in me."

"I'm going to have them fix you up with something really good." Molly scooted out of the booth when the bell on the door chimed. They both looked to see who entered. Nick's eyes found hers and a dashing smile appeared instantly. "Looks like you got yourself a dinner date, darlin'." Molly winked as she left. "Evening, Detective."

"Do you mind if I join you?" Nick asked Charley politely. He looked tired and rejuvenated all at the same time, which she found odd. He carried an unusual nervous energy about him.

"Sure," Charley replied. Dinner alone had been more of what she had in mind—or possibly chatting a bit more with Molly. She was such a neat lady and Charley enjoyed talking with her.

"I have a confession to make," Nick started.

"Okay, is everything all right?" Charley studied him for answers.

"I read one of your books."

There it was. She hadn't expected him to say that. "Oh dear. Really?"

"You were right, Charley."

"How so?"

"The murders and your books, which are excellent, by the way," he rambled. Nick pulled his phone out and began scrolling.

"Thanks. Wait, books? How many did you read, Nick?" Charley asked with concern. "You never mentioned you had read any of them before."

"I read a couple last night or this morning. I didn't even know what time it was." He laughed awkwardly. That would explain the utterly tired look in his face. "See? Here is the murder with the lipstick stain on the victim." He handed her phone.

"I know. I tried telling you." Charley gave him his phone back. She didn't need to see the words. She had written them and knew them well enough. They were traced in her heart and mind.

He continued in a serious tone, "This one here? You don't even know the details of the case but you wrote it almost exactly as it happened." Nick handed her the phone back.

Charley scanned the words carefully. Her words described a brutal stabbing. She remembered that story quite well.

"We found the victim in his truck and the murder weapon was left behind like you said in the book. We weren't able to get anything back from the prints yet." He looked discouraged. "But you were right. These murders are connected."

She nodded and found it difficult to remain calm. "Yep, because of me, some whacko is out there reenacting my books."

"Oh, babe, I didn't mean it like that. It sheds some more light into the case now. Maybe it's a deranged fan or someone who could be committing these murders." He reached across the table. He gently stroked her hand with his fingers. "I didn't mean to upset you."

The tender way he spoke to her softened her heart, but Charley pulled her hand away. "I'm just done." She was confronted with a confused expression.

"What do you mean?" Nick asked.

"Just everything, Nick. I appreciate what you're trying to do. I just hate that I'm responsible because of an angry fan. I shouldn't have written that last book. I really wanted to do something different and actually enjoyed writing that cheesy romance."

"This is *not* your fault," he said sternly.

"But it is. These people wouldn't have died if it weren't for my books. It's like killing someone twice, Nick. It takes a lot out of me to write fictional murders. Just imagine how it feels when they become a reality."

"You didn't kill these people," Nicked tried to convince her.

"They're dead, aren't they? It doesn't matter if I was holding the knife or not. I'm responsible." Tears streamed down her cheeks. Charley was so angry. She was mad at the world, the killer, her publisher, but mostly at herself for believing she was the reason behind these murders. A rational person would see that of course she hadn't actually killed anyone, but the way she saw it, she played a huge part in this.

Nick got up from the booth and swiftly scooted next to her. He pulled her into the arms and she inhaled his scent. He smelled wonderful, a spicy mix of aftershave and laundry soap. "Babe, we will catch this son of a bitch. But I need you to understand that you didn't do anything wrong. You are a talented writer and have a gift. You got a guy like me to read, and that says a lot."

"I don't think I want to write anymore," she sniffled.

"You don't have to, honey. You need to do what's best for Charley—not for your readers, publisher or anyone else. If you want to stop writing, then stop."

His words held so much weight. No one, not Victoria, her mother or Pamela had given her the permission she secretly wanted, someone to tell her that it was okay if she stopped writing. Everyone had kept pushing her to continue, but it was his support in that moment that meant the world to her. It was as though he truly understood her and her reasons for wanting to quit. That might not be the answer or the way to fix the awful things that had been done, but Charley just wanted someone to give her that option. She looked up at him, and his eyes shone with rich compassion. She saw it. *Love.* A genuine storybook romance kind of love, the weak-in-the-knees and butterflies-in-the-gut sort of emotion that made Charley very nervous.

Her father had been right. Nick loved Charley, and from the way she was staring up at him, he could swear she just might love him too. He knew traumatic situations could alter emotions, frame them into something they weren't. But this moment felt more real than anything else. Charley's face softened and her eyes glowed in a way he'd never noticed before. *Did Cupid just strike her with his trusty arrow?*

"Nick, I needed to hear that…more than you know."

"What did I say?" He was so lost in her eyes he couldn't recall what it was that he said.

"That I don't have to do this anymore." She squeezed him tighter. "It's like you're granting me my wish."

"Your wish is my command," he teased. "Plus, you'd have more time to teach me how to fish."

Her laughter was the prettiest sound in the world. "It's a nice thought, but I'd be breaking my contract. I can't even begin to imagine the nightmare I'd be facing with the publisher and Pamela."

"You get one life to be happy. If writing doesn't make you happy, then stop writing."

"That's the thing… Most of the time writing is what brings my soul joy. It's this book — the pressure around it, these deaths and just everything."

"I'm here for you. You do know that, right?" Nick reminded her in a near whisper.

"You were hired to be," Charley joked. "If not by Pamela, then definitely by my father."

"This is a total pro-bono case now." He pressed his head to hers.

Charley slapped his chest lightly. "You should at least get paid for putting up with me. I'm such a mess." She wiped her wet cheeks with the sleeve of her shirt.

"I'm here because I want to be." Nick kissed her forehead and she snuggled closer. "I'm finding I need you a lot more than you need me," he confessed. "Ruger? Now he's kind of on the fence."

"Nick, I'm sorry for being an ass this whole time," she apologized.

"Like I was any better. I'm a surly bastard at times."

"It's probably the lack of sleep."

"That cabin bed is awful," he replied. "The couch isn't much better."

"I figured Tucker hooked you up with the deluxe suite since he likes you so much." Charley moved closer to the window and ran her fingers through her hair and smiled. "Isn't this all so damn crazy?" Her eyes sparkled and it was if she were seeing him in a new light. "Like, even with all these horrible things happening around us, we somehow have managed to find one another. I never would've predicted that one — the silver lining, so to speak."

"So, are you saying we're going steady now?"

"Oh please." Charley giggled at his silliness. Who knew he even had that side to him?

"Are you asking me to be your boyfriend, Charley Vanderberg?" Nick couldn't resist lightening the mood. Charley rolled her eyes and let out a hearty laugh. But her blush gave away how she actually felt.

"You wish."

* * * *

She sat in front of her laptop and couldn't get Nick's words out of her head. *Boyfriend.* Charley couldn't help but giggle at the notion, nor could she dismiss the butterflies in her belly. It was enough to make a girl want to write another cheesy romance. Her fingers grazed the plastic keys as she touched them seductively. Charley opened a blank page and stared at the endless possibilities in front of her. That was often her favorite stage in the writing process. That first step, and there was nothing quite like it. Sometimes it took her a paragraph or two and hundreds of words deleted before she found her footing. It was the beginning of her new adventure, that place before she would fall down the rabbit hole and get lost. A fond place before she would be consumed by menace.

Charley smiled as her fingers stroked the keys lovingly in the way that only an author can. Black font filled the white screen. She wasn't writing. She was living. That was the part that no one truly understood unless they were a writer. It was when a writer was the most connected to themselves. The words were so tightly wound around Charley, almost suffocating, but she wouldn't trade that feeling for anything in the world.

Coming off her high, she reread the words. They were nothing like those found in her current manuscript or honestly, in any of her other novels. These were gentle, like the most perfect breeze on a sunny day, the kind that softly tickled your face. They held the promise of all things sweet and wonderful, but they were all the wrong words.

This isn't what my publisher wants but what my heart does. Charley knew who inspired her to write this. *Nick.* Too much had gone on and her heart was having a difficult time keeping up with her brain. If there hadn't just been several murders in this quaint town, and she didn't have her publisher breathing down her neck, Charley could dip her toes in the dating waters. She closed her eyes and toyed with an idea, a ridiculous one. Charley wondered what would happen if she actually did retire. *Would I be happy? What will I do for the rest of my life?* The fear of boredom washed over her. Then panic set in as Charley entertained the idea. She had been a writer for so long that she wasn't entirely sure what else she could do with her life. The thought that she was so cemented in her career was overwhelming. Being bound to contracts, deadlines, and the other insanity that came with it, why would anyone want to do this professionally? Maybe Charley was just a glutton for punishment.

Her mind traveled back to her earlier conversation with Victoria. *Why did my publisher demand the book earlier?* Charley exhaled and knew she needed to contact Pamela in the morning. Maybe she could beg for an extension. Again, if she retired, this kind of pressure wouldn't be there.

* * * *

He lay there on the lumpy old couch with a loudly snoring Ruger and pondered his next move. Nick wanted to ask Charley out and take her on a real date. He wanted to show his intentions and that he was far from joking about them seeing about the possibility of a relationship. After dinner, when he'd walked Charley back to her SUV, Nick had kissed her and his world had stopped rotating. Everything had felt good. Other ideas had crossed his mind as well.

Charley had been right. After all the awful things that had been happening of late, it was strange that they had found each other. *'A silver lining,'* she'd called it. It felt like a lot more than that to Nick — destiny, fate, a wish granted from wishing on a star long ago. They seemed meant to be, despite the circumstances. Now, if he could just catch the killer then Nick would whisk her far away from Crescent Lake and give this whole love thing an honest try.

He closed his eyes and pictured them doing mundane tasks, cooking and washing dishes together. God, what was wrong with him? One would think he'd imagine her naked in his bed, spending a gloriously night worshipping her sexy body. Nope, instead, his warped brain went to grocery shopping, walking their adorable dog and lazy Sundays lounging around doing nothing. For once in his life, he had someone who made him want a normal and happy life, someone to grow old with—and that was a thought that had never crossed Nick's mind.

Chapter Fifteen

She had slept the best she had since arriving at the resort. Maybe it was because Charley had gone to bed with romantic visions in her mind. It was nice to pretend that there weren't any other pending issues or pressures. Her dreams were pleasant, and she actually felt renewed for the first time in ages. Her reflection shared the results of a good night's sleep, and there were no dark bags under her eyes today. Charley felt good. It was as simple as that. She showered and dressed quickly to see what the day would bring.

Feeling encouraged by this energy, Charley decided to take her coffee out to the lake and maybe see if the fish were biting. The morning met her with a perfect shade of blue sky, the air was cool but the glorious sun promised it would be hot later on. With her pole clutched in one hand, a mug in the other and a paper sack tucked under her arm with a few supplies thrown in, Charley walked the deck with a sense of purpose. She spotted two majestic eagles circling over the tops of tall pines and took it as a good omen. Despite all that had happened here, this place was beautiful. Charley settled in and readied her hook. Peace washed over her as she cast out the line into the water.

"They biting?"

Charley turned to see Nick standing there with Ruger. She had been so lost in her own tranquility that she hadn't heard him approach.

"We're about to find out," she answered as she reached for her mug. Charley was happy he was there, and the man was looking particularly sexy this morning. He wore dark jeans and gray pullover — to her surprise, something besides black. She hadn't been sure he owned anything in any other color. Ruger stopped at the edge of the dock and looked down at the water. "Maybe this little chunk can help me catch them."

"He might scare them off or hightail it outta here if he sees one. You never know with that guy," Nick joked.

"You're such a ferocious beast, aren't you?" Charley stroked his soft fur and was rewarded with a lick on her hand.

"You interested in taking a day off?" Nick carefully sat down next to her armed with his own coffee.

"What did you have in mind?"

"I was thinking maybe we could go for a drive or something."

"Something? Like, a date kind of something?" Charley teased as she reeled her line back in.

"Something like that." He laughed. "You did ask me to be your boyfriend, after all. I figured I should probably take you out on a date."

Charley cast it out again and Ruger let out a bark. The idea of actually going on a real date with Nick excited her. This sweet side of him was hooking her. She was a sucker for a handsome man who could be a gentleman. Chivalry was one way to make Charley swoon.

"You're pretty good at that," he commented.

"I learned everything about fishing from my dad." Charley smiled at the memories. "It's kind of neat we got to fish together when they were here."

"Yeah, my old man wasn't really the outdoorsy type. Hell, he wasn't really the father type. We didn't do much together and definitely weren't close," Nick opened up.

Charley listened on as he explained more about his childhood. As Nick told the stories of how his father had never showed love or any kind of affection, her heart broke. The beatings he and his mother often received at the hands of his father turned her stomach sour.

She couldn't imagine her own father ever doing anything like that. Her parents loved Charley and her siblings and made sure they knew how proud they were. From the stories Nick shared with her, his mother seemed loving enough but was nothing remotely close to hers. In Charley's opinion, his mother hadn't protected her precious boy. Nick defended her, nonetheless. He explained how resilient children are and that he had survived.

He went into further detail about the reason for his transfer to Crescent Lake and hearing the pain in his voice as he told her how he'd witnessed his partner and his son gunned down in cold blood brought her to tears. Nick felt a tremendous amount of guilt for not having been able to save them and took full responsibility for their deaths. That was such a heavy burden to carry. Nick shifted the conversation to why he decided to be a cop and his passion to help people. That was something completely new, Nick talking about himself. She rather liked it and found herself completely enthralled with his stories, even as sad and dark as they were. Charley hoped she would hear some happy tales. She knew they had to be in there somewhere.

Charley wasn't paying attention when she felt her pole shift next to her. She wasn't fast enough to grab it. "Oh shit," she screamed in horror as her pole sailed into the water.

Nick pulled off his shirt and removed his shoes. In a fluid motion, he quickly dove into the chilly water. Charley got an eyeful of his body as he emerged from the lake. His abs and pecs were nothing like she'd imagined. The man was undeniably gorgeous. Nick sprang out of the water just as quick as he had dived in. His jeans were heavy with water and hung low on his hips. Charley found Nick truly mouth-watering, the dark trail of hair leading into the waist of his jeans, the droplets of water that decorated his sculpted chest. His shaggy hair was now slicked back, and Charley noticed he was shivering as he handed her the pole.

"I know this means a lot to you."

She set the pole down and it was as if everything paused. Her heart was moved by the chivalrous gesture but it was her body that was reacting to seeing a soaking-wet Nick in front of her. She closed in on him, his face inches from hers. Droplets dangled from his lashes and the desire to kiss them away filled her. *Is this what he felt like the first time he saw me dripping wet?*

Maybe it was that he didn't hesitate to rescue something that meant the world to her or because he had let her into his world. Vulnerability had a funny way of creating other emotions. Charley grabbed Nick by the hand and led him to her cabin. She didn't stop to reconsider things. She knew exactly what she wanted — and that was Nick.

Once inside, Nick seemed cautious, clearly unsure if this was their current reality. To reassure him, Charley pulled her top over her head. She stood before him with just her bra and jean shorts on. Nick licked his lips and looked more like a hungry wolf. "Ruger, you be good and take a nap." The pug snorted and found his place on the couch.

Charley giggled and pounced on him and he was quick to catch her. She wrapped her legs around his waist and kissed him. His skin was still cool from the lake.

"A thank-you would have been fine," he whispered into her mouth.

"Are you complaining?" she teased back.

"Definitely not."

Charley was driven by lust as Nick carried her to the bedroom. He laid Charley on her back and stood at the foot of the bed. He seemed to be soaking in the moment. She wanted nothing more than to be rid of their pesky jeans — hers, but especially his. He must have sensed her frustration and shucked his off, giving her an ample view of his naked body.

Charley bucked her hips impatiently and tried to remove her shorts as she eyed her prize. Nick laughed as he pinned her legs. He moved his hands from her calves and stroked the length of her legs. Nick continued slowly and expertly, softly massaging her as he inched his way up her thighs. Her core was heating up fast and Charley was going crazy with anticipation. She gripped at the sheet. It had been too long since she'd made love to anyone. She was terribly desperate with want, and Charley felt like a teenage boy, ready to come at the slightest touch. She tried to move her hips and whimpered, "Please."

He worked her legs even slower, torturing Charley while giving her a wicked grin. He kissed her ankle and gently nibbled her flesh. He finally moved his hands up to the hem of her shorts. Nick crawled onto the bed with her. "Do you realize how beautiful you are?"

Nick's voice was rough as he remained in control. He slowly removed her bra and gazed down at her while he traveled his hands down her ribs. Nick dipped his head to her chest. The stubble on his jaw was rough against her skin as his nuzzled her breasts. He flicked his tongue against her erect nipples, then he sucked hard and caused Charley to moan loudly. While he lavished her breast with attention, he circled her swollen clit with his finger then traced her center as he found her entrance under her shorts. They sighed in unison.

"I thought I was the one who was supposed to be wet?" he asked.

Charley didn't have the verbal skills to reply. She grabbed his face and kissed him deeply. Charley was done playing games, and this teasing had gone on long enough. Charley managed to move higher on the bed, her back almost on the headboard. She needed leverage, but Nick was too busy pleasuring her with his fingers. Nick departed from their kiss and ventured lower, stopping to adore each part of her with feathery soft kisses. He finally removed her cumbersome shorts but left her panties on. Charley attempted to slide them off but he stopped her. Nick winked and lowered his head. He nipped at her throbbing pussy through the thin fabric. Charley almost came when she felt his breath on her. He slid the panties to side, not taking them off her. "These are cute," he said before he flicked his tongue against her clit. He then sucked her until stars burst behind her eyelids. She tugged at the sheets, balling them into her fists as she rode out her first orgasm. Her body was on fire.

Nick teased her delicate skin, blowing air on her clit and letting his tongue work its divine magic. Charley gripped his head with her fingers as his mouth claimed her. Nick feasted on Charley until she was nearly limp from release. No one had ever eaten her out like this. Nick devoured her was as if she were his last meal and he wasn't going to let a single drop go to waste. But she needed to feel him inside her. The hunger to feel his cock became too much to bear. Charley was renewed with energy, and in some sort of acrobatic spin move, maneuvered her way out from underneath him.

She gripped his warm, hard cock, and the girth surprised her. Nick released a throaty moan. He looked up at her longingly as she twisted around on the bed then clutched the headboard as she spread her legs farther, inviting Nick to take her from behind. Without hesitation, Nick held on to her hips and drove himself deep inside her. Charley gasped as her body adjusted to him. They worked together to find release. Charley was sweaty and needy. Nick cupped her breast and tugged at her nipple, causing her to release a sharp breath. He moved his other hand to her clit and began pinching it gently. The sensation sent Charley to another plain, as she begged Nick to fuck her harder.

They picked up more speed. She was blinded by another hard orgasm and this time screamed out his name. It must have been just what he'd needed to hear for him to explode.

"Fuck," he muttered as he bit her shoulder and pushed himself even deeper inside of her. They were both still for a moment, unsure if it had actually happened. Charley collapsed onto the bed. Nick lay on top of her and they were both quiet, almost as if each of them was waiting for the other to speak and not wanting to disturb the dream. There was no way this was reality.

He was still hard, even after having made love to Charley. God, he wanted more of her. Charley was now snuggled up next to him as they shared the sheets. She gently toyed with his chest hair as she seemed lost in her own thoughts. He hadn't expected any of this but now felt even more connected to her. This beautiful creature was his now. Their chemistry was undeniable. The sex had been incredible, to say the least. Her body was his new temple of worship. Charley had tasted like heaven and he fit so perfectly inside of her. He felt himself growing thicker at just the thought. Charley must have sensed his need and began to stroke him under the sheet.

Her breasts were exposed, as the sheet only covered her lower half. He found a nipple and sucked it hard. With closed eyes, Charley threw her head back as she climbed on top of him. With a devilish smile she asked, "You ready for round two?"

* * * *

"A Care Bear? Seriously?" Charley couldn't stop from laughing.

"Hey, I was like, five," Nick defended himself.

They had spent the better half of the day in her bed—talking, kissing, touching and more touching. Her naked body was happily sore from all the lovemaking.

"I think it's adorable. So, were you the pink one?" Charley teased.

In a sweet retaliation, Nick kissed her neck and caused her to squeal. "Gosh, I bet you were such a cute kid. I still can't believe you went as a Transformer. I would've had such a crush on you." Charley's stomach growled loudly. "I guess someone needs some nourishment." Nick kissed her forehead before wrapping the sheet around his waist. "Got anything to eat here?"

"Probably not," she answered honestly.

"Well, I did intend to take you out until you seduced me." Nick shrugged playfully.

"I guess I kind of did, didn't I?" Charley replied innocently. "We could clean up and go to the diner, if you want," she suggested.

He seemed to mule over the idea. "Or we can go to the store, pick up some things and go on a picnic?"

"That sounds romantic. Where at?"

"Well, I'd suggest my bed but I'm think you've used me up pretty good."

"Oh crap, I completely spaced it. My pole and your clothes are probably still on the dock," Charley remembered.

"I can grab them," he offered.

"Like that?" Charley eyed his body wrapped in her sheet.

Nick looked down. "Good point. I will run over to my place and change." He bent down to kiss her again. He inhaled her scent and nuzzled her neck. "God, I can't get enough of you," Nick whispered. Her body grew warm. "I better go or neither of us will be leaving this bed, Charley," Nick said with a sly grin, caressing her thigh. The way he said her name was velvety smooth, like a red-carpet welcome with a side of champagne. She was drunk from all the wonderful lovemaking.

Once Nick had put his clothes on and left, Charley raced to the shower. The hot water soothed her as she lathered a fragrant bodywash onto her skin. She replayed the morning and didn't feel one ounce of guilt. Charley reasoned that she was a grown-ass woman and deserved to have a little fun, except this didn't feel at all like just a little fun. This seemed so much bigger. Charley let the water beat on her back and shoulders as she imagined where this new romance might take her. Was she truly open to being with Nick or was this her brain's desperate attempt at escape?

She toweled off and dressed when her phone rang. "Hello," Charley answered happily.

"I haven't heard from you and was starting to get a little worried," Victoria supplied on the other end.

"Well, I was a bit indisposed," Charley teased.

"Oh my God, with Tucker? Yuck."

"Um, please no, not Tucker," Charley answered. She hadn't thought of Tucker in a few days and all notions of anything romantic had disappeared.

"Oh wow. Nick? Damn, girl. I'm glad my little pep talk helped."

"Vic, I don't even know where to begin," Charley sighed happily.

"Uh, from the beginning and do not, I swear do not—leave out a single sordid detail."

Charley proceeded to tell Victoria the entire story, spanning the last few days and how things had developed. As she revisited the moments she had shared with Nick, Victoria would interrupt with a dozen or so questions. Charley had no problem answering all of them. As strange as everything had been, being with Nick was the only thing that seemed normal and right.

"I'm so proud of you."

Charley laughed, "Why?"

"Because you made the right choice. And feel free to thank me at any point here."

"Well, who knows where it will actually go, if anywhere. But I do have to admit it was really nice."

"Nice?"

"Okay, it frigging hot and hands down the best sex I've ever had," Charley truthfully admitted.

"Damn. Told you, girl. I knew the man could lay it down."

"You weren't wrong." Charley giggled as her mind wandered to their love-drenched afternoon. "I'm supposed to see him again tonight."

"I'm glad, but do you think you have any strength left?" Victoria joked before her tone shifted. "So, the reason for my call."

"Book shit?"

"Yep."

"Total mood killer, Vic," Charley groaned. "But what's going on? Just hit me with it."

"So, I talked to Pamela, and the publisher is not budging a single inch on when they want the manuscript. They're planning an over-the-top launch. We're talking *huge*."

"I'm not anywhere near finishing that book. In fact, I'm considering pulling the plug on it," she replied truthfully.

"That, ma'am, is a big fat no."

"I'm just not feeling it," Charley conceded.

"Well, you'd better. Look... I'm glad you got laid, but it's time to focus now. After the book is done then you can explore things with Nick."

"I'm not sure I have it in me to write this kind of shit anymore."

"I know you've been struggling, but I know you have it in you to finish this novel. Maybe afterward you can try your hand at something different."

"Like last time?" Charley pushed back. "Because that worked out really well. No, I'm thinking about possibly hanging up the towel for good."

"You can't be serious. You're a writer, Charley. You'd be miserable if you weren't up at all hours destroying fictional lives, you little sadist," Victoria joked.

"No, I'm thinking that this book is just too much and that maybe I want different things in my life now."

"Like what? A little house with a white picket fence. A family and kids? Come on now... We both know that isn't what either of us want. Writing is our life."

"I know, but I just don't know if that's all *I* want anymore. I don't want to have any regrets, Vic," Charley said with conviction.

"Why now of all times?" Victoria sounded exasperated. "I mean, I get it. I truly do and don't want you to think for one moment that I don't want you to be happy and to have everything you want. But this book is so important. Everything is sort of riding on it."

"See? It's this kind of pressure and demand that I'm over." Charley felt her frustration grow as a knock sounded on the door. "Someone's at the door. I'll call you back later and we'll figure out something."

"Maybe you're too distracted there, girl."

"I gotta go, Vic. We'll chat later." Charley disconnected the call and walked to the cabin door.

She opened it and found a freshly showered Nick standing there.

"So, your pole wasn't on the dock."

"Crap." Charley huffed. "Maybe someone turned it in."

Nick handed her the discarded coffee mug from that morning. "My sweater was there and shoes. Our mugs were also there. I'm really sorry."

"It's my fault. I should have taken it with me."

"Well, you were sort of on mission," Nick said playfully as he went to reach for her. Charley pulled back. "Hey, what's wrong?"

"I just got off the phone with Victoria."

"Book stuff?"

"Yep. So, I'm just a little irritated right now and losing my pole is kind of the cherry on the top. Maybe I'll go to the lodge and see if anyone turned it in."

"I can go with you," Nick offered when his cell phone buzzed loudly. "Capra," he answered. "Yes, I can be at the station in like ten." Nick's eyes narrowed in on Charley. "The sheriff wants to go over a few leads that just came in. This could be big, honey."

"Yeah, you totally should go." Charley tried her best to hide her disappointment. The reminder of what their actual reality was hit her. She had spent all day playing in a fantasy world, pretending that there wasn't a murderer on the loose.

"I'll try to hurry," Nick said as he kissed her cheek. "We can still have that picnic, but it might be in my bed after all."

Charley feigned a smile, but making love was the last thing on her mind. As Nick left, Charley noticed a small slip of paper on the ground.

Charley, I have something of yours. Tucker

The note must have fallen from the door and Charley was hopeful it was about her pole. She watched as Nick hopped into his pick-up and drove off to the station. Charley walked toward the lodge. The late afternoon sun was hot, and the ground felt warm through her flimsy sandals. Children were splashing at the shore while adults were sunning themselves without a care in the world. Summer was in full swing at the resort now. Boats were out on the water and some men were fishing from the dock.

The air inside the lodge was drastically cooler and a welcome relief from the outside heat. She spotted Tucker behind the counter. He was wearing an icy-gray shirt that brought out the stunning color of his eyes. There was no doubt that Tucker was a gorgeous man, but it didn't hit her like it normally had when she saw him. Any feelings she'd harbored for him were now gone. That ship had sailed and she was perfectly okay with that.

"Hey, Tucker, I got your note," Charley announced cheerfully as she waved the slip of paper. She moved closer to the counter.

"Yeah, I found something I believe belongs to you on the dock this morning." Tucker disappeared through a small doorway. Charley peeked over the counter onto the desk, and she noticed two paperback copies of her novels on the desk. A chill traveled up her spine. Could he be somehow involved? *God, is Tucker the killer?* Tucker reappeared with her childhood pole in hand. "I found it kind of funny that you'd leave it there."

"I got distracted," she mumbled. "Thank you."

"Charley, are you doing okay?" Tucker studied her with concern.

"Uh, yeah, I'm all right." Charley had a million questions stampeding her brain at the moment and found it difficult to have a conversation. "Too much sun."

"If you need anything, please know that I'm here for you," Tucker offered sweetly.

"Yeah, I appreciate that." Charley scurried off as quickly as she could, getting an odd look from Tucker as she exited. Charley questioned if she should tell Nick, knowing how much the two men despised one another. Maybe it wasn't as sinister as Charley imagined. But what were the odds her books would be there? Tucker had admitted early on that he wasn't much of a reader, so why her books? Maybe that was why the sheriff had called Nick into the station. Charley's mind went into overdrive. Sometimes being a writer was the worst thing. Only a writer could imagine all the horrible scenarios and exaggerate them.

Charley raced back to the safety of her cabin and instantly felt trapped. She was lightheaded and hungry from all the lovemaking that morning. Charley went to the small bathroom and splashed some water on her face. She felt refreshed and less dizzy. Charley decided to make a run to the diner. Maybe she'd have a little chat with Molly and make some sense of things with a full belly.

The diner's patrons consisted mostly of elderly locals and a few visiting families from the resort. It was noisy but smelled delicious. Charley smiled the second she spotted Molly taking an order. She quickly found an open booth and waited patiently.

"Hey, darlin'," Molly greeted her. "Where's ya boyfriend?"

"Molly, you know he isn't," Charley shot back playfully, feeling the need to keep that little secret to herself. Had Molly known of this morning's adventure, Charley would look even more like a liar. "Do you have a few minutes?"

"You look a little pale, Charley. You feeling okay, sweetie?" Molly examined her carefully.

"Just hungry." Charley feigned a happy smile.

"Let me get you some food then I'll take my break and we can chat."

Charley stared out of the window. It was beautiful outside, hot and sunny. Yet, Charley couldn't shake the chill that had settled into her bones. It's funny how in a matter of hours so much had changed. This morning had been sexy and the start of a new adventure with Nick. She had learned so much about him in such a small span of time. Then by afternoon, she was back to feeling tormented with the reality and pressures of completing the novel, thanks to Victoria's phone call. To top it off, her Spidey senses were making her think that Tucker was possibly the one behind these copy-cat murders. That was all in one day, and the day was far from over. She almost feared what news Nick had learned from the sheriff.

Molly returned with an enormous plate with a mountain of golden fries and a fried chicken sandwich. Iced tea with a wedge of lemon was sat down in front of her. "I'll be right back." Molly came back with a plate with half the portion and an iced-tea for herself. "Okay, girlie, what's going on?"

Charley nibbled on a fry. It tasted like heaven. "Where do I even start?"

"The beginning is as good a place as any." Molly took a bite of her sandwich. "Let's start with Nick," she prodded.

Charley played with her straw and stabbed at the ice cube. "Things with Nick are complicated but interesting."

"Most things with men are," she agreed with raised eyebrows.

"Then there's this book."

"The 'stupid book', as I recall you saying last time we chatted," Molly added sweetly. "The publisher still on you about hurrying it up?"

"Yes, and my assistant and friend Victoria called this afternoon. You remember her, right?"

"Yeah, the pretty city gal. What does she have to say about the book?"

"Just how important it is that I finish it. Honestly, my heart isn't in it anymore," Charley admitted as she reached for another fry. "You and Nick have been the only ones who have supported my decision to just be done."

"Bless his heart. He's not a quitter either, but he must have sensed that it wasn't truly what you wanted."

"So, my last book was a romance novel and it sort of tanked," Charley explained. "This book is sort of my come-back novel. There is this enormous expectation and I'm just so overwhelmed."

"Why did the romance novel tank? I love me a good trashy story."

Charley laughed before taking a sip of the delicious iced tea. It was sweet and the lemon was strong, a perfect refreshing beverage for summer. "No, mine was a bit more of cheesy sweet romance. Maybe if it were trashy, I would've been successful."

"So, your readers hated it and now you're having to make amends by writing one of your crime novels but your heart isn't in it. What do you want to write?"

"It's more than that." Charley stared at Molly. "The murder at the resort was literally a scene out of one of my books."

"Get out!" Molly's eyes were wide with surprise. "Are you kidding me?"

"No, of course not," Charley replied quietly. "I'm serious."

"How are you not freaking out?" Molly's voice pitched to a higher note. "My God, that's awful."

"Yeah, I know. It's been horrific and I feel so incredibly responsible."

"You do realize this is not in any way, shape or form your fault."

Charley sighed before taking another sip of tea. "That's what Nick says. But here's the thing, it wasn't just the one murder."

"And the others are like the ones from your books?" Molly bit her bottom lip.

"From what Nick said. He told me after he read a few of my books and saw the similarities. Somehow, it's all connected. Nick's actually at the station right now. The sheriff called him this afternoon," Charley shared before sinking her teeth into the sandwich.

"Wow. I'm shocked. The whole thing seems like a good premise for a book, doesn't it?" Molly joked.

"It feels a little more like horror movie."

"Honestly, I'd watch it," Molly answered as she chewed on a fry.

"But then this afternoon, I went to the lodge and saw some of my books on Tucker's desk," Charley began to explain.

"Really? Maybe he's just curious about you. It's not every day we have a celebrity in our neck of the woods, darlin'."

"You don't think it's creepy or somehow connected?" Charley asked.

"That Tucker is the killer? Your mind is really runnin' wild." Molly released a loud laugh. "God, I've known him for ages. He's not really the killer type, I'd say. He might be a bit of a snob at times—I mean, he does come from money—but he's not evil by any means."

"So, you don't find it a little weird that my books were there?"

"Honestly, no. I could see how with everything you just told me how your mind would go there. But as much as I don't really care for Tucker, I don't peg him as the one behind all this."

"Then who?" Charley asked. It made sense that Tucker might not be the killer after all. Who would just leave potential evidence lying about?

Molly shrugged. "That I don't know. Maybe some nut from the city who followed you out here?"

"No one knew I was coming here," Charley pointed out. "My agent is the one who arranged everything so secretly."

"People who want to know things will find a way. Do you think you're in any kind of danger?" Molly's face was etched with concern.

"My agent evidently thought so at one point. She's the one who asked the sheriff to have Nick babysit me," Charley scoffed.

"I could think of a worst babysitter, honey. And it looks like he did a damn fine job," Molly joked and it lightened the mood slightly. "Charley, everything will work out. Have a little faith, honey. I don't like seeing you all worried like this."

"I'm sorry. I guess everything is hitting me sort of all at once."

"Just stay true to your heart. If you don't want to write this book anymore, then don't. They can't force you."

"But they can sue me," Charley countered.

"Oh, come on. You're rich enough to pay off those buzzards." Molly reached across the table and patted her hand. "At least you'll be rich in love."

Charley rolled her eyes. "If only it were that simple."

* * * *

Charley peeked outside to see if Nick had returned yet. It was late and she was starting to worry. Charley let out an exhausted yawn. The moon was casting its solemn glow over the lake. Charley had returned earlier from the diner and kept her door locked. She couldn't shake her uneasiness and wanted nothing more than for Nick to come back. Charley hoped maybe he had answers to all the questions that swarmed her tired brain. She reasoned that since he had been gone all night, he surely must know something. Or maybe she'd scared him away. Perhaps all that intimacy had been too much for him. Charley was still processing it herself. It had been pretty mind-blowing, but she would be an idiot if she didn't acknowledge the sexual tension they'd been fighting since she had arrived.

She stepped away from the window and planted herself on the couch. Charley wrapped a blanket around herself in a childish attempt to keep the monsters at bay. She needed a distraction and decided to go onto her phone, where she aimlessly scrolled through her feeds on several social media sites and lost track of time. Her eyes grew heavy and she still had not heard from Nick. Maybe he regretted letting her in and sharing everything about himself. Now she knew his hurt and perhaps he feared she'd play those against him in some way. She let her mind wander into enemy territory as she created more ridiculous assumptions for his absence. Doubt ensnared her and Charley was irritable as she finally crawled into bed.

Chapter Sixteen

The small bedroom was flooded with the golden light of morning. Charley blinked hard but knew the fight was futile. Her body was stiff from the old mattress and she was beginning to miss her comfortable bed back home. Her legs were tangled in a mess of sheets that made her skin itch. After a night of tossing and turning, Charley wondered if she should just pack it up and admit defeat, that it was time to wave the white flag and seek refuge back home. It wasn't like her to just give up. She'd always had more tenacity than that.

Charley sat up in the bed and contemplated her next move. The walls felt like they were closing in and her anxiety was mounting. The air was too hot in her room and she felt short of breath as another wave crashed over her. This room had held romantic memories from yesterday but today it felt cumbersome and was the last place Charley wanted to be. She said a small prayer and tried to steady her nerves as she left the bedroom. She peeked at her phone and saw that it was early in the morning, early for her anyway. It was a tad after eight.

Charley brushed her hair and threw it up in a messy bun. She went onto autopilot as she made her coffee and raided the cupboards for anything edible. She couldn't seem to escape the trapped feeling. Charley grabbed her mug of coffee and decided she needed some clarity as she left the cabin. The air outside was cooler and was a welcomed relief. She inhaled deeply and was grateful that her lungs no longer felt as though they were coated with sticky air.

Her flip-flops were quiet on the weathered wood of the dock. Once at the end, Charley took a leisurely sip of her coffee and sighed. The vanilla and cinnamon creamer was the perfect blend of sweetness and spice. Charley looked at the dark water before her, and the morning sun danced on top the lake, creating a golden shimmer. A few boats could be seen in the distance, but the resort was silent, and for a moment, Charley felt so incredibly alone. Her mind supplied her with ample entertainment of negative thoughts and cold, leftover doubts. She shuddered and fought the tension that was trying to pull her under. Charley had come to a decision.

"Morning."

Charley jerked at the sound and her coffee splashed from her mug. The hot liquid burned her skin as it hit her legs and feet.

"God, I'm so sorry. I didn't mean scare you," Nick started to apologize.

"It's fine." She wasn't in the mood to deal with him right now. Charley wiped the coffee off herself. She carefully lowered herself towards the water to wash the stickiness from her hands and didn't hide her annoyance. With her luck she'd probably fall into the water. Nick moved closer and she could see the concern heavy in his brow.

"I wanted to stop by last night but it was so late."

"Well, I was up," she growled.

"I'm sorry, babe. I should've called you," Nick apologized but she wasn't the least bit interested to hear it. "I didn't mean to upset you."

"I don't really care. I just think it's time for me to leave," she explained in a voice she didn't recognize as her own. "It's this place. I'm just over being here, you know?"

He nodded and shoved his hands in the pockets of his jeans. "Is this because of yesterday?" His questioning glare put her at unease.

"Not really. Maybe."

How was it possible to feel like the walls were closing in on her again when there weren't any boxing her in?

He hadn't ever seen her look so miserable. Charley didn't seem like herself and Nick felt responsible. He had been eyeballs-deep in the cases the previous night. There had been several tips called in that they'd followed up on. Dead ends were all Nick had wound up with, but he had desperately hoped something would've come from them. He wanted to come back to Charley with an answer. All he wanted was to make her feel safe again.

"Baby." He reached for her hand. Nick saw her hesitate for a moment but she allowed him to grab it. "I didn't mean to put any kind of pressure or expectation on you." She looked away and avoided his eyes. "I can't explain it, especially after everything, but I'm falling for you. Hard." There... He had said it. Nick was being open and transparent with how he felt, leaving no question. This was new for him and scared him to his core.

Charley looked up at him, her sapphire eyes pools of beautiful emotion. Nick froze as he saw her waging an internal war. Charley bit her lip and turned her gaze toward the lake. She suddenly wrapped her arms tightly around his waist and yanked him to her. From the tips of her toes, she stretched up to meet him. Nick stood there, a bit surprised by her but all the same time pleased. Charley finally reached his mouth and kissed him hard. The force of the kiss almost knocked Nick back.

All his nerves caught fire as Charley assaulted his mouth with such passion and something else Nick couldn't quite read. She tasted of sweet coffee and desire. Nick couldn't get enough of her. This delicious woman was everything he wanted. It took every ounce of control he had not to swoop her up and carry her back to his cabin. Charley broke their embrace without any warning. Her cheeks were flushed, and those eyes were now overcast with lust.

"I'm sorry," she said softly.

"For what?" Nick kissed her forehead. "Charley, I promise we'll figure things out and..."

Charley held her hand up and stopped him. "Nick, I need to go. I really wish this could have worked out, but it isn't meant to be. I want to go home." Her bottom lip quivered. Charley turned and practically ran away from Nick.

He stood there watching at her jog back to her cabin and felt terribly alone. The air was gone from him. There was so much he wanted to tell her, but maybe he wasn't supposed to have a happy ending after all. His feet kept him planted and was completely frozen. *Run after her, you fool.*

* * * *

She carefully folded her clothes and placed them in her suitcase. Charley moved slowly. She wasn't in the biggest rush to leave this cabin but knew the time had come. She had spent too much time debating whether to stay or go. It's not like she was writing anyway. The previous night, Charley had been too preoccupied with matters of the heart that writing was the furthest thing in her mind. Maybe if she went home, she could hammer out the damn novel and be free. Staying here meant dealing with all that had happened here — the murders, wrestling with writer's block and falling for Nick. Charley didn't possess the coping skills necessary to carry on here. She wished someone would come to rescue her, make all the difficult decisions for her. But she realized the only knight in shining armor here was her. Charley was her own hero, and sometimes giving up was actually anything but. Charley wasn't surrendering or waving the white flag, though it seemed very much like it. She needed to go home and get herself back to normal, whatever that was these days. No one could do that for her, only herself.

Charley wiped the tears from her face as she gathered her toiletries from the bathroom and shoved them into a bag. She swept the cabin for anymore of her belongings. Would she miss this place? Charley knew she'd definitely miss Nick, but romance was the last thing Charley needed right now. Her world felt off kilter. It was like all stability had left her little world.

Making love to Nick had been wonderful and a sweet escape. Learning about him and seeing the deep hidden nooks that were full of vulnerability and broken bits made Charley want to take care of him and protect him. But Nick was stronger than her. He had overcome so much. Nick had told her yesterday morning that she had brought him out of the darkness, but he was giving her far too much credit. She was not the light he thought she was. The darkness was where she had lived for so long, and she wasn't sure light even existed anymore. The only way to ever be free from its clutches would be to finish this novel and be done.

It was living in the depths of heinous acts of monsters, a cruel existence for a soul who couldn't hurt a fly. If she were being truly honest with herself, it had taken its toll on her. It was one thing to write about it, but to see her exact descriptions showcased in front of her had proved to be too much. Lord knew she'd tried to bury all her feelings, but the guilt she harbored would probably never leave her.

Charley shoved a suitcase in her SUV, her fishing pole was laid carefully next to it, and her heart was heavy. She looked toward Nick's cabin and noticed his truck wasn't there. Charley wanted to tell him and even Ruger goodbye, though it probably would've killed her to do so. Without another thought, Charley got into her SUV and left the resort in haste. As she cruised into town, she spotted the diner and found herself parking. Charley felt as though she needed to at the very least say goodbye to Molly. Also, a chocolate milkshake would mend her broken heart.

The drive to the diner had made her heart sad. She mentally said goodbye to this place that had been home for almost two months. She parked her SUV and worked up the nerve to say farewell to one of her favorite places.

"Why so glum?" Molly asked as Charley slid into an empty booth.

"Actually, I'm leaving and wanted to stop in for one more of your amazing milkshakes."

"I'm sorry you're leaving. Was it something I said yesterday?" Molly looked incredibly sad.

"No, I just realized that nothing good was coming from me staying. If anything, Molly, you helped me sort through some of problems."

"It sure doesn't feel like it. Well, that milkshake is on the house. You want anything else?" Charley shook her head and Molly slipped her notepad back into her apron. "I'll be back in a jiff."

The diner was the busiest she had ever seen it. The lunch rush was loud and orchestrated chaos. She would miss this. Charley stared out of the window and recalled when she had first arrived, seeing cruisers fly past and her words that she had missed finally returning. It was a strange sensation. She hadn't even been there for two months, yet it felt like years. Charley was tired, emotionally drained, and knew that going home was the right decision. Molly delivered the milkshake and hurried to her other customers.

Charley tried to suck the shake, but it was too thick. She opted for a spoonful of the whip cream and savored the sweet taste.

"Well, hello, Charley."

* * * *

"I really screwed up royally, pal," Nick said to Ruger as he sat on the tailgate and crushed the can in his hand. Ruger looked up at him with concern in his soulful eyes, his wrinkles only adding to the little worried face. "I know... You miss her too."

After spending yesterday with the sheriff, they hadn't gotten any closer to figuring out who was behind the killings. Now Charley was leaving, not that he blamed her. It was a wonder that she'd stayed this long after learning of the horrific killings. Nick didn't know how to fix any of this. He felt like he'd let her down and broken his promise to catch this fucker. Nick grabbed another can and popped the top off, hoping to numb his feelings. He had driven to a field surrounded by aspen trees, their leaves rattled as a strong breeze assaulted them. He hadn't felt this familiar sense of isolation in weeks and had hoped those days were behind him. Evidently, they weren't. He was crazy to believe he deserved someone wonderful in his life but had hoped he had snuck under the universe's radar. When he was with Charley, Nick felt as though he was getting away with murder, that he had somehow tricked his way into making someone fall in love with him — to fall in love himself.

Nick had been positive he and Charley were starting something wonderful. After having made love and been brutally honest with Charley about who he truly was, Nick believed their future was cemented. He had never opened up about his childhood to anyone. Nick didn't want pity or judgment. Charley simply held him and said nothing as he drained his heart of all the stagnant emotions from the past. He knew he would never find anyone else like her but didn't know how to keep her here. Nick was more than aware that he couldn't force Charley to be with him, hold her hostage and make her love him. What could he do? His mind was empty of any solutions. This was proof that he couldn't just sneak past the universe, which was definitely out to get him.

Chapter Seventeen

"Pamela, what are you doing here?" Charley was surprised to see her agent standing next to her.

"Do you mind?" She motioned toward the empty side of the booth.

"Of course not. Please sit." Charley wrung her hands together. Her nerves were rattled at seeing her. *This can't be good.*

Pamela was dressed in pale gray-colored suit, and the soft pink scarf she wore around her neck brought out her rosy complexion. "I figured I would drop in for a visit since I hadn't received any Chapters this week. Plus, Tucker has been hounding me to come to the resort. I thought, *what a wonderful way to kill two birds.*" Pamela flagged down Molly. "May I have an iced tea?"

"Certainly," Molly answered politely as she eyed Charley. "Anything else for you?"

Pamela looked thoughtfully toward the ceiling. "I know I shouldn't, but how about some fries?"

"I'll be back with your order." Molly left them.

"So, were you just popping in for lunch? Taking a little break from writing the next bestseller?" Pamela sat upright in the booth and looked completely out of place.

"Actually, I was on my way out," Charley replied as she attempted to suck on the straw. She managed to get some of the shake this time.

"On your way out?" Pamela seemed confused. Her hazel eyes grew darker. "Meaning?"

"I was headed back home," Charley admitted. She felt like a child who had been caught sneaking out.

"And why would you be doing that? Charley, we had an agreement," Pamela said coolly.

Charley released a heavy sigh. "I know. But I don't feel like I'm being very productive here. I haven't been able to write for a few days and I felt like it was time to go home."

"And why is that?" she asked. "Is Tucker still quite the distraction?"

"No, not at all."

"Who then? That detective?"

"Nick, the one you originally hired to babysit me, remember?" Charley added with more sass than she'd intended. She sensed how angry Pamela was with her, not that she entirely blamed her. To be fair, there was a deadline approaching and Charley hadn't sent any Chapters. Of course, her agent needed to protect her investment and get things back on track.

"I wonder if our detective is doing a little more than babysitting you. So, stop with the theatrics, Charley." Pamela glared at her. "I won't beat around the bush. I'm concerned about the book."

"Which is why I feel I need to go home to finish it," Charley defended.

"Because creating distance between you and the detective is so utterly impossible? I don't believe you'll finish the novel if you go home — or at least not on time, Charley. You seem to forget that's why you were sent here."

Charley bit the inside of her cheek as she struggled with telling Pamela. "If I'm to be one hundred percent honest with you, I don't know if I want to finish this damn book," she announced.

Pamela's eyebrows rose high on her face. "That's not an option. Do you realize what is at stake here?"

Molly arrived with a plate towering with fries. "I figured you both could share."

"Thank you." Pamela waved at Molly dismissively. She then stared hard at Charley. "When I sent you here, your assignment was to finish this manuscript. It was not to roll in the sheets with the detective or try to seduce my nephew," Pamela growled.

Charley about choked as she listened to Pamela. How could she possibly know about her love affair with Nick? And seducing Tucker? What the hell was she talking about? Charley grew angrier by the second. "First off, it's none of your business. Secondly, I didn't try to seduce your nephew."

Pamela shook her head. "Truthfully, it is my business, considering I'm the one who sent you here. You had one job, to write the book."

"I don't understand why you're even talking to me like this, Pamela. You don't actually own me, and I could just hang up the towel and call it quits if I truly wanted to," Charley snapped back.

"I've been more than patient with you. I had your back when the publisher wanted to drop you after your last release. This isn't just about *your* career, Charley."

Charley felt the weight of everything crush her. "I'm sorry. You should have let me go."

"Not when there are contracts involved and money to be made," Pamela rebutted. "Look, Charley... I apologize for being gruff with you. I've been doing all the heavy lifting while you stayed holed up in your apartment writing little stories." Pamela bit into a fry and appeared to be readying for battle. "I don't feel you entirely grasp the gravity of this situation."

Charley didn't appreciate Pamela talking down to her. "Are you kidding me? Victoria explained how the publisher is pushing the date up and isn't budging on the issue. You made it crystal clear how terribly important this is, which has only added to my stress."

"You think you're the only stressed one here?"

"I realize they're probably breathing down your neck as well. But I'm the one expected to write this novel."

"Exactly. Because you, my dear, signed a contract. Have you forgotten that you agreed to these terms? That there is legal recourse in addition to the scandal this could possible cause?"

"Pamela, I don't know what else to tell you except I will get the remaining Chapters to you. I can't guarantee they won't be total shit, but I can promise you they will be the last that I ever give you." Charley scooted out of the booth and threw a twenty-dollar bill on the table. Pamela's face was scrunched with anger. In all the years they had worked together, there hadn't been one time that Pamela had ever talked to her this way. Charley was livid as she left the restaurant.

Once inside her SUV, Charley felt something stab her and reached into her pocket. "Shit," she said out loud. The key to the cabin. She would need to return it to the lodge. It dawned on her she'd left something else very important behind. She beat her hands on the steering wheel and cursed under her breath. *Can this day get any better?*

* * * *

What did he really have to lose? After sobering up, Nick drove back to the resort. He needed to talk some sense into Charley. She was too special for him to allow her to get away. Being with her was like breathing under water. It seemed impossible and an incredible feat, but it was amazing and downright magical. It had been difficult for a cynic like himself to believe anything this good was possible. Nick loved her and she needed to know that. He was willing to risk everything to make sure she knew.

The advantage of being a cop was that your buddies don't pull you over when you were racing down the highway. The sky was the color of cotton candy with wispy pink clouds strewn over perfect blue. In the distance there was a patch of gray clouds moving in. Nick drove through the sleepy town with a mission. He steered toward the resort and spotted her SUV in its usual space. He parked and Ruger hopped out and bounded for Charley.

"Charley," Nick called out to her as he jumped out of the truck. She turned and he could see she had been crying. The skin around her eyes was swollen and rimmed with red. But she was still as beautiful as ever to Nick. "What's wrong?" Nick rushed to her.

"Everything," she answered as he gathered her in his arms. She let her head rest on his chest, and he savored the feeling of her. In their short time apart, he had already missed this.

"Look… I know everything seems messed up right now," Nick started.

"You have no idea." Charley pushed back and the tears in his eyes broke her heart. "Pamela is in town."

"Your agent?" Nick was confused as he studied the worry on Charley's face.

"Yes. She surprised me at the diner," she explained. Charley went on to tell Nick how their conversation had gone, how she'd forgotten to turn in her key and had left her laptop, of all things, behind. It was evident to Nick that the universe might not only be out to get him.

"See? It was meant to be. You aren't supposed to leave yet. A little divine intervention." Nick reached for her hands. "There's so much I need to tell you."

"I really just want to get my laptop and go home."

"Fine, then I'm coming with you," Nick said firmly. Ruger stood on his hind legs and stretched on Charley's legs.

"You can't be serious," Charley replied.

"Completely."

"Oh, Nick," she whispered.

"Besides it's already getting late and we should talk. What if you stayed with me tonight?" he offered. Nick needed to buy himself some time to convince her that they should be together.

She knew she should decline his offer, but Charley was too exhausted and angry to be driving. She knew the statistics of what happens when one drives when upset or tired. Spending the night with Nick would probably only add to her problems, but Charley couldn't deny the comfort she felt in his arms.

"We can leave in the morning, okay? I want us to talk and see if we can figure this all out," Nick said.

Charley shook her head. "I honestly don't know what to do anymore."

Nick kissed her on the top of her head. "I don't either, but whatever it is, I only want to do it with you."

Deep down that was exactly how she felt too. It was fear that was devouring her. Was it crazy to think that maybe this was actually meant to be? Why was it that she kept ending up in Nick's arms? She was tired of being wishy-washy. Charley wanted things to be easy and not to have to think about the *what ifs*. She cared about Nick and there was no denying they seemed to share some special connection. If she had to pick any guy to be stuck running around in this nightmare with, it would be Nick.

"Let's go back to my cabin and sort some of this crazy shit out." Nick linked his fingers with hers and gave her hand a gentle reassuring squeeze.

"Let me get my laptop and see if I left anything else behind."

"Want me to come with you?" Nick offered.

Charley shook her head. "No, I'm good. I'll come over to your cabin in a bit."

"How about I run to the store and grab us some food and drinks for tonight?"

Charley smiled at the sweet gesture. "That works." Nick hugged her again before getting inside his truck. Charley watched him drive off and headed inside her cabin. She felt a tiny light of hope spark inside of her as she went to retrieve her stuff. Her laptop was exactly where she'd left it. She moved past it and decided to stretch out on the couch to rest her eyes for a little bit. They were raw and sore. The beginning of a headache was starting to hammer her tired brain. Charley snuggled into the couch and felt herself drift off.

The sensation of being watched penetrated the odd dream she was having and forced Charley awake. Pamela was seated on the coffee table, with her legs elegantly crossed. Her suit didn't have a single wrinkle and her expensive pumps shone.

"What are you doing here?" Charley shot up into a sitting position. She felt vulnerable and confused.

"I came here to make sure you finish what you started."

Charley stared hard at her and studied Pamela's eyes. There was definitely something off about all this. "I think you need to leave. There's really nothing left for us to discuss. My attorney will be in touch."

"That won't be necessary. There's plenty for us to discuss now," Pamela retorted as she drew a small pistol from her back and pointed it at Charley.

"What in the actual hell?" Charley screamed as she scurried into the corner of the couch. "Have you lost your damn mind, Pamela?"

"Desperate times call for desperate measures, as the old cliché goes. I've been more than patient with you, Charley." Pamela rose slowly, the gun pointed directly at Charley. "I gave you ample opportunity to complete this project, and I've gone out of my way to help you with this writer's block you've been suffering from. You've done nothing but squander that."

Charley's brain sputtered every possible scenario that could come of this situation. None were going to end well if she didn't play this right. Fear burrowed its way into her heart as she thought that this could be the end of her life. It was true that her entire life flashed before her. Charley could see glimpses of her childhood. The faces of her parents and siblings became clearer than ever before. She closed her eyes and let the images burn into her brain. They would be devasted at the news of her death. Nick appeared in her mind. *Where is he?* He'd blame himself for this. The idea of a bullet penetrating her frightened her more than she'd ever imagined. Sure, she had seen gunshot victims, but the idea of that metal ripping through her body ignited a new fear. *Pain.*

"So, here's what's going to happen," Pamela explained. "First, you're going to finish this novel. Here." Charley remained frozen on the couch. She didn't dare argue with Pamela, who opened the laptop and pointed at the empty seat. "The sooner you finish, the sooner this will all be over, Charley."

* * * *

After grabbing three burgers from the diner, a case of beer, dessert and flowers from the grocery store, Nick drove back to the resort. He anxiously drummed his fingers on the steering wheel of his truck. His hope was to get Charley to see reason. He'd screwed up a lot in his life and didn't want to make a mess of things with her. He felt as though this might be his last chance. The resort came into sight and Nick began to grow nervous. The tall pines cradled what was left of the sun. The lake moved in a steady motion as gentle waves slapped at the rocky shore. Those clouds he'd seen earlier seemed to have vanished and all seemed calm. He took that as a good omen and released a grateful sigh. Everything was going to be all right. It was as if the universe was finally sending out a positive cosmic message and Nick was happy to receive it.

He pulled into the resort and passed by the lodge. Nick snickered as he looked at the luxurious building. The thought of Tucker thinking he could have Charley almost made him laugh out loud. *Let him try.* Charley was a girl worth fighting for, and he'd love for Tucker to challenge him. Nick parked the truck at his usually spot and headed to his cabin. He put the sack of food on the table and the case of beer in the fridge. He supposed he should tidy his tiny bachelor pad up before Charley came over. Nick grabbed a trash bag and started to dispose of the empty beer cans that littered the small space. He recited in his mind what he planned on saying to Charley. Ruger danced underfoot and seemed more excited than ever. "You need to be a good boy when she comes over, okay?" Nick advised sweetly.

When the cabin was cleaned, Nick waited as patiently as a man on a mission could. He looked at the time and decided to go over to her cabin if she didn't arrive soon. Maybe she had fallen asleep. The poor girl had looked like hell—still beautiful to him but absolutely drained.

He looked out of the window and saw that her SUV was still there. He'd worried for a brief second that maybe she'd fled again. The food was getting cold, and Ruger was growing anxious. Nick opened the cabin door and felt a strong breeze hit him. So much for the perfect weather. The lake looked angry as the dark water now violently slapped the shore. Dark clouds were devouring the calm sky. He could smell raining coming, hurried next door and knocked at her door.

"You will answer that door and tell whoever it is to go away," Pamela instructed.

Charley had been sitting in front of her laptop with a gun pointed at her from the couch. She was so utterly rattled, and her hands kept trembling as she tried to type. Charley knew it was probably Nick at the door. Now seeing how crazy Pamela was, she didn't dare risk telling Nick she was in trouble. Charley worried Pamela might kill them both.

She slowly pulled the door back. There stood her handsome Nick, clueless of the dangerous situation inside.

"Hey, I was getting worried about you. You ready? I got food," Nick announced happily.

"I'm not feeling that well after all. I think I'm going to nap," Charley lied carefully. The nose of the pistol was wedged into her ribs as Pamela stayed out of Nick's sight.

"I thought we were going to talk," Nick pressed with a sexy and hopeful smile.

"Nick, please." Her voice cracked. She tried to keep her composure but if he didn't leave soon, they both were going to be killed. "My head really hurts and I just want to rest."

Nick studied her and she feared he suspected something. Pamela poked her hard and Charley knew she desperately needed Nick to leave.

"I guess I can't force you out," Nick replied, the disappointment evident in his voice. It nearly broke Charley 's heart.

"Unless you got a warrant," she teased nervously. Pamela prodded her more forcefully and Charley had to bite down on her lip to avoid letting out a whimper.

"Maybe I have probable cause," he joked as he kissed her cheek. Nick frowned. "You sure you don't want to come over? You could rest there."

Charley could only manage a slight nod and fought tears that were threatening to bubble to surface. "I love you, Nick." She couldn't believe how the words had tumbled out of her mouth with ease. The shocked expression on his handsome face would forever be locked in her mind. Her soul must have felt the need to tell him, just in case she never got the chance again.

"I love you too," he said — and he left.

Though he was going back to his cabin without her, his heart was full. They had said those three magic words. At first, he didn't think she'd really said them. He'd figured his ears had played a vicious trick on him. The sincere and almost frightened tone in which she'd said them had hit him so hard that he didn't hesitate repeating it back to her. He wanted to hold and kiss her but there was like an invisible force-field keeping them apart. Nick couldn't quite understand exactly what it was. He would probably spend the remainder of the night trying to figure it out instead of riding on the high that Charley loved him. Nick reached his porch and paused to gaze out at the water. The water slapped hard against the shore and pine needles fell as the wind whipped faster through the trees. There hadn't been any storms since he'd moved there. In some ways it seemed fitting, everything considered.

The small cabin shook as the wind continued to beat against it. Rain now pelted the metal roof, creating a loud ruckus that had Ruger hiding under the covers on the bed. Nick was stretched out and trying to soothe his very frightened pup. He couldn't dismiss the irony of how the day had played out. Nick should be spending the night with Charley, discussing their future and making love. Instead, he was here alone with his pug. His eyes grew heavy and his body gave in to the exhaustion.

He wasn't sure how long he'd been asleep, but the knock at the door jolted him awake. The cabin was mostly dark now, except for a small lamp in the living room. Nick felt around in the bed for Ruger and couldn't find him. "Ruger," Nick called for him. He could hear a soft growl in the other room. Nick left the bed, grabbed his gun and carefully walked to the door. Ruger bared his teeth and stood in an aggressive stance. Nick waited for another knock and opened the door cautiously. He was hopeful it was Charley, but Ruger wouldn't act this way if it were. He gripped his gun and opened the door enough to see who it was. *Tucker. What in the hell does he want?* Nick was tempted to point the gun at Tucker but thought better of it.

"Can I come in? We need to talk."

* * * *

She stared at the screen of her laptop while Pamela kept the gun trained on her. It had only been a couple of hours but it felt like an eternity. This was pure hell. Her nerves were fried and Charley prayed harder than she'd ever prayed before.

"You're making this far more difficult than it needs to be," Pamela accused from the couch.

"How do you expect me to write when you have a gun on me?"

"Need I remind you that it didn't have to be this way." Her arrogant tone pissed Charley off.

"This is ridiculous, Pamela," Charley spouted angrily. "I can't believe you'd ever do anything like this."

"I wouldn't have to hold you hostage if you'd just finish the damn novel. You were too busy fooling around with that detective and not putting in the work. When you first got here and sent me that Chapter, I felt like we had finally beat that terrible writer's block of yours," Pamela explained. "Your writing was fantastic. Better than anything else you've written."

"If you let me go, I'll write the novel," Charley begged from the chair.

Pamela let out a sinister laugh. "You know the deal. Finish the book and you'll be set free." There was something in the way she said it that spooked Charley. Why would Pamela even let her go? Of course, Charley would run right to Nick, and Pamela had no intention of letting her leave alive.

* * * *

Nick ran his hands through his hair and tried to make sense of what Tucker had just told him.

"I thought it was crazy too."

"You knew she was here?" Nick asked. Ruger eyed Tucker suspiciously and never left his station at Nick's feet.

"Yes. She doesn't seem like herself, though. I saw her at my desk the other morning and she had Charley's books all laid out. It just seemed really strange to me."

"She ran into Charley at the diner. From the way Charley described it, it was a complete disaster."

Tucker shrugged. "Maybe she's just stressed out because of this book. Charley hasn't exactly been a ray of sunshine lately. I guess there's a lot of pressure in the publishing business."

Nick smiled at the thought of Charley giving Tucker the cold shoulder. It had only been hours earlier that she had told Nick she loved him. He was feeling pretty confident about where they stood in their relationship.

"Do you think my Aunt Pam could have anything to do with these murders?" Tucker asked nervously. Nick could see a few beads of sweat glisten on Tucker's forehead and he seemed uneasy as he broached the question.

"Did she say something to indicate that?"

Tucker hesitated. "I mean, not really. But when we talked about the lady who was murdered here, it was like she already knew exactly what had happened. She mentioned details I hadn't shared with her."

"What kind of details?"

Tucker made a disgusted face. "That lipstick smudge on the lady's forehead. I'm not sure how my aunt would know about that. I certainly didn't tell her."

Nick's brain went into full-on detective mode. He started to consider Pamela's motives. What he couldn't understand was why Pamela had chosen now of all times to show up. Had she been in the area during the murders? It didn't make much sense. "The first murder was well over a month ago, and do you know if she was the area around that time?"

"No, I think she was actually somewhere in New York with one of her other authors. She arrived barely two days ago," Tucker supplied. "Granted, I wasn't exactly expecting her, but I've also been hounding her for a visit." Tucker rose from his place. "I think I'm

302

going to head back now. Maybe I was wrong for coming here. I'm sure she has nothing to do with any of this." Tucker appeared anxious. "She's a nice lady, Nick."

Nick nodded. "If you can think of anything else, just let me know." Nick shook his hand as Tucker started out of the door.

Tucker looked Nick straight in the eyes. "Take care of Charley. She's special." It was an unspoken treaty. He hadn't expected any of that from Tucker, especially his last words. At least Tucker knew he was out of the running now and he'd handled it like a gentleman. Nick respected that.

Chapter Eighteen

I watch as the last customer leaves and she smiles sweetly as they exit. Her grin is wide and happy, but there's exhaustion in her eyes. My guts twist inside of me but I know what must be done. It almost pains me to do this. This lady was so very nice to me earlier. This is all her fault. She has put us in a peculiar position. I gave her back the inspiration she had been missing for so long. I fixed her. She wasn't strong enough to do it on her own. I've been watching her more closely. Her time is being wasted with the detective and chatting with this lady. She should have been writing.

I enter the building quietly and am met with a confused and slightly irritated expression.

"Hello again."

Please don't speak. That makes all that I have to do much harder. She is not part of the plan but is now a necessary deed.

"We're just closed, darlin'." Her words twang sweetly as I approach closer.

The lighting is dim all around us and the restaurant is still warm from all the meals cooked. I can smell the residue of burgers, patty melts and fries hanging in the air between us. I'm queasy as I grip the blade firmly in my sweaty palm. She tosses a white dish rag on the counter with annoyance and comes from behind it.

"Here... I'll let you out."

I move swiftly and close my eyes as I plunge the knife into her belly. She screams as she attempts to push me off her but I keep my stance firm as I dig the blade deeper. I embrace her as she claws at my arms. Despite her will, we find ourselves tangled together in some kind of boxer's ballet. We're both sweaty and exhausted. She clings to me, in shock and bleeding onto the checkered floor. Her apron is soaked through, the crimson color shiny and glistening in the peaceful lighting. She is gasping in my ear and I wait for her to accept what is happening. The weight of her slips out of my tired arms and she falls onto the floor. I crouch above her and stare into her eyes. Her faraway expression is haunting, more so than any of the others. I snatch her hair up in my hand and aim for her throat. I slice through her skin and find the muscle and meat difficult to carve. I struggle to cut along her neck to free her head from her body. Charley had made this out to be a lot easier in her story. The meat is tough, like an overdone steak. The blade gets caught and my hand hurts. The blood from her belly has made the handle slippery. I am near her nape when I hear a pop. It's the air escaping her or maybe her soul. I can see Charley's words as I hold my prize over its body.

My eyes connect with her and she smiles approvingly at me from the corner. I feel my body tremble with rage, pride and a hollowness that hasn't been there before. The blend of weakness and power makes my guts sick. In a different reality, I'm not sure I'd be doing any of this. I walk past her with a new feeling of resentment. My fingers are laced through bloody blonde hair and I almost feel disconnected from myself as I walk away.

Chapter Nineteen

The ropes dug into her skin and caused a burn like she'd never felt before. Charley had spent the last hour trying to wiggle her way out. Pamela had tied her up and informed her that she would return shortly. Charley worked on the knots and her skin was sore and raw from her efforts. She cried out in frustration. *Why do movies make escaping look so damn easy?* Charley hadn't managed to even loosen the rope even a tiny bit. She continued to struggle in hopes that she might somehow become magically free. This was a nightmare. She had all this time to escape and couldn't. The mental torment was almost too much to bear. Charley paused when she heard voices outside the door.

The door opened and a large man entered. She didn't recognize him at first. Charley couldn't contain her scream or confusion when she spotted what he carried. His face was solemn as he walked toward her desk and released his grip. It gently rolled in front of her. Charley couldn't tear her eyes away, bile immediately rose to the back of her throat and she felt faint. It became difficult to control her breathing as panic washed over her.

Pamela stood next to Charley and stroked her hair. Her perfect suit had blood splattered all over it. "I believe you've met my husband before." Pamela smiled proudly. "He has been working tirelessly to help you. Haven't you, dear?"

The man smiled sheepishly but there was a cold darkness about him. Charley closed her eyes and prayed that this was one enormous nightmare she would soon wake from. She blinked hard and reopened her eyes to find Molly's head still on the table, staring back at her, the pain forever frozen on Molly's pale face. Dry crusted blood clung to the uneven, carved skin. How could anyone be this utterly cruel? Charley squeezed her lips tightly but the vomit forced its way out of her mouth and spewed all over her. Charley thought she might choke. Her eyes stinged as tears streamed from them.

"Oh, now you're making a complete mess of yourself," Pamela complained. "Dear, can you bring me that dish towel over there?" Her husband quickly did what he'd been told. He avoided Charley's stare.

She was too paralyzed to move. There was no possible way any of this could be happening right now.

Pamela began to wipe Charley's face clean of vomit. "I think we need to have a little chat, dear," Pamela said in an exasperated tone.

"I have nothing to say to you, you awful bitch," Charley spat as she strained against the rope.

"Let's not be so vile." Pamela moved to the couch. Her husband followed her after he repositioned

Charley to face them. He loosened the ropes slightly and whispered an apology to her. His hot breath against her ear almost made her vomit again. She was repulsed by the very sight of these monsters.

"I think we need to start from the beginning." Pamela began to unfold the most horrific tale Charley had ever heard. Pamela didn't spare any of the graphic details of the murders committed. Pamela hadn't killed one soul, but her hands were soaked with their blood. She had orchestrated it all. Her husband was simply a pawn in her evil game, though Charley could see his eyes light up as Pamela recounted each murder in detail, singing his praises. He ate up the compliments like an affection-starved animal. It was pathetic.

Charley's stomach went sour as she learned Pamela's thought process. She truly believed this would motivate Charley in some sick way. "We did this for you. We wanted to inspire you, to remind you of the amazing work you've done," Pamela said sweetly with a crazy glint in her eye as she patted her husband's knee. "It was awful seeing you struggle the way you were. You were like a lost little puppy who needed our guidance to find your way back."

This was a scene straight out of an insane horror novel—Pamela's soiled suit, casual talk of brutal murders and the loving smiles exchanged between the husband and wife. Charley wouldn't be surprised if Pamela had offered to make them tea next. Her smile was full of pity, but then not a second later her face morphed into one of pure disgust. "But you just tossed our commitment to you back in our faces like a spoiled brat. You only think of yourself. It's rather selfish, if you ask me."

Charley didn't even know how to respond. She wanted to end this nightmare, but no matter how hard she tried, she couldn't think straight. She was the writer here, but her brain was stalled for inspiration. Charley wasn't able to wrap her mind around this entire wicked situation.

Something caught Pamela's attention as she turned her gaze to the small window. "Is that Tucker leaving the detective's cabin?" She shot up from the couch.

Then an awful thought hit her. What if Tucker had a part in this as well? Nothing else could possibly surprise her. A family of psychos on a murdering spree would be completely normal at this point and now he'd just left Nick's cabin. Had he killed him? Charley's heart splintered at the very thought.

"Dear, we have to deal with him."

"Pam, please, no," her husband implored. "He doesn't have a clue about any of this."

"What reason would he have to pay the detective a visit? He might be on to us. We can't have any loose ends," Pamela explained in an icy voice. Her husband slouched in defeat. "We're going to have to deal with this one eventually." She motioned toward Charley. "This has become more complicated than it needed to be." Pamela glared at her. "All thanks to you."

Charley began to cry, learning that Tucker was actually innocent in all of this and that Nick was still alive. She didn't know what they planned to do to Tucker but she prayed they showed him mercy. He was their nephew, after all.

Her thoughts went to Nick. She feared they would be after him next. She felt hopeless as everything went through her mind. Charley knew the grim reality of her situation. There wasn't much chance of escaping here with her life, either. She was beginning to accept her fate as Pamela walked up to Charley with the gun present in her hand. She raised it toward Charley and everything went black.

* * * *

It is as though my heart has been crumpled into a messy wad inside my chest. Discarded and forgotten, I watch as Pamela, my beautiful wife, takes my nephew's life. She doesn't hesitate as she shoots. There is a darkness and trained precision I have never seen in her before. I close my eyes and will everything to go back to how it was before — before she'd decided this was the way it all needed to be.

I own my part in this. Being in the same room as Charley sparked a completely different feeling than I had anticipated. I felt ashamed when I gave her that woman's head. She didn't deserve this. None of them had. Pamela had insisted that it was the only way. I feel the beast claw inside of me. I envision snapping Pamela's neck, and I can almost feel the pleasure of her bones breaking. I'm instantly consumed with guilt. The torment is alive in me. I deserve this punishment. I could blame Pamela for awakening the monster inside me, but the truth is that it was there long before she was in my life. It lay dormant, waiting for the opportunity to do its bidding. She'd simply disturbed the sleeping beast and unleashed it. She'd lit the path for it to embark on this journey when the time was right. They had both needed me. I was simply the vessel.

I hear Pamela order me to follow her. I can't seem to pull myself away as I watch the crimson pool around Tucker's head grow, saturating the carpet with its rich color. Images from his childhood play in my mind and I begin to weep, his life staining the fabric as I try to leave his body. Anger simmers just below the surface as I attempt to hush the beast. Pamela calls my name again, annoyance present in her voice. I remind myself that she knows best.

* * * *

It still didn't make much sense to Nick. He feared that perhaps Tucker was trying to throw him off the scent. What if Tucker was actually the killer? As much as Nick disliked him, he didn't take Tucker for much of a murderer. The man who had committed these crimes had to be a big son of a bitch. Nick reviewed his notes from each crime scene to see if he could make heads or tails of it. Nothing added up or pointed him in the direction he'd hoped. With too many unanswered questions, he decided to head to the lodge to follow up with Tucker. He wanted to get a look around and see if maybe something would jump out at him. Nick grabbed his holster and a jacket. He knew it was still pouring buckets out there. Ruger was under the covers again hiding from the storm. What a night this had turned out to be. Maybe if Charley's light was on, he'd check on her.

"Hold down the fort, Ruger," Nick ordered his pug as he shut the door.

The wind whipped at his face as he pulled his jacket tighter. The temp was warmer than he'd expected. The rain had slowed some, but the path leading to the lodge was muddy and slick. As he passed Charley's cabin, he saw that the cabin seemed quiet and dark. He hoped she was getting rest and feeling better. Nick planned on surprising her first thing in the morning with coffee and breakfast. Maybe they could spend the day in bed. He'd love to hear her scream his name again. That was the sexiest sound next to the sweet moans that had escaped her pretty mouth when they were making love. Damn, how he wished tonight had gone differently. What he would give to have her in his bed right now.

He steered his mind back to his mission and continued on. Nick saw the lights were on at the lodge. The large structure looked like an ominous beacon in the darkness. Nick shook off any water on him before entering. "Tucker," he called out, "I thought of a couple more questions." Nick walked around the lobby and waited for a response. He eyed the creepy taxidermy. He had never been interested in hunting animals. It was the human variety he hunted. "Tucker, man, where are you?"

Nick decided to check things out while he had the chance...a little investigating while the opportunity presented itself. He didn't see anything out of order in the lobby. The furniture was even dust free. Everything appeared clean and in its proper place. Nick wandered past the counter and saw the books strewn out on the desk, just as Tucker had described earlier. Nick reached into his pocket for a glove. He carefully looked at the books and some of the papers on the desk. There were mostly invoices and nothing of interest. Nick ventured farther down the hall that led him into living quarters. It was dimly lit but seemed just as orderly. Nick continued to look around. As he rounded the corner, he stopped in his tracks. Before him was an enormous pool of blood and Tucker was face-down in it.

"Shit."

The killer had been there and must've seen Tucker coming from Nick's cabin. He needed to act quickly. Nick searched his pockets to call this in and discovered he hadn't brought his cell phone with him. He needed to radio the station from his truck. Questions whirled around in his mind. How had he not heard any gunshots? He reasoned the loud wind must have filtered them.

He was fueled with adrenaline as he jogged to his truck. Nick threw open his door and grabbed the receiver to get in touch with dispatch. He was able to get in contact, though the storm was making it difficult to relay the message that he needed backup. Nick decided to get his phone then he'd check on Charley. When he reached his porch, he noticed his door was slightly ajar. Nick reached for his weapon as he slowly entered. There on the couch was a woman tightly gripping Ruger. A giant of a man stood protectively behind her. Ruger began to wiggle like a crazed demon once he saw Nick. His eyes were wild as he bucked and scratched. Ruger managed to free himself from the woman's grasp and ran straight to Nick. Nick wanted nothing more than to scoop up his little buddy and calm him, but something about this scene filled Nick with dread. Nick steadied his aim.

"I wouldn't do that if I were you," the woman said. She aimed a pistol in his direction. "So, Detective, you couldn't just leave well enough alone."

"I have no idea what you're talking about. Ma'am, you need to lower your weapon." Nick's instruction was met with a laugh.

"Not a chance," she retorted. "You see, we had a simple plan, and it would seem you assisted in ruining everything," she spat. "Why couldn't you just do your job?"

Nick realized this must be Pamela, who'd insisted on him being Charley's bodyguard for the duration of her stay. He hadn't figured out who the large man was yet. Maybe some kind of sad-looking henchman? Did he have tears in his eyes? Were they responsible for Tucker's death? Fear crawled all over him as he thought of Charley. Had they killed her too? He didn't know what he'd do if she were gone. He'd lay down his life for Charley. He needed to get control over this situation then he could rescue her. Nick said a silent prayer asking God to keep her safe until he could get to her.

"Instead, you decided to distract our little author," Pamela continued as she waved the pistol in the air. "I only needed her to write this novel. My job and reputation were on the line. Did she tell you that?" Pamela was seething. "Probably not… She's a selfish, ungrateful little bitch."

Nick's anger boiled as this woman insulted Charley but he kept his focus.

"What did Tucker say when he was here earlier? Because of you, he's dead now."

A confession.

"Put the gun down," Nick attempted to reason with her. "We can work this all out." He wanted to deescalate the situation as quickly as possible. His finger rested on the trigger like the trained professional he was. Adrenaline flooded his veins while he remained in control. He focused his breathing and kept his eyes trained on them. Nick needed to wait for his shot, because it didn't appear that this woman was going to go down without a fight.

* * * *

She heard a loud bang somewhere in the dark corner of her mind. She was confused where it had come from. Had she just been shot? Was it thunder? Maybe she hadn't heard anything at all. Her head ached and her vision was slightly blurred as Charley opened her eyes. For a moment, Charley had no idea where she was. Her arms were stiff and sore. As she attempted to move, she realized she was bound. Hazy bits began to come back to her. *Pamela. A gun.* Charley turned toward the table—Molly's head. That hadn't been a nightmare. Charley screamed and began to thrash about in her chair. Soon the ropes loosened around her and she was free. Her legs were slightly numb and clumsy as she raced for the door to escape. She needed to get to Nick. She instantly remembered Pamela and her husband were going after Tucker. Charley prayed she could stop them somehow. Maybe Nick could radio for help. She hoped Nick was safe.

When she opened the door of the cabin, she was greeted with wind and complete darkness. The only illumination was from the porch lights. Charley moved as quickly as she could but stumbled along the way. Anger fueled her small journey to Nick's cabin. She spotted his truck and suddenly her feet went out from underneath her. She fought getting back up. The mud was slippery as Charley tried to get her footing. Everything felt as though it were in slow motion. A loud sound erupted, and Charley ducked. *Nick.* With renewed energy, Charley raced onto his porch.

His patience had worn thin. "I'm not going to ask you again."

The man moved swiftly from behind the couch and pulled a knife from his waistband. Nick pulled the trigger and fired. The man went down hard from the shot. Another shot exploded and Nick felt a sharp sensation burn through his shoulder. It was a searing pain like nothing he'd ever experienced before. He stared at Pamela, who was now standing with the pistol trained on him. Nick slunk down against the wall, barely able to hold his gun.

"What have you done?" Pamela screamed as she raced toward the man. "You killed my husband, you rotten bastard." Tears steaked her shocked face and Pamela aimed her pistol once again at him. Her eyes darted past Nick, and he looked to find Charley. A brief moment of relief coursed through him, followed by fear and the realization of the grim situation they were in. He noticed a dark bruise near her eye. She was covered in mud, and looked petrified—but she was alive.

The sound echoed in her brain and hurt her ears. There was no mistaking it this time. That had definitely been a gunshot. She rushed through Nick's door without any hesitation and saw Pamela standing with a gun pointed at Nick. *Am I too late?* Her gaze moved to Nick, who was slumped against the wall and bleeding. He also had a gun, which was trained on Pamela. Charley saw Pamela's husband on the floor, then her eyes connected with a pair of very scared eyes. Ruger cowered under a table. It was as though time had frozen. She saw the man she loved injured and helpless. Knowing that Pamela was only seconds away from killing him ripped through her soul. Could she save him? Charley ran full speed at Pamela, knocking her to the floor.

After all these years, Charley never would have imagined Pamela would betray her and cause this much hurt. She had considered her family and had worked hard for this woman. All her rage and frustration shot out from her fists as she began to punch Pamela. It was as though she were in a tunnel, her sight narrow and focused. Her body didn't feel like her own as it moved with a strength and speed she didn't recognize. She felt like a spectator in all of this.

He managed to push himself up the wall as he watched Charley tackle Pamela. Pamela lost her grip on her pistol, and Nick seized the opportunity, kicking it away from her reach. Charley, in a crazed fit, was beating Pamela. Nick feared Charley might actually kill her. The sound her fists connecting to Pamela's face and chest echoed loudly in the room. The disturbing sound of knuckles pummeling bone and tissue caused Nick to wince. The sheer animalistic anger that came from Charley perfumed the air — a mixture of sweat, blood and hate.

The sound of sirens wailed in the distance and flooded Nick with hope, as he knew help would soon arrive. Nick had learned a few things that night — getting shot fucking hurt and he loved Charley even more than he thought possible. He wasn't certain he was going to make it out alive. If it hadn't been for Charley, he would be dead. She was stronger than he'd ever given her credit for and had survived whatever torture they must have inflicted on her. The very thought made him sick.

The sheriff soon entered the cabin with his gun drawn. "You okay, Capra?" the sheriff asked with genuine concern as he eyed Nick's bleeding shoulder.

"I know you probably didn't think your message got through to dispatch, but we tried to hurry, son."

Nick nodded at the two deputies raced in. One quickly pulled a flailing Charley from Pamela, who sat on the floor looking like a defeated boxer, bleeding with a swollen face. He could see the shadowy bruises claiming her face. Charley was handcuffed and placed on the couch as the deputy desperately tried to calm her down.

Unsure if the crazy-looking and filthy creature resisting the deputy could possibly be the famous author, the sheriff asked with hesitation, "Is that Vanderberg?"

"The one and only," Nick answered proudly.

"I hardly recognized her. I didn't think she'd be much of a fighter either." He walked toward the man Nick had shot. "What in the hell happened here?" The sheriff was taking in the scene. "This our killer? Or is it that one? Nothing would surprise me at this point." He pointed to a now-handcuffed Pamela.

"She killed Tucker. Her husband begged her not to. Her husband killed all those other innocent people, but Pamela made him do it," Charley yelled from the couch. "It's all her fault."

Even with her being covered in mud and blood, Charley was beautiful. "As you've probably guessed, that's Pamela, Charley's agent," Nick supplied as his shoulder throbbed.

"Oh, we know her and her husband." The sheriff shook his head in disbelief. "We know the Mansfields pretty well around here. I just can't believe they had a hand in anything like this."

"I'm just glad it's over. I think we have a pretty clear-cut case here." Nick's heart broke as he watched her struggle with her arms behind her back. "Is it really necessary to cuff her? She's lucky to even be alive. Shit, she saved my sorry ass."

The sheriff nodded. "Go ahead and uncuff her," he ordered the deputy. The sheriff looked closer at Nick and laughed. "I guess it's a good thing she was here to protect you."

Nick nodded in agreement and wanted nothing more than to hold her.

She winced as they uncuffed her, her skin raw and sore. Charley immediately ran to Nick. She needed to touch him, to know that he was really all right and to know that this nightmare was finally over. As she circled her arms around his waist, Charley looked up at him as she tried to hold in everything she felt. Nick was bleeding and his face couldn't hide the pain he was in, but that didn't stop him from kissing her. She felt that familiar sensation of the world pausing again. This man had the ability to stop time while sending a sexual electrical current through her. Charley focused on the unique connection they shared and knew Nick was the only one who had ever made her feel this way. He would be the only man who could piss her off and make her fall helplessly in love at the same time.

"I thought I was too late," Charley whispered. "I thought they'd killed you too." A flood of emotions bubbled to the surface and she couldn't stop the torrent of tears.

"Turns out I was the one who needed a bodyguard," Nick joked as he kissed her on top of her head. "You ever consider a career in the MMA? My God, you kicked her ass! Remind me never to piss you off."

"Hey, I warned you from the beginning not to mess with me." They both laughed nervously.

Ruger whimpered and Charley picked up his chubby body. He was shaking badly as he licked her face. "You poor baby," she cooed and hugged him tightly.

"I thought I was supposed to be getting all the attention. I guess I have some competition now," Nick teased as Charley tried to calm the scared pup.

The EMT walked inside and took a quick look at Nick's wound. He then escorted Nick outside to the ambulance. Charley followed closed behind with Ruger in her arms. It had finally stopped raining and the wind had died. The storm in many ways had passed. A small crowd was huddled together watching them as they exited the cabin.

Nick was instructed to sit at the back at the ambulance. She wanted to stay close to him and refused to leave his side. Charley watched as a gurney was wheeled past them. She was grateful it wasn't for either of them. Her gaze shifted to the police lights down at the lodge. The red and blue glow reflected off the water and her heart sank. It brought Charley pure joy as Pamela was led out and put in the back of the police cruiser. At least tonight one monster had been destroyed and another would be locked away. She would make sure justice was served and that Pamela wouldn't see the light of day again.

Charley leaned against the ambulance and she lost control of her emotions. She sucked in the warm, moist air and tried to steady her racing heart. Her body shook as another wave slammed into her. It was finally all over, but would she ever be okay? That was a question she wasn't entirely sure she knew the answer to. She was alive but had she lost Nick, Charley might not have ever recovered from that. All the awful thoughts that ravaged her mind were quieted once she felt Nick next to her. Charley let herself fall into him and she relaxed slightly. She was utterly exhausted and physically and emotionally spent. Charley wanted nothing more to be in a warm bed with him.

"I'm sorry," Nick whispered sadly as he kissed the top of her head.

"Why?" Charley looked up at him in confusion. She could see tears in his eyes.

"Did you mean what you said earlier? Because the way you said it, I should have known something was wrong. I feel like I failed you, Charley. I should have protected you." Nick looked away.

Charley didn't pause. She replied, "Yes, I did very much mean it." She reached for his handsome face and pulled him gently back to her. "Nick, I was scared. I didn't want anything to happen to you, but I wanted you to know." She couldn't look at him. Charley had feared she was going to die. "I think I've been in love with you a lot longer than I wanted to admit."

"I know. Well, actually I think your parents knew first." Nick dipped down and pressed his forehead to hers.

"They kind of did, didn't they? Let's not tell them, though. They'll never let us live that down."

They both laughed, and for a split second, life felt almost normal. As if only moments earlier they hadn't been in death's crosshairs.

Nick bent down and crushed her lips with his. It was like the first they had kissed on that dock — that familiar sense of time being suspended as the world paused around them. But this time there was an unspoken promise in their kiss, and Charley smiled. Things would definitely be okay...someday soon.

Epilogue

Two years later

"Please don't lift that, babe."

"Good grief, are you serious? I'm fully capable, thank you very much," Charley retorted as she set the box down on the table. "Plus, I have to get these ready for my signing."

"I know, but I'd rather you not. Just boss me around, and I'll do whatever you want," Nick whispered as he nuzzled and kissed Charley's neck. He wrapped his arms around her, his hands resting on her belly. "How is it possible you're even more beautiful today?"

Charley laughed and relished being held. "Because being as large as a house is so damn sexy. I can't even see my feet anymore."

"Well, you're gorgeous to me—you and your missing feet." Nick kissed her on the cheek and went to open the box. He pulled out a book and examined it.

"Isn't the cover great?" Charley beamed with pride. The bright cheery yellow cover was glossy and simply gorgeous. "It looks just like him." Charley peered down at Ruger, who had taken the opportunity to snooze at her feet.

"Look at that awesome new pen name," Nick added playfully with a sexy grin.

"*Charley Capra*... It does have quite the ring," Charley agreed.

"Well, so do you," he teased, which resulted in a playful slap on the arm.

Charley held the shimmering diamond on her ring finger up in the air to catch the light. He was right, it was quite the ring. She'd picked it out, after all. "I never imagined I'd be writing children's books, but I'm so happy."

"You make *me* happy." Nick kissed her cheek again.

Charley finally had her happily ever after. It took a while to happen, and some of it she had to do on her own terms—such as proposing to Nick. The poor guy had asked her to marry him plenty of times, but it wasn't until she had finally healed from the trauma that she had endured before she was ready to say *I do*. But when Charley did, she did it big and their wedding had been wonderful. They had been surrounded by family and friends who loved them, though their adorable little ring bearer had stolen the spotlight. *Is there anything cuter than a pug wearing a bow tie?*

Life had changed so much since that summer at Crescent Lake, a place Charley hoped she'd soon forget. It would take time and Charley might never end up forgetting. Once Pamela had been taken away in handcuffs, Nick had been taken to the hospital to get his wound treated and Charley had taken care of

Ruger. Ruger had been terrified and Charley had held the poor shaking pup all night. That in itself had created an unbreakable bond. Once Nick had been released, they couldn't get out of there quick enough. The media had already begun to storm the area and the high-profile case was already front-page news.

Charley had wanted to get as far away as possible from her old life. She had gone back to Seattle and made plans to move nearer to her parents. She hadn't been alone. Nick and Ruger had never left her side, especially Ruger. The adorable pug who used to drive Charley crazy followed her everywhere. She could barely go to the bathroom unattended. He now took up residence in her new writing cave with his very own bed, though he did prefer to lay by her feet. He was her little shadow now and had been the inspiration for her first ever children's book.

Charley decided she'd had enough of murder and mayhem, but deep down she knew — *once a writer, always a writer*. Her own real-life ending was far better than any cheesy romance novel she could've written. It was real and honest — a truly crazy adventure with someone who needed her as much as she needed him. Charley felt a kick and smiled. They were soon going to be on another adventure — *parenthood*.

Want to see more from this author? Here's a taster for you to enjoy!

Single in Seattle: Reeling in Love
Gloria Herrmann

Excerpt

"I think we got it," Molly said confidently to the almost naked man standing in the corner, wearing nothing but a stark white towel draped across his tan waist.

"You sure?"

Molly nodded as she scrutinized her work. "Yeah, the lighting was brilliant. I don't think we could have done any better."

"If you say so. You're the expert with that thing." The model pointed at the large camera Molly cradled in her hands, the screen displaying the digital shots from the day of working with him.

Molly loved her job as a professional photographer. Her friends were insanely jealous. What woman wouldn't be? She spent her days in her studio behind the lens of her trusty camera, capturing sexy images of some of the most gorgeous men from all over the world. Either she was paid to travel to them or they flew to Seattle to have her work her magic. Authors in the romance industry adored her photos. Her attention to detail had won her awards over the years, but what she loved the most was bringing the characters from books alive. Sure, it didn't hurt to look at well-defined muscles and sculpted abs that begged to be touched and to know what was hidden beneath the scrap of cloth that usually covered these men, but that wasn't how the business worked. Her friends would argue it was just because Molly didn't throw herself at these scantily clad men that she was missing out on these valuable opportunities.

If they only knew how nervous most of these men were, their fragile egos stripped down for her. It took Molly the first half of the shoot to calm them, easing them out of their shells, getting them just to loosen up enough for the right shot. It was more like babysitting rather than staring at a buffet, despite what her best friends thought. Not all the models lacked self-confidence, however. There were some who would stroll in, look directly into the camera and own it. But, for the most part, a lot of the guys were unsure and needed coaxing. Molly often felt more like a counselor than the world-famous photographer that she was.

Today, the Seattle sun was shielded behind soft, white clouds, filtering its rays into her studio that overlooked the Puget Sound. Her tall, glass windows provided the most stunning views of the shimmering water and the bustling city. Molly had worked hard for this view. It hadn't come easy or cheap — or without her busting her ass to make her name known in the photography industry. She had the scars — mostly emotional, but scars, nonetheless — to prove the struggles she'd endured, climbing to the top. Now she was one of the most sought-after photographers. Models from all over the globe wanted her to shoot them. *New York Times* and *USA Today* bestselling authors and publishers almost begged for her to shoot their covers. They wanted the best and…well, Molly was. Her skills proved that she had something special and everyone knew it.

Not bothering to sit down at her desk — bending over, instead — to focus on the images she was uploading to her laptop to edit, she almost forgot to say goodbye to the model she had just worked with. It wasn't until he was standing close to her, now fully dressed, that she realized he was still in her studio. Having him near her like that shifted the atmosphere in the room. His dominating presence was invading her space, creating nervous waves in her stomach. She inhaled his expensive aftershave, looked up from her screen and smiled.

Molly managed to say, "Great shoot today. Thanks again."

Remember to breathe, Molly.

"Yeah, it was amazing. You're amazing." The man paused, running his fingers along his day-old beard, the perfect blend of refined and unkempt sexy. His voice was silky and oozed well-practiced enticement. Molly watched him stand still, contemplating his next move. She was tempted to grab her camera and snap another shot. The light was hitting him just right and his pose was thoughtful and natural. This man was gorgeous.

He turned his mesmerizing gaze toward her and asked, "Do you want to grab a drink?"

Molly swallowed. It wasn't the first time she had been asked out by a model after a shoot. Sometimes it was the result of having bonded over their frail vulnerabilities. Sometimes they figured she was as good a lay as any while they were in town — another stamp in their romantic passport, so to speak. Molly wasn't so sure about this one. He wasn't overly emotional or guarded about his body, nor did he seem to really desire her. *So, what is he after?* She watched him scan the large studio. There was her answer. This type of square footage didn't come cheap and he knew that.

"You know, maybe another time. I'm really excited to get this edited." Molly pointed at her sleek silver laptop, delivering a fake smile in hopes it would put him off.

He nodded and thanked her again as he saw himself out. *The nerve.* Molly rolled her eyes and released the air she had been holding in her lungs. While she was in mid sigh, her cell phone chirped.

"Hello," she answered, a little more gruffly than she'd intended.

"Wow, so what's with the 'tude, lady? Bad day?"

It was one of her best friends, Tiffany.

"Just got done working with a model."

"Well, then why do you sound all cranky? Was he awful? So good-looking that you couldn't handle it?" Tiffany teased, causing Molly to laugh and her mood to lighten.

"You know the type. He wanted to go out for drinks—"

Tiffany cut her off quickly. "And you said, yes, right? Because if you didn't, you honestly need to have your head examined."

"I'd have to say he was more interested in my real estate than me." Molly frowned.

"Like real estate, as in the prime location between your legs? You know, it's all about location, location, location, baby."

"I wish." Molly huffed in frustration. "No, more like the prime location of my studio."

"That sucks."

"Tell me about it. He was gorgeous and he smelled divine. He was totally your type—tall, dark and devilishly handsome."

She heard Tiffany's disappointment through the phone. "Really? Oh, I just don't know how you do it, Molly. I have to give it to you. I would simply come undone working with those gorgeous men and not taking advantage of them every chance I got."

Tiffany always acted like she was some aggressive sex kitten, but they knew the truth. She was actually quite timid, which was a huge reason why she was single. All three of them were single and not dating anyone special. It didn't usually work that they were unattached all at the same time, but they were now. Their other best friend, Mackenzie, was the mother hen of the group. Well, more like the bossy one—completely overbearing, but with an absolute heart of gold. She, too, teased Molly about her line of work, but Mackenzie loved being a teacher, as it helped fill her maternal void. They had biological clocks that had gone haywire over the last couple of years, but everyone had warned them as they entered the dirty thirties that baby fever would hit soon after, and it had for Tiffany and Mackenzie. Every time they passed a stroller, neither could resist the temptation of peering in to catch a glimpse of some infant swaddled in fuzzy pink or blue blankets. Molly? She had her moments. They were brief and passed quickly when she heard the wail of a newborn or the shrill sound of a tantrum from a toddler. That didn't tempt her to want to rent out her womb for nine months.

She looked at her spotless, chic studio. Her smile went deep into her soul, masking the want for a baby. Her space sparkled and gleamed with the afternoon

Seattle sunlight, illuminating sleek lines and utterly contemporary taste.

If she were being completely honest with herself, yes, she did indeed want a child, eventually. But Molly also realized she was missing a very important part of the equation—a man. She didn't want just a sperm donor, though she and her friends had discussed that over far too much wine and Chinese food one night, considering it as a last resort. That had left them laughing for hours. No, Molly wanted the real deal. They all did. They wanted a man—a sexy, successful and simply wonderful man. *Is that really asking for too much?*

Being single, especially in Seattle, came with its challenges. Molly thought the enormous Emerald City should be plentiful with eligible bachelors, but Molly assumed that, as with any place, being single was a mixture of bad luck and an overly detailed list of the personality traits she wanted in a boyfriend. As time passed, her list had grown a lot shorter. She'd crossed off quite a few of her must-haves and was looking to review her available options. Now she figured it was mainly the bad luck that was keeping her single. Molly had been unattached the longest out of her friends, who were more like her sisters. Tiffany had been on a dating spree recently, but Mackenzie and Molly had known that none of the guys were Mr. Right for their friend. Mackenzie also had a pretty extensive list of requirements for her ideal mate, and she was even more stubborn than Molly when it came to sacrificing the qualities she was willing to live with, so she dated very little.

"Well, since you didn't want drinks with that sexy model, how about meeting up with us?" Tiffany asked.

Molly smiled. Yes, a drink with her best pals she could do. "That sounds lovely, actually." She could use some cheering up. The best cure for her bruised ego was some quality time with her besties.

"Great. I'll pick up Mac and we'll swing by the studio and grab ya. Sound good?"

"Perfect. I have some edits I want to go through, so just buzz when you guys get here."

Molly said goodbye and hung up. She stared at the monitor in front of her, the images of the model in various poses looking back her.

* * * *

Lost in her work tweaking the images with an array of filters, Molly was so engrossed that she almost didn't hear the loud buzzing that echoed off the large studio walls. She got up quickly from her desk and jogged to the massive double doors to let her friends in.

"Jeesh, what were you doing? I have been ringing that dang buzzer for, like, *forever*," Tiffany complained as she slipped past Molly into the studio. Mackenzie frowned and hugged Molly.

"We've only been standing outside the door for a minute," Mackenzie assured her.

Tiffany walked over to one of the large windows facing the Puget Sound. The sun was setting, casting a tangerine hue over the haze of the city. "God, do you ever get tired of this magnificent view?"

Molly shook her head as she joined her, staring out at the glittery lights in the surrounding buildings that seemed to stretch up toward the sky. "Nope."

"Yeah, I didn't think so." Tiffany laughed as she faced Molly. Her dark hair was loose on her thin shoulders. Tiffany's large eyes were a soulful brown and she had the best cheekbones. Tiffany was gorgeous in a unique and completely unexpected way. Molly's brain acted as a camera, capturing shots of her friend's delicate features as the sunset cast a shadowy light on her face. Tiffany sensed what Molly was doing and threw her a pouty look.

Mackenzie stood next them. The willowy blonde towered over Molly, making her feel short and stubby. Mackenzie had the figure of a teenager, slim and athletic. Her sun-kissed hair was cut in a sleek bob, framing the sharp angles of her face. She was another beautiful woman. Molly couldn't help but snap mental pictures of Mackenzie, too. She searched Molly curiously with soft mocha eyes. They all had brown eyes in varied shades of the common color, but resembling their different tastes in coffee. Tiffany had the espresso, dark and bold. Mackenzie was more of an iced mocha with an extra shot. Molly's resembled the instant crap coffee variety that no one really liked. Molly hated her eyes. They were plain. Her friends had tried to convince her otherwise, but they both had spectacular depth and richness in theirs. Molly thought hers looked like a muddy puddle after a typical downpour in Seattle—watery, with a sad, muted tone. Nothing special.

"What's going on with you?" Mackenzie reached for Molly, concern swimming in her eyes and worry creasing her otherwise wrinkle-free face, the result of fabulous genetics.

Molly sighed. *Is there anything going on with me?* They usually accused her of being moody, but she was an artist. *Isn't that sort of the job description? Acting the part of the tortured soul?* They sure never let her play that role for very long.

Tiffany stared at her hard and added, "Yeah, you seemed cranky on the phone. So what's up?"

"I don't know. I mean..." Molly really couldn't explain how she felt. She had a blessed life. Granted, she had worked for it, but, regardless, she knew she was lucky. Happy? Well, that was a different ball of wax.

"Drinks. That's what we need." Tiffany perked up, her hand on her hip, taking a sassy stance. She reached for the oversized purse that was slung over her shoulder. A Louis Vuitton knock-off, but it looked as real as they came. It was their little secret. Tiffany dug around and retrieved a bottle of Prosecco, holding it up for them to all gaze at her prize.

"You were carrying that in there? Oh dear. Seriously, Tiffany," Mackenzie scolded.

Tiffany winked and answered with a wicked grin.

"I, for one, am thrilled our friend is lugging around a bottle. You never know when you may need it." Molly grinned happily at Tiffany. "It does make you look a little like a wino, but you're my favorite drunk."

"No, you have me mistaken. I'm fun, not a drunk." Tiffany defended as she moved toward a long table that was against the wall opposite the windows. "Besides, at least I bring the good stuff."

"I have an idea. Let's stay in. Want to order some food?" Mackenzie suggested.

"Yes, let's do that. Molly's got one of the best views in all of Seattle. Let's just hang out here," Tiffany replied while she peeled the label away to get to the cork.

"Chinese?" Mackenzie whipped out her cell phone and started to dial their favorite takeout.

"Hell, yes," Molly and Tiffany answered in unison.

These were her girls. It didn't matter if they stayed in or went out on the town. As long as they were together, they were guaranteed to have fun.

Shortly, they were seated around a large glass table that Molly normally used to lay out prints from shoots. They dined on their fill of chow mein, pork fried rice and more Kung Pao shrimp than any woman should ever eat. White cartons, soy sauce packets and chopsticks were littered around them as they chatted about everything—mostly about the lack of sex or romance in their lives. Biting into a crispy fortune cookie—her favorite—Molly surveyed her beautiful friends. She couldn't understand why any of them were single. Tiffany was gorgeous, sweet and sassy... What was there not to love about her? Mackenzie was stunning, witty and full of love... She had so much to offer. Then there was her. She knew she might not be the sexiest thing on the planet, but she was successful, caring and everyone constantly complimented her on how pleasant she was, even telling her she was sort of hot, especially when she wore her glasses. *So how is it that I haven't landed the perfect guy yet?* Cracking open another cookie, she read the thin slip of white paper. Bold red font stared back at her, reading, *'There is nothing truer than the company of friends.' How right is that fortune?*

More wine flowed and, to keep the mood light, Molly blasted the radio. She and her two best friends danced barefoot in the empty studio, singing their hearts out and putting on a drunken performance that could rival the best pop star's. Tiffany swayed her hips to the song. Mackenzie took a while to loosen up, but then started to bop to the beat. Molly busted out some goofy moves that reminded her of middle school dances, her favorite being the 'running man'. They laughed hard, clutching their sides when Tiffany took a spill on the slippery wood floor. In their feeble attempt at helping her up, they all ended up on the floor somehow, spread-eagled, staring up at the vaulted ceilings. Music continued to play, filling the wide and open space, but the mood had shifted. That was when the laughter died and the deep realness of their friendship was exposed.

"I love you, guys," Tiffany whispered, her dark tresses fanned out against the honey-colored bamboo floor.

"Me too," Mackenzie added softly.

Molly tried to swallow the lump that was forming in her throat, feeling tears starting to surface. "I love you both. Thank you for tonight."

They all stayed on the floor, listening to several more songs before Tiffany said, "God, this floor is killing my back. I feel old."

Mackenzie and Molly both laughed.

"And for the record, we *are* old," Mackenzie replied.

"I wanted to say the same thing, but figured I would tough it out until one of you cracked." Molly started to get up.

Mackenzie and Tiffany groaned as they eased themselves off the floor. Working quietly as a team, they cleaned up the remnants of their dinner.

"I would totally live here, Molly," Mackenzie commented as she tossed several cartons into a waste basket.

Tiffany was wiping up some sticky Kung Pao sauce. "Seriously. This studio is so fabulous. You need to let me move in here."

"I do love this place." Molly looked around at her kingdom. An enormous clear-glass shelf that held her many awards was against one of the walls. Expensive frames that contained some of her best work were hung precisely in the perfect locations. Various shades, light fixtures and tons of other photography gear were set up in one corner. The room celebrated her. It showcased all of her efforts but, more importantly, it proudly displayed her passion for this form of art.

After every last morsel was cleaned and the work space was back to being immaculate, they made their way back to the window. The sun had long since disappeared, leaving the city lights to twinkle silently as the three of them stared out at the busy traffic below.

"Thank you again, guys. I really needed this tonight."

Mackenzie and Tiffany linked their arms through hers as she stood in the middle.

She would be lost without them. They knew all her secrets and her fears. They had supported her during her moments of crippling self-doubt. They'd loved her when she was at her worst. They'd dried her tears when critics had given her harsh reviews. They were her cheerleaders. They'd pushed her to continue to pursue her dream so many times when she'd just wanted to give up. They had been the first to celebrate when she finally did become successful and had told her countless times how much she deserved it.

These women were more than just friends. They were her tribe, her sisters. They were Molly's everything.

Home of Erotic Romance

Sign up for our newsletter and find out about all our romance book releases, eBook sales and promotions, sneak peeks and FREE romance books!

About the Author

Gloria Herrmann is a contemporary romance author originally from California but now lives in the Pacific Northwest with her family and pug Rizzo. Her stories are a reflection of the love she has for family, friends, and real-life moments.

Gloria loves to hear from readers. You can find her contact information, website details and author profile page at https://www.totallybound.com